Life's not like the movies . . . or is it?

An avid knitter and manager of a yarn store in New York City, Caitlyn finds herself at loose ends after getting dumped by her long-time, live-in boyfriend. What better way to move on then to find a man like the old-school movie stars that she dreams about? But her first attempt at online dating is a disaster. Especially when the date turns out to be the new renter of a room in her apartment.

Wall Street powerhouse Ben needs a place to crash while his condo is being renovated. Love is the last thing on his mind since he's just getting over a breakup. But he can't resist a challenge, especially one like his prim and proper new roommate. A do-gooder with a heart of gold, Caitlyn is spearheading a fight to save an old theater, while Ben is working for the developer trying to tear it down. Sparks will fly, but they may not be enough to ignite big-screen romance . . .

Visit us at www.kensingtonbooks.com

I0677549

Books by Maggie Dallen

The Chance Series
The Accidental Engagement
The Accidental Boyfriend
The Accidental Elopement

Reel Romance Series
Her Leading Man

Published by Kensington Publishing Corporation

Her Leading Man

A Reel Romance

Maggie Dallen

LYRICAL PRESS
Kensington Publishing Corp.
www.kensingtonbooks.com

Lyrical Press books are published by
Kensington Publishing Corp. 119 West 40th Street New York, NY 10018

First Electronic Edition: February 2017
eISBN-13: 978-1-5161-0141-2
eISBN-10: 1-5161-0141-3

First Print Edition: February 2017
ISBN-13: 978-1-5161-0144-3
ISBN-10: 1-5161-0144-8

Printed in the United States of America

Chapter 1

Seeking Cary Grant, that's what her online profile had read. The guy sitting across from her at the bar was attractive, had a British accent, and… Well, that was where the similarity ended.

"So what do you *really* do then?" he asked with a mouth full of bread. They hadn't ordered dinner but the waiter had kindly brought them a basket of warm bread, most likely in a vain attempt to sober up her obnoxious date, who stank of whisky.

Caitlyn let out a weary sigh. She was way past caring if her disgust was obvious. This man had tested her patience from the moment he'd sat across from her.

"What do you mean, what do I *really* do?" she repeated.

She hated that question. *Hated it.*

He shrugged and tossed back a large gulp of his beer. "So you just work at a yarn store then?"

Caitlyn's hands clenched together in her lap as she prayed for patience. So maybe managing and teaching at a yarn store wasn't the career she'd dreamed of when she'd gotten her art degree in college, but she liked it there. "Isn't that enough?"

Her date shrugged again and leaned over the table so the smell of whisky was nearly overwhelming. "Not much of a career path, is it?"

He let out a belch that nearly knocked her out with its gaseous fumes.

"I like it." She squelched the urge to qualify her life decisions. She certainly didn't have to explain herself to this man, who wouldn't know art or passion if it hit him upside the head. Being surrounded by gorgeous textures and fibers, and sharing her passion with others—it made her happy. She'd made a home for herself there over the last five years and she refused to apologize for it, especially not to this drunken jerk.

"And what about you?" she asked, fruitlessly attempting to make eye contact with their waiter so she could pay the bill and get out of there.

When that failed, she shoved her empty wineglass toward the end of the table so the waiter could see that they were done. One drink had never felt so interminably long.

"I'm a venture capitalist." Though with his drunken slur it came out more like *vent captlish*. "I build companies from the ground up." He shoved a piece of bread into his mouth and leaned in even closer, lowering his voice as if sharing a state secret. "I make a lot of money."

Caitlyn actually flinched in the face of such a gauche remark. "Good for you."

He pointed a finger in her face. "You could learn something from me. I could help you."

Oh, wonderful. "I don't need any help, thanks."

His eyes narrowed to the point where she suspected he might just fall asleep and land face first in the breadbasket. Part of her hoped he would. At least then she wouldn't have to hear him speak. He wobbled in his seat. "Yeah. You need me."

"Check, please." She was a little louder than intended, but it did the trick. The waiter looked in her direction and raised a finger in the "one second" gesture before racing off toward another table that was beckoning.

Her date seemed oblivious to her quest for the check. He was currently leaning over the table, his bleary gaze fixed on her. "Want to know what I think?"

"Not really." She fumbled through her purse for her wallet. So far, she'd heard everything this man thought on a myriad of topics and was thoroughly disgusted. How this soulless, aggressive, alpha male had managed to come across as sensitive and thoughtful in their e-mail exchanges was a mystery. To think she'd actually been excited when she'd first spotted him sitting there. Sensitive, thoughtful, *and* hot as hell? For a split second she'd honestly thought she'd found the one. Mr. Right.

She couldn't have been more wrong.

"I think you need someone to add some excitement to your life," he said matter-of-factly before popping another piece of bread into his mouth.

Her hands froze inside her bag as those words shredded her last bit of patience. "What does that mean?" The words came out through gritted teeth, and she glared at him across the table. He continued to chow down on his bread as he explained—loudly and with an excessive amount of hand gestures, not noticing or caring that his running commentary on her life had struck a nerve.

"Look at you." He waved a hand toward her, nearly tipping over the condiments in the center of the table in the process. Caitlyn picked up her purse again to look for her wallet, hoping that by ignoring him, he would stop speaking.

It didn't work. Ben continued on with his explanation undeterred. "There's probably a hot piece of ass hidden under all those layers, but no one would ever know it."

A sudden jolt of anger made her nauseous. Caitlyn clutched her purse, and for one brief moment she envisioned slugging him with it.

He kept going, apparently unaware that he was in danger of being smacked upside the head with an oversized handbag. "This whole look you've got going is so Plain Jane. Are you trying to come across as frigid and matronly? Because if so, you've succeeded."

She tried to hold on to the initial rage, but his words hit too close to home. He was all but echoing everything her ex had said. Oh, her ex had never been quite so crass—aggressive and crude had never been his style—but the basic message was the same.

"You need to spice it up a bit," he was saying. She was vaguely aware that her date was still talking, but his words were partially drowned out by the rush of blood pounding in her ears.

Taking a deep, steadying breath, she tried to rein in her raging emotions. *Do not listen to him. He's a drunken asshole who has no idea what he's talking about.* Despite her mental pep talk, her hands were shaking. She stared at the jumbled contents of her bag. She needed to find her wallet so she could pay and get the hell out of there.

"I mean, I get it if you're going for the whole sexy librarian thing but trust me, love, if that's the case, you really need to focus on the *sexy* part of that equation." He laughed at his own joke, and it sent little crumbs of bread flying out of his mouth. "And no offense, but a yarn store? Sounds painfully boring."

The waiter walked past—without the bill—but with an apologetic smile that said he heard every word and felt sorry for her. Great, stranger pity. That was exactly what she needed after being mocked mercilessly by the man who was supposed to be perfect. She didn't need pity; she needed the damn check.

Mr. So Not Right leaned over the table and lowered his voice. "You know what you need?"

She ignored him, focusing instead on fishing out the leather wallet that had gotten wedged beneath a tattered romance novel and a skein of yarn. Wallet found! Now where, for the love of God, was the check?

"You need to get laid."

Caitlyn gasped, her cheeks burning and her stomach sinking with revulsion at the crude remark. "That's it, I've had enough."

Screw the check. After digging into her wallet, she pulled out enough cash to cover her drink.

"I'm serious," he said, one hand reaching out as if to grasp hers. She pulled back just in time. The man was repulsive enough to listen to—she sure as hell didn't want his hands on her.

"I'm serious," he slurred again. "You look like a woman who needs a little excitement…in the bedroom." Leaning back in his chair, his lips turned up into what could only be described as a leer. "I could help you."

Bile rose in her throat at the repulsive, offensive offer, and she didn't attempt to hide her cringe of horror. The waiter finally set the bill down on the table between them. *Thank the freakin' Lord.*

They reached for it at the same time, but Caitlyn was faster. Her date lurched forward to snatch it out of her hands. "I got this." He fell back into his seat, knocking the rest of his beer over in the process— directly into her lap.

Yup, it was official. Worst. Date. Ever.

* * * *

Caitlyn stomped through the snow on her long walk from Manhattan's Murray Hill neighborhood to Alphabet City. It was quicker than waiting for the bus at that time of night, and the exercise helped her work off some steam.

That man was infuriating. And worse, a complete and total waste of time. She could have gone out with her friends tonight. Or made some progress on her latest knitting project. *But no.* She'd spent the last hour listening to some jackass from London explain in excruciating detail why he was God's gift to women.

If that had been the extent of it, the night wouldn't have been completely intolerable. But then he'd insisted on challenging—no *mocking*—her life decisions, and apparently doing his very best to make her feel bad about herself. As if her self-esteem wasn't already at an all-time low after the breakup.

She had nothing to feel bad about, she reminded herself. Just because she didn't have a sexy career or a boyfriend didn't mean she was a failure. She liked working at the knitting store, and she loved sharing her craft.

It wasn't so easy to dismiss his comments about her sex life, however. Or rather, the lack thereof. But it wasn't like she wasn't trying to get back on the horse. Yes, she had taken some time to recover from her heartbreak, but she hadn't joined a nunnery. She'd gone along with

Meg's great Internet dating plan, hadn't she? And look how well that had turned out. She blew a strand of hair out of her face. Clearly online dating was not for her. She'd stick with the tried and true method of meeting a man in her everyday life. Well, probably not at the yarn store. But at a bar, or when she was out running errands. That kind of thing happened, didn't it? That was it. This was the last time she'd let her friend talk her into online dating.

Her phone buzzed in her pocket. Speak of the devil.

"I am never going to forgive you for putting me up to this," she greeted her best friend, pouting into the phone despite the fact that her friend couldn't see her.

Meg sounded annoyingly amused. "I take it the big date didn't go so hot?"

"I don't want to talk about it."

"Fair enough. Would a drink cheer you up? I'm at Cagney's and need some company."

Halfway between Murray Hill and home, Cagney's was an old-school pub that offered the sweet, sweet temptation of blissfully mind-numbing alcohol. "I'll be there soon."

Meg and her husband, Jake, had bought the bar several years before, and at the time it had been as run down as the old movie theater it neighbored. Caitlyn spotted Tamara in the ticket booth as she walked by the theater. Her friend was bundled up, her long blond hair tucked into an oversized hat, and her slim shoulders hunched over beneath a puffy winter coat. She looked freezing and miserable, but she gave Caitlyn a smile and a wave as she passed by. "How was the date?" Tamara mouthed through the glass.

Caitlyn scrunched up her nose in disgust and gave her the thumbs down signal. Tamara's face fell, but she didn't look surprised. As a fellow single lady, she was adamantly opposed to blind dates or online dating… or dating at all, for that matter. She would most likely take Caitlyn's failure and use it as yet one more reason why dating was not for her.

And maybe she was on to something. Her friend seemed to be quite content with work and friends. Maybe that's all she needed too. Inside Cagney's, a fire roared in the giant fireplace and couples cuddled up against one another in the booths. Loneliness made her throat tighten. Okay, so maybe she wasn't like Tamara—she *wanted* to find someone and she couldn't deny it. And not just any someone, she wanted to find the one. A partner, a friend. Someone she could count on. Her parents had found it. They'd been lucky in that regard. Even if they hadn't had a full lifetime with one another, the time they'd had together had been perfection. Or at least that was how Caitlyn remembered it. They died when she was a teenager, but all of her memories were of her parents as a united, contented team.

She slumped onto a barstool beside her very pregnant best friend. "I just want *that*," she said, nodding toward a nauseatingly cute couple to her right. "Why can't I just fast forward to that? I'm tired of all this online dating."

"You've been on one date so far," her friend reminded her.

"Yeah, but it was the worst."

Jake set her drink in front of her and leaned over the bar, apparently eager to hear a horror story. "How bad was it?"

Caitlyn sighed. "The only thing more depressing than wasting an evening on a date from hell is having to relive said date for one's happy couple friends."

Meg rolled her eyes. "Oh, stop whining. We could use a good laugh."

They were watching her with expectant looks, and Caitlyn resigned herself to the inevitable. "Fine, but you two are buying my drinks tonight."

By the time she was finished recounting the story, Caitlyn found herself laughing alongside her friends. "God, how pathetic am I that I actually sat there for an hour?"

Meg nodded and picked at the bowl of popcorn sitting between them. "Mmm, I would have walked out immediately."

Jake leaned against the bar with a mocking grin. "So he was no Cary Grant then, huh?"

Meg stifled a laugh as Caitlyn tipped up her nose and pointedly ignored the comment. All of her friends thought it was hilarious that she was actually seeking her dream man. Granted, her dream man had died decades before, but still—was it too much to ask to find a sexy, chivalrous, self-deprecating, gallant, charming, and witty single man in the city?

Apparently so.

When her ex had dealt the deathblow to their long-term relationship, she'd fallen into a bit of a depression, if she was being honest. She'd thought they were happy, that they'd had a future. He was supposed to be *the one*. Her life partner. The man she would grow old with. They'd never really talked about marriage and kids, but Caitlyn had assumed it was just a matter of time. Once he grew up a bit, surely he would want to settle down. After all, they were *happy*—or content, anyway.

Or at least she'd thought they had been. But looking back, she was no longer sure. The day he'd broken up with her was the day the rug had been pulled out from under her feet. Her perfectly content world tipped over. It was all over. Like someone had snapped shut a book they were finished reading and moved on to the next one on the shelf.

Her friends had done their best to drag her out of her funk, but for a solid six months she'd grieved for the life she wouldn't have. No longer able to envision her future, she'd found it hard to know where she was in the present. For the first time since her parents died, she'd been aimless. Lost.

It still wasn't easy, but at least she'd fallen into a rhythm and forged new habits and pastimes over the past few months.

When she'd finally caved and let her friends convince her that it was time to get back on the horse, she'd felt the first glimmer of hope. Maybe her ex wasn't the one. Clearly he wasn't or he wouldn't have left. Maybe there was someone better out there—someone who fulfilled her wildest dreams. Sitting in front of her computer, staring at all of the limitless options, the huge unseen universe of potential mates—she'd finally been able to see that there might be a new and exciting relationship in her future.

So why not aim for the best? Why not set out to find the ideal man of her dreams? And that was Cary Grant. It had been since she was eight and she'd stumbled upon *Bringing Up Baby* one rainy weekend afternoon. She'd known then and there that he was her perfect man—always had been and always would be.

She was certain there were men out there that embodied his charm and chivalry—his kindness and warmth. She just hadn't met one yet. But he was out there, she knew it. And this time when she fell for someone, she would make sure he was the spitting image of her perfect leading man.

Caitlyn let out a wistful sigh and Meg patted her arm. "Cheer up, buttercup. Maybe if you're this pathetic tomorrow, Tamara will pick Cary Grant for the next weekend double feature."

Caitlyn's eyes widened with excitement. "Ooh, you think?"

Every other Saturday for the past two years, Caitlyn, Meg, Jake, and a few of their friends volunteered alongside Tamara to keep the Ellen Theater in some semblance of working order. The current owner had let the place fall into disrepair over the past decade, which was not only bad for the neighboring bar's business, but just plain sad. There wasn't much they could do as far as restoring the architecture of the old theater, but they did what they could to keep the interior clean and functioning.

Meg had recruited her younger sister, Alice, and Tamara had enlisted her roommate, Marc. They'd named themselves "Operation Petticoat" for the Cary Grant movie of the same name, thanks to a comment by Jake about how they were attempting to save a sinking ship. It turned out to be a rather fitting name for a bunch of classic movie nerds. Like the film, they were a motley crew, to be sure. But they shared a love of old movies and that, plus the free drinks that Jake provided at the bar next door, had been enough to cement the crew's friendship.

"Jake has been trying to sweet talk Tamara into picking a James Cagney lineup this week," Meg said, nodding toward her husband, who was pouring a draught beer at the other end of the bar.

"I can't compete with that. Jake has the whole 'I'll give you free drinks for life' edge," Caitlyn whined.

Meg cocked her head and made a show of studying her friend. "Normally I'd say you're right, but you are so pathetic right now that you just might win."

Caitlyn laughed and smacked her friend on the arm as she finished off the last of her drink. "Gee, thanks."

* * * *

Ben's hangover was officially into its second day. Which was unfair, really. When had he gotten so old that hangovers were multi-day events? But then, he'd been on an epic binge the other night, so it was only fair that his hangover be equally epic. He just wished the night had been epic. He assumed it hadn't been, since he could barely remember it. Surely if it had been epic, it would have been memorable.

As if a two-day hangover wasn't bad enough, the sound of his oldest friend being yelled at by a shrieking demon was definitely not helping. He tried to block out the sounds of the couple fighting in the other room of the penthouse suite, but it was no use. His best friend's girlfriend was so loud the neighbors on the first floor must have been well aware of her fury. Though their fighting was preferable. He couldn't even imagine how painfully awkward it would be to be crashing with a happy couple after a breakup.

He'd even put on some earphones to drown them out with music, but the sound of his name thrown out like a weapon was inescapable. Cringing, he pulled off the earphones and gave in to the urge to eavesdrop now that the conversation had turned to him.

It wasn't exactly breaking news that Vanessa was pissed he was staying with them. But to be fair, it had only been a few weeks, and it wasn't his fault that his condo wasn't ready yet or that he'd been forced to leave his own pleasant, cozy home thanks to his cheating skank of an ex.

Still, he'd known from the beginning that he couldn't take Gregory up on his offer to crash for too long, not with the state his relationship was in. Jesus, at least he and Olivia had skipped this kind of toxic despair. Finding your girlfriend in bed with your workmate was not ideal, but at least it had managed to end their relationship quickly and all at once. It had been a swift deathblow rather than this slow torturous death that Gregory seemed to be suffering through with this on-again, off-again relationship.

But still. He'd never intended to stay as long as he had, and he certainly didn't want to add any more issues to his friend's full plate. So he dialed his executive assistant at the office. "Hey, Natalie."

"Are you coming in today?" she answered. He could hear the sounds of the office and was struck with a hint of homesickness.

Ben rubbed his eyes with his palms. She'd asked the same question every day since *the incident*. He didn't know how much she knew, if anything. Their office was small, and gossip had a tendency to spread like wildfire. But, if she did know about the breakup and about how his ex had been sleeping with one of his partners, she had never let on. In fact, his assistant of the past two years seemed hell bent on nagging him until he returned to the office.

No thanks.

Knowing how Alejandro had betrayed him was bad enough, but he definitely didn't trust himself to face him in person. Not in an office setting, at least. A good bar brawl, that he could do. A quick session in a boxing match? Sure, he'd be there. But having to sit across a conference table and see that smirking, smug face and not be able to hit it? No way.

Still, it was kind of sweet that she kept trying. "Any updates from Darren?"

One of his newest clients, Alexander Darren III, was an up-and-coming real estate developer who was looking to Ben and his firm to provide the capital for his next venture. So far the pitches Darren had sent over looked promising and the numbers seemed to add up. But there was still a long way to go before they signed a deal.

"Nothing yet." Natalie sounded bored by that topic. Oh, heaven forbid they ever get through a phone conversation that solely revolved around business. "Where are you staying?"

Natalie may not know the details—or maybe she did, his assistant seemed to know everything—but she'd helped book him a hotel for those first few hideous nights and was well aware that he hadn't returned thanks to her assistance having movers pick up his belongings and all.

"Still at Gregory's."

Natalie let out a sigh that could only be described as dreamy. "Mmm, Gregory. Is he single yet?"

Ben couldn't help but laugh. "No, and neither are you."

She sighed again, but it was only to make him laugh. His assistant was almost twice his and Gregory's age and was happily married with three kids. But, as she liked to point out whenever Gregory stopped by to pick him up for lunch, a girl can dream at any age.

"That's actually why I'm calling," he said.

"Because Gregory's single?"

"No, you vulture, because I'm going to need to find a new place. Soon. I think I may have overstayed my welcome."

"What are you thinking, another hotel?"

Ben made a face even though no one could see him. Those nights at the hotel had been miserable. Alone and self-pitying, he'd had nothing to do but wallow. He was an inherently social creature and he needed to be around people—or a person at the very least—now more than ever.

"Why don't you see if there are any temporary sublets available out there. Maybe with a roommate?"

If his assistant found that request odd, she didn't let on. She knew him well enough at this point that little he did or said fazed her.

"Will do. I'll send you some options by end of day."

Gregory walked into the room, his normally put together look more disheveled than Ben could ever remember seeing him.

"Gotta run, Nat, your dreamboat just walked in."

"Natalie?" Gregory asked as he hung up.

"The one and only. Did Vanessa leave?" His question was followed by a loud slam of the front door and he and Gregory both winced.

"I'll take that as a yes," Ben said.

Gregory plopped down into an overstuffed chair in the corner of the study, opposite Ben who was slumped over the desk. He'd been poring over numbers all morning—or at least until the fighting had started, making number crunching impossible.

"You doing okay?" Ben asked.

Gregory's head snapped up in surprise. Understandably. Ben wasn't exactly known for being touchy-feely, and Gregory was definitely not one to talk about his emotions.

"Do I look that bad?" Gregory joked, although there was little humor in his expression.

"You look like shit." Ben was also not known for mincing words, and right now his friend—who was rather notorious for being suave and debonair—looked like he'd been through battle. His normally clean-shaven face bore a five o'clock shadow and his eyes were circled with dark shadows.

Gregory let out a little laugh as he thrust a hand through his already disheveled dark hair. "That's about how I feel."

An awkward silence hung between them as Ben debated whether his friend needed a sympathetic ear or a diversion. Gregory made the decision for him. "So, have you heard anything from this new client?"

Ben shook his head. Unlike Ben, Gregory came from money. Serious money. He was the guy that everyone loved to hate. Even Ben, although he counted Gregory as one of his few true friends. Definitely one of a small number of friends who weren't also work acquaintances.

The thing that was most annoying about his friend was that he had it all. Not only did he inherit a sum that most would never dare dream to see in their lifetime, but he was also ridiculously handsome, intelligent beyond belief, and had managed to quadruple his inheritance by the age of thirty.

He was also whip smart when it came to real estate, a fact which Ben had knowingly taken advantage of during this deal with Darren. He knew numbers, and the numbers told him that real estate was the next route his company should take. But it was unchartered territory for the small, private firm, and Gregory had been a wealth of information.

Ben wasn't above using his friend and his connections to get ahead. Unlike Gregory, he had most definitely *not* come from money. His father may have been a bastard, but he'd made sure Ben knew the value of hard work and the benefits of having money. To get to the point he was at, one of the youngest partners in his firm, he'd had to be driven. Easy to do when your one and only goal in life was to succeed in business. His father had drilled it into him long ago—the only way to get ahead was to stay focused. His relationship with Olivia had been a distraction. All the drama had made him lose his focus. He was still considered ruthless and sharp by his colleagues, but he knew he could do better. This deal with Darren was his chance to get ahead of the pack.

It was a *good* thing that Olivia had cheated on him. Now he could go back to focusing on the things that mattered. He should have stuck with one-night stands and casual flings like he'd always done in the past. He'd vowed ages ago that he'd never allow a woman or a relationship to interfere with his goals. He'd seen the bitterness that had developed between his parents. The resentment had eaten away at their marriage because his father blamed his mother—and her children—for holding him back from success.

He'd been raised to believe that he could have one or the other in life, that was the lesson he'd learned all those years ago. Love or money. Family or freedom. Relationships or power. He'd chosen the latter every time and had never regretted it. The former were fleeting, untrustworthy. But money and the freedom and power that came with it... That was tangible, controllable. The only factors involved in success were effort and determination, whereas love was a fickle beast, victim of the whims of others.

But even knowing all that, what had he done? He'd gone and broken his own rule. He'd gotten involved, like an idiot. He'd become sloppy, forgotten his own rules and the reason they existed because he'd been swept up in Olivia's intoxicating passion. Any relationship would have been stupid, but one like that? One that stole his energy and took away his focus, that had been a gigantic mistake. One he wouldn't be making again anytime soon.

Ben pulled himself back from that train of thought. Every time his mind turned to his ex and her betrayal, he was on the verge of losing himself in a shame spiral. Betrayal, jealousy, pain... These were all the reasons he avoided relationships in the first place. He should never have been in a position to be hurt to begin with. He'd let her get too close and he'd suffered as a result. Served him right.

Gregory cleared his throat, pulling him back from the maudlin thoughts that had been haunting him for the last few weeks. "And news on Darren?" Gregory asked again.

Right, business. Darren. The new deal. "Waiting on Darren and his team to get back to me with the revised contract."

Gregory nodded absently, apparently lost in thought. Ben had a pretty good idea where his friend's mind had gone. Such a shame. For a man who had everything, Gregory was bloody miserable, thanks to that howling banshee of a girlfriend. He'd watched from the sidelines all these months as Vanessa twisted him around her little finger and then tied him in knots over and over again. It wasn't his place to intervene. All he could do was watch and wait and hope to hell that his friend came to his senses and ended the toxic relationship once and for all.

He could all but see his friend pull himself out of whatever dark place he'd gone to as he focused on Ben once more. "So, how'd your date go the other night?"

Ben shrugged and made a noise that was something akin to "eh." It seemed preferable to admitting the truth. He had no idea. The whole night had been a bit of a blur.

It had been a stupid idea in the first place. Hooking up after a breakup was one thing—that was expected and therapeutic—but a date? He blamed Natalie for sending him the link to a dating site. He'd never done online dating before, and he had to admit, the online part was kind of fun. You create this profile that is basically just an ego-boosted best version of you and then you chat with all these women. Countless women. And some of them were pretty great—one in particular was interesting, eloquent, funny, and fucking hot, if the pictures were anything to go by.

So he'd asked her out. Not that he was looking to get into another relationship or anything. He'd learned that lesson. But online dating seemed like the most efficient way to find his next hookup so he could start to move on. He should have just stuck with the old tried and true method—go out to a bar and hit on the ladies. Buy a few cocktails, throw out a few compliments, and leave the rest up to Mother Nature. It had never failed him before. But no, he'd allowed Natalie to convince him that online dating was the wave of the future. Online was one thing but going on a date was a totally different matter. Maybe that was why he'd started on the whisky before his date had even arrived.

Gregory took his non-answer to mean that the date had only been so-so.

It was possible it had been amazing, but Ben would never know. And he sure as hell wasn't going to reach out to her to find out. Even if he'd wanted a second date—which he didn't—how the hell would he explain the fact that he had almost no memory of their first date. Bloody embarrassing. He'd learned his lesson. From here on out he would stick with what he knew. Sex. Pure, simple, meaningless sex. That was what a rebound was supposed to be.

Besides, that black hole of a night was over, a thing of the past. He hadn't gotten any e-mails from his date hinting around about meeting up again, so more likely than not she'd moved on as well. No use giving it a second thought.

Chapter 2

Caitlyn tried to focus on mopping the floor of the theater's lobby, but yet again her traitorous brain was replaying the date from hell. It had been nearly a week. She should be over it already. But every time the memory came up, she thought of new, cutting remarks she should have said. Comebacks that were so witty and scathing he would have walked away in tears.

But no. Instead, she'd run away like a coward. God, sometimes she was so tired of being passive.

"Whoa, watch it there." Marc laughed as her mop nearly tripped him. A tall and lanky ballroom dancer, Marc deftly dodged her mop with a little dance step.

"Sorry," she mumbled. Marc was Tamara's roommate and an official member of the crew. It was just sheer luck that Tamara had found herself a nice gay roommate who also happened to adore old movies. Why couldn't she be so lucky with her subletters? She had yet to really click with one of the many renters who'd temporarily shared her apartment after her ex moved out.

"How is it that our resident morning person is the grumpiest of us all?" Tamara asked. The petite blonde gave her a teasing nudge as she passed and swatted Marc's hands away when he attempted to pull her into a dance when a new song came on the radio.

"Sorry," Caitlyn said again.

"Tell me you're not still moping over one bad date," Alice said. Even at seven-thirty on a Saturday morning and with a dirty rag in her hand, Meg's younger sister looked like a supermodel. Her long auburn hair pulled into a messy bun, her face was clean-scrubbed, but she was still gorgeous. Add the fact that she had a super successful career as a PR specialist and a slew of men at her beck and call, and Alice was a walking reminder that life was incredibly unfair.

Pushing a stray lock out of her face, Alice turned to her. "I know you're new to dating so trust me when I say that good dates are the exception to the rule. You'd better get used to the lousy ones."

Alice's lips turned up in a small smile as she added, "Although a night that ends with insults and a lap full of beer is pretty bad as far as bad dates go."

Caitlyn turned to Meg, who was sitting in the corner flipping through the chore list for the day—the only task her big belly would allow. "You told her?"

Meg shrugged. "She's my sister."

Caitlyn rolled her eyes as the others laughed. Clearly her bad date had been the source of everyone's amusement this week. She bit back a weary sigh. *Wonderful.*

Tamara passed her again, lugging a full trash bag, her face screwed up in a sympathetic pout. "I'm sorry you had such a terrible experience. That is exactly why I don't date."

"You don't date because you're too shy to speak to the opposite sex," Marc called out. Marc had taken it upon himself to break Tamara out of her shell but hadn't had much success. They'd been roommates and friends for more than three years, and so far his "interventions," as he called them, had yet to pay off. Tamara was pretty in a fragile, ballerina type way, but she hid her looks behind her long blond hair, which tended to act as a veil she could duck behind, and baggy clothes that did nothing for her figure. Marc still had his work cut out for him.

Tamara kept wiping down the refreshment stand, unfazed by her roommate's comment. Caitlyn supposed Tamara heard remarks like that night and day since she lived with her biggest cheerleader.

"I'm too busy to date. This theater doesn't run itself, you know," Tamara said with a toss of her hair. It sounded like something she said more out of habit than anything else. Marc gave a snort of disbelief but let it drop.

"How's the mission going?" Caitlyn asked.

"The mission" was Tamara's ongoing quest to get the old theater on the list of N.Y.C. landmarks. The current owner was not exactly aware that Tamara was pursuing landmark status from the Landmark Commission—and if he knew, he most likely wouldn't be pleased. It was a not so-secret-secret that the barely-there owner was hoping to sell, and it was clear he didn't care what the new owners did to the place. He hardly took an interest in the Ellen Theater now, and he was the sole proprietor. Tamara, the woman who actually ran the place, was determined to keep the integrity, not only of the architecture but also of its original purpose.

"It's not," Tamara said. "I filed all the paperwork, but I'm still playing the waiting game."

"Do you think the owner found out and is using his connections to stall?" The owner wasn't exactly a real estate mogul, but he owned enough properties to have connections where it counted.

Tamara sighed. "I honestly don't know if he's intervening or if the red tape is just so thick that this wait time is normal."

Meg chimed in from her seat in the corner. "While you're waiting, you could be dating."

Tamara and Caitlyn shared a grin. They were both on the hot seat these days. Marc and Alice were persistent, but as fellow single people they weren't nearly as bad as Meg and Jake, who thought everyone should be as happy and content as they were.

They'd met first semester freshman year of college at a dorm mixer and had been together since. Meg and Caitlyn had been roommates at NYU so she'd been witness to the whole disgustingly perfect romance from the very beginning. Sometimes Caitlyn was convinced the two lovebirds had no idea just how lucky they were to find one another at such a young age.

"You heard Alice," Caitlyn said. "There are no good men left."

Alice's red head popped up from behind the concession stand. "I did not say that! I just said that good dates were hard to find."

Jake cut in. "Alice has a point, Cait. Most men aren't worthy of your time."

Caitlyn rolled her eyes, but his sweet words made her heart ache. Caitlyn caught Meg's eye and struggled not to laugh as her friend made a face. Jake was a few years older than the rest of them and had a tendency to act like a big brother to all of Meg's friends. Although, she and Meg joked that at times—like this one—Jake had a tendency to sound like a dad. Which, Caitlyn liked to point out, was just another sign that he was going to make an excellent father. He had lots of practice.

Ignoring their giggles, Jake added, "You know what they say—you've got to kiss a lot of frogs…"

"But she didn't even get a kiss out of this one," Alice chimed in. "And what Caitie needs isn't a kiss. She needs to get laid."

Caitlyn's cheeks burned. Her friend was teasing, of course, but the words scraped her nerves more than she cared to admit.

"Here, here," Marc said.

"Amen to that," Jake called out.

Caitlyn stopped her lame attempts to mop and stared at them, not sure if she should laugh or chastise her friends. She was so not the type to sleep around and they all knew it. They'd been mocking her for years for being the prude of the group. It wasn't like she was opposed to sex or anything. She just didn't see it as a high priority. Romance, love, partnership—that was what she needed.

Which was probably why her ex thought she was boring. He'd always teased her about being an old lady, with her knitting and her homebound ways. But over the last year or so his teasing had grown more caustic, and he'd made more than one pointed comment about her lack of enthusiasm in the bedroom.

Her friends didn't know about that, of course. The fact that her ex thought she was frigid was too embarrassing and private to share. But for Alice and the others to think that she would throw herself into the arms of some stranger was ludicrous. Laughable. Yet somehow all she could do was gape at them, speechless.

Alice caught her open-mouthed stare. "What? Even a serial monogamist is allowed a fling or two between healthy, long-term commitments." Alice feigned an exaggerated yawn as she trailed off, making Caitlyn laugh along with the others.

"Not all of us are looking for casual sex," she reminded her friend.

Alice sighed melodramatically, but she was smiling when she said, "Suit yourself."

The fact that Alice had echoed the exact words from her date was not lost on Caitlyn. *You need to get laid.* While Alice was clearly teasing, that jerk had been serious. More than that, he'd all but offered to be her lover. As if she would ever stoop that low.

Her traitorous brain flashed on the ruggedly handsome face, with his sharp features and the scruffy beginnings of a beard. And then there were those sexy dark eyes and that cocky smile. Too bad he had to be such a jackass. She shook her head to come back to sanity. She pulled her phone from her back pocket to check the time and moved to put away her cleaning supplies. "Much as I'd love to hear all of your thoughts on my love life—or lack thereof—I've got to head out of here a little early. My new subletter is showing up this afternoon and I've got to get the place ready."

Meg's head snapped up. "A new one?"

Anxiety laced her friend's voice and Caitlyn held back a sigh. If Jake was the self-appointed dad of the group, Meg had definitely adopted the role of their mom.

"Are you sure it's safe to have a stranger in your apartment?"

"For the hundredth time, yes." Caitlyn gathered up her oversized purse. "The site I use verifies the candidates and does background checks. It's totally safe."

She glanced over to see Meg gnawing on her lip and looking pleadingly at her husband, silently begging him to appeal to Caitlyn's good senses. Caitlyn interrupted the silent exchange with a laugh. "Meg, aren't you the one who's constantly telling me to do online dating? Those men aren't verified, you know. You're being a hypocrite."

"Am not." Meg crossed her arms over her big belly, her mouth pulled down in a stubborn scowl. "That's totally different. You're meeting those men for one evening. In public. It's not the same thing at all."

Exhaustion swept over Caitlyn, even though her day had just begun. They'd been over this time and again since the breakup nearly a year ago. "What do you want me to do? I can't afford that place on my own."

As soon as the words were out of her mouth, Caitlyn wished she could call them back. She knew the answer all of her friends were itching to give. She'd heard it more times than she could count.

They'd tell her it was time to look for a new place. Give up her home. Start fresh in a place with no memories, no ghosts of boyfriends past. As if it was that easy to let go of everything comfortable and safe. This apartment was the first true home she'd had since her parents died. The dorms didn't count and neither did her first apartment straight out of college—a one-bedroom dump out in Queens that she'd shared with three other girls. The apartment she'd found with her ex—the ground floor apartment of a townhouse-style apartment building in a nice, quiet neighborhood—that was a true home. She'd dumped all of her money into furniture and decorations. She finally had a space of her own that was exactly the way she liked it. Losing her boyfriend was hard enough, thank you very much. She wasn't about to let go of her home too. Her apartment was the only stable thing she had left…other than her friends and her job at the store. Not to mention—did they have any idea how hard it was to find a decent apartment in her price range?

Shouting out her good-byes, she practically ran out of the theater to avoid hearing the lecture. Besides, she had an apartment to clean.

Unfortunately being alone did little to help with her brain's frustrating tendency to relive *that night*. She worked herself into a tizzy as she did laundry just thinking about the comments her date had made. Then she worked herself into a royal rage at the fact that she was still thinking about that man in the first place.

By the time she had moved on to cleaning the bathroom, she was in the midst of a sick cycle of anger. And all thanks to *him*. She found herself giving a silent lecture to the toilet as she scrubbed it clean. Who did he think he was? The man was a complete stranger who knew nothing about her. Cynical, rude, and crass. He was an affront to British men everywhere—particularly Cary Grant, may he rest in peace.

A jerk with a drinking problem, that's what he was. He was in no position to pass judgment on her life or her job. The jackass wouldn't know about artistic integrity if it smacked him upside the head. She scrubbed the toilet even harder. He was exactly the type of Manhattan, alpha-male, misogynistic a-hole she went out of her way to avoid.

He'd actually asked her what kind of car she drove within the first two minutes of meeting. She lived in Manhattan, why would she have a car? Or a driver's license, for that matter. Of course he'd followed that up with a bragging session about his sports car—as if she'd be impressed. *So you're destroying the environment with your emissions so you can feel better about the size of your penis? Good for you.* Dammit, why hadn't she said *that*?

She fell back on her heels, her hand aching from the intensive scrub job. But the car comment and the derogatory remarks about her career— that wasn't even the worst of it. She could practically hear his irritatingly sexy British accent in her head. *Are you trying to come across as frigid and matronly? Because if so, you've succeeded.*

Who the hell did he think he was? Who even *said* that?

The toilet did not have an answer.

She was losing it. *Let it go already.* But she couldn't. And it didn't take a genius to figure out why his words were still ringing in her ears after so many days. He'd hit the nail on the head. She was boring. Why else had her ex walked away? He'd all but said those same words. Oh sure, he'd phrased it in nicer, more flowery language, but the message had been the same.

She wasn't exciting enough. Their life together was too comfortable, he wasn't being challenged, blah, blah, blah. At least the asshole hadn't beaten around the bush.

Moving on to the rest of the apartment, she made a concerted effort to stop thinking. Swiping the last of her yarn stash into an oversized bag at the end of the couch, she vowed that she would *not* think about the jerkface and his rude comments anymore. She had work to do. Ben, the guy who was subletting her extra bedroom for the next month, was due at any moment and she wanted to make her cluttered two-bedroom apartment at least somewhat presentable.

Her buzzer squawked like a dying pigeon and reminded her that she really should have the super take a look at that. She plastered a pleasant smile on her face and threw open the door. The air rushed out of her lungs in a whoosh and blood drained from her head, leaving her dizzy.

"You," she sputtered to the man who was grinning at her on her doorstep.

"Well, well, if it isn't the darning spinster from the other night," he said in that same sexy British accent she'd been hearing in her head all week. He gestured toward her living room. "Aren't you going to let me in?"

"What are you doing here?" Her mind was spinning with possibilities. How had he found her address? Wasn't that information supposed to be private? Had she even given the dating Web site her home address? No, definitely not. Which meant...what? This guy was a stalker?

She took a wary step back so she could shut the door, but her date from hell was blocking the door's path with a giant duffel bag. She blinked at it for a moment, and the reality of the situation set in with a dawning sense of horror.

"Oh no," she whispered.

"Which way to my bed, *roomie*?"

The bottom of her stomach gave way as a rising tide of nausea swept over her. "But you're not—my new roommate's name is Ben, not Matthew."

He looked at her like she was insane. "My real name's Ben."

"But your profile said Matthew," she argued.

He gave a small shrug. "Everyone lies in online dating."

"I didn't."

His eyes widened. "Seriously? Caitlyn's your real name?" And then, as if it bore repeating, "You actually used your real name?"

Why did he make it sound like *she* was the crazy one? Surely she wasn't the only honest person to ever create an online profile.

She shook her head. That was not the issue here. What mattered was the jerk who'd been haunting her thoughts for the past week was standing on her doorstep, waiting to move into her apartment. *This could not be happening.* Her mind was struggling to keep up with this turn of events. Why hadn't she requested a picture? She'd checked references, and they'd exchanged some e-mails....

"How did you not recognize *my* name?" she asked.

He outright laughed at that. "My assistant set this up. Besides, I figured Caitlyn was a made up name for you anyway."

"It wasn't." She would have thought they'd covered that already, but it was all she could think to say as her brain struggled to make sense of this scenario.

She had to be the unluckiest woman on the face of the planet. Either that or she'd been a horrible person in her past life and karma was out for revenge. Those were the only explanations she could think of. Because, really—what were the odds that in a city of eight million, her date from hell and her new subletter were the same man?

And what were the odds that man was a bastard?

Chapter 3

There were worse fates than finding oneself the temporary roommate of a beautiful, if prickly, former date. It certainly beat Ben's last temporary living arrangement with his best friend and his psychotic, man-hating, verbally abusive girlfriend. *Poor Gregory.*

Besides, the shocked look on Caitlyn's face when she'd opened the door was well worth the discomfort of running into a woman he'd failed to call.

He didn't think he'd ever actually seen someone's mouth drop open in surprise. And if her eyes had widened any more they would have popped right out of her skull. It was actually rather adorable. *She* was gorgeous with those cupid bow lips, delicate features, and wide pale brown eyes. She looked like a doll—a fragile, perfect china doll. Had she been this pretty on their date? His memory of that night was embarrassingly fuzzy, but he seemed to remember a slouchy hat and an oversized coat. He was certain she hadn't been this attractive.

This he would have remembered.

After several moments of staring at one another, Ben broke the silence. "Are you going to let me in?"

Caitlyn's mouth snapped shut as he moved toward her, attempting to get himself and his bag off of the frigid front stoop and into the warm, lovely smelling apartment she was guarding.

"You can't come in," she said.

Now it was Ben's turn to stare at her in surprise. Everything about this woman screamed sweetness and light, from her big brown eyes to her angelic little mouth. To hear an unpleasant remark coming from her was like hearing Santa Claus curse like a sailor.

"I beg your pardon?"

She started to push the door closed. "You can't come in here." She sounded panicked, and he realized for the first time that her look of surprise was rather more like a look of horror.

Oh no.

He scratched his head and considered the woman before him. "Look, about the other week…"

Her eyebrows lifted and her lips set in a grim line.

"I'm really sorry I never called."

Her cheeks turned a rosy pink. Ah hell, now he'd gone and embarrassed her. His brain scrambled to think of a version of the "it's not you, it's me" speech that wouldn't get him into even more trouble.

"I just don't think I was ready to start dating. I thought I was but then—"

"I'm not mad that you didn't call," she interrupted. Her look of annoyance belied her statement.

"Okay then," he said, gesturing toward the apartment. "So can I come in?"

She was still watching him expectantly, as though waiting for him to say something. He wished he knew the magic words because it was goddamn freezing out there.

"Look, I know this is a bit uncomfortable for both of us." Mainly for him as he was the one freezing his ass off. "But if we could be adults about this—"

"You were…*rude*." Caitlyn spit the word out and Ben looked at her in surprise.

"I'm sorry?"

"You should be sorry, you were a…a…" He watched her with more than a little amusement as she struggled to come up with a curse word to describe him. The amusement was tempered by a vague, and unfamiliar, sense of guilt.

Why couldn't he remember that night? Well, he knew why he couldn't remember that night, but it was frustrating as hell. He would kill to know what he said to make this gorgeous woman spitting mad. Unless it wasn't something he'd said. The vague guilt erupted into a horrible fear. "If I did anything inappropriate"—he waved his hands vaguely, at a loss for words, which was an even more uncommon sensation—"if I kissed you or touched you in a way that—"

"You didn't." She'd crossed her arms in front of her chest and was looking at him now like he was crazy. He exhaled in relief.

"You don't remember," she said. It was not a question, and he was grateful for the lack of judgment in her eyes. He felt rotten enough without a guilt trip.

"No, I'm afraid I don't." He watched her nibble on her lip as she studied him. "Judging by your reaction to me and the fact that I have very little memory of that night, I'm inclined to believe you when you said I was an asshole."

Her brows drew together. "I didn't call you an asshole."

"You were going to," he said.

"I wasn't. I was going to call you a jerk."

"Asshole is better. More vivid. The efficacy of cursing is all about the mental image it summons."

He thought he saw the corner of her mouth twitch upward, and a jolt of pleasure shot through him at the realization that he'd nearly made her smile. He found himself dying to see that smile. So he fell to his knees.

* * * *

"What are you doing?" Caitlyn's voice sounded shrill, even to her own ears.

Still on his knees, Ben clasped his hands together and looked up at her with comically wide eyes. "Please let me in."

Caitlyn didn't know whether to laugh or shout for help. Her elderly neighbor, Mrs. Dubois, came out of her apartment and stopped dead in her tracks at the sight of this handsome man on his knees on her doorstep. And now that stupidly sexy face was turned up to her, his dark eyes looking pathetically like a puppy dog.

She clapped a hand over her mouth to smother the giggle. "What are you doing?" she asked again, this time while tugging on his arm to get him to stand up before Mrs. Dubois came over to investigate.

He didn't budge. "My dearest..." He paused and Caitlyn raised a brow in disbelief.

"*Caitlyn*." Seriously? The man had mental issues.

"Caitlyn. Of course." He cleared his throat to start again. "My dearest Caitlyn, I unfortunately have very little memory of our lovely night together, but I suspect from your demeanor that I truly was a complete and utter jackass. Am I right?"

She nodded, unable to stop the grin that was spreading over her face at his insanity. He may be a jackass but he was entertaining, at least.

He concluded with a bowed head. "For my behavior that night, I apologize with all my heart."

Before she could reply, his head snapped back up. "If you could find it in your heart to let this jackass into your apartment so he doesn't freeze his balls off, he would be forever in your debt."

She opened her mouth to say no, but stopped as the reality of her situation set in. What alternative did she have? She couldn't afford rent on her own for this month and it could take weeks to find a new subletter, especially one who was available to move in right away.

This guy was an asshole—that much they'd firmly established—but being obnoxious was not the same as being a sociopath or a murderer. And his references *had* checked out. More importantly, so had his credit check.

She glanced over his head to see Mrs. Dubois watching unabashedly. "Good evening, Mrs. Dubois," she called out. The old woman scowled at her and she turned her attention back to the man who was prostrate at her feet.

She conceded with a sigh. "Come on in. But don't make me regret it."

* * * *

She watched him unpack his toiletries in her bathroom and tried to reconcile the jerk from her horrid date with this Ben whose references raved about him. Maybe he'd paid them off. But then, she'd had the same issue trying to figure out how horrid-date-guy was the same man who had sent her all of those thoughtful, funny e-mails. The man was an enigma. Or he was just very good at paying people off. One of the two.

He turned then to see her watching him and she felt heat flood her cheeks. Great, now she looked like a creepy stalker. "Uh, I just wanted to make sure you're settling in all right."

One side of his mouth twisted up into a grin that made her heart beat double time. He was sexy, there was no doubt about that. Handsome too, and he knew it. He had unruly, short, dark brown hair, rugged features, and a large build—not stocky but solid and well built. *Like a lumberjack.* A five o' clock shadow only managed to make him more attractive, which was rather annoying. She didn't want to be attracted to this man—not only because he was a conceited jerk but because she was going to be sharing a small apartment with him for a month, at the very least.

Physical attraction made her uneasy, it always had. With her last two boyfriends, the physical attraction had grown slowly, a result of their mutual affection. But this kind of sexual energy... It made her nervous. She hated the fluttery feeling it brought on, and she dreaded the thought of being uncomfortable in her own home. Her sanctuary.

She would just have to get over it.

She pointed him to the spare bedroom, and when he went back there to unpack she followed before coming to a stop in the doorway. "If you need anything, just let me know." The moment the words came out of her mouth, she wished she could pull them back. Hovering in the doorway of his bedroom was weird enough, but somehow the simple offer sounded like she was offering something dirty, or at least that's what his sexy grin insinuated.

Heat flooded her cheeks. She was just being polite, dammit. She gave this speech to all the new roommates, and there was nothing salacious about it. With that thought, she straightened her shoulders and ignored his childish smirk.

"Towels are in the hall closet, and if you need anything for your bed…"

One of his brows shot up at that.

Oh, why was she still talking? Backing away from the bedroom, she gave a little wave. "Okay, then. Good night."

She was just about to turn when he stopped her by reaching out a hand and grasping her arm. Flames ignited at the simple touch, and Caitlyn held her breath as she stood frozen in place. It was harmless touch, but the electricity that shot through her was palpable…paralyzing.

Ben dropped his hand and Caitlyn was once again able to inhale.

"Sorry," he muttered, looking down at her arm. In a gesture that was adorably cute and boyish, he ducked his head and ran his hand through his hair, mussing it further. "I just wanted to say sorry. Again. For…you know."

That night.

"I really appreciate you letting me stay here and giving me another shot." He looked up and their eyes met.

Her heart fluttered in her chest at the sweet sincerity she saw there. His gaze was warm and direct. It felt…intimate. *Damn.* This man was sexy as hell when he was a jerk, but as a good guy? She was certain the temperature in the room rose by another ten degrees. She had to resist the urge to fan herself.

Not trusting herself to speak lest she accidentally put her foot in her mouth, she gave him a smile before turning away and heading back to her room. Once there she let out the breath she'd been holding.

She absolutely needed to find a way to get over this stupid attraction. There was no way she could spend the next month walking on tiptoes around this man just because he had a ridiculous, inexplicable effect on her. This was her home, her asylum, her sanctuary.

Deep breaths. Still leaning against her door, waiting for her heart rate to return to normal, Caitlyn reminded herself yet again that she would get over this initial, crazy reaction. He'd stunned her, that was all. Of course seeing your date-from-hell was going to cause a bit of a disturbance. But now she could move on. Treat him like she would any other temporary roommate. Temporary, that was the key word here. He wouldn't be here long—a month, that was what they agreed on. Besides, they were both busy professionals, and they would probably rarely see one another while he was there. That much she knew from experience.

She'd had a steady stream of temporary roommates to help her make rent every month in the year since the breakup. She'd always managed to keep a friendly distance, ensuring that the relationship was a professional one. A landlord and tenant, to a certain degree. Friendly but not friends, that was what she wanted out of a roommate. And she certainly didn't want sexual tension. She inhaled deeply, finally calm enough to fully enter her room and start getting ready for bed. It was settled then. They would just have to do their best to stay out of one another's way.

* * * *

That proved to be much easier said than done. Two days into her new living situation and Caitlyn was ready to strangle her roommate. She came home from a morning class at the shop to find him sprawled out on her couch, still in a T-shirt and boxers he'd clearly slept in, his hair a mess of bedhead.

And he looked incredible.

He was typing away at a laptop on the coffee table and was surrounded by dirty dishes and stacks of notepads and books, which she assumed were part of his work. She paused in the entryway, and when he looked up, she knew she still wore of look of disgust. She was far from a neat freak, but it was disconcerting to see someone else's clutter take over her space. Not to mention the disaster he'd made of the bathroom. She was half convinced this guy had lived his life with a maid to pick up after him—but then, if this guy could afford maid service, what the hell was he doing subletting at her rundown place?

"Welcome back." He glanced up from his computer. "Something wrong?"

Yes. From the moment he'd moved in, he hadn't left the apartment. He was always there, in her way, every time she turned around.

"No. Just… Don't you have an office to go to?"

He shook his head and went back to typing. "I typically work from home. I'm more efficient if I'm home alone."

"That would have been nice to mention in your application," Caitlyn muttered.

"What?"

"Nothing." *You heard me.* But she let it drop—the only thing more uncomfortable than his presence would be a confrontation.

As she went about her routine over the next few days, she assumed he would at least leave the apartment in the evenings to go out with friends. But every night he plopped down next to her on the couch where she was knitting and watched TV alongside her. To her horror, she soon found that he wasn't the type who merely watched TV. Oh no, her charming houseguest had to comment on every little thing that occurred on the screen as though television was an interactive sport.

During one commercial break, he'd turned to her with a sudden, avid interest in her knitting project that she had been diligently working on for the past two nights that they'd been camped out on the couch. It was a delicate lace shawl made with fine yarn and tiny needles and she had to knit every stitch with great care.

"Who's that for?" he asked.

"One of my students commissioned it. It's for her daughter's wedding."

He studied it for some time, inspecting the edges with a surprising gentleness. "It's beautiful."

A lightness filled her chest. The compliment made her far happier than it should have. But it was always nice to have her work appreciated. "Thank you."

And then he had to go and ruin the moment. "How much is she paying you?"

Her hands stopped their monotonous task so she could look up at him. "I beg your pardon?"

He was turned toward her with an interest that was alarming. No male ever had taken such an interest in her knitting. "How much are you charging?"

"A hundred dollars and the cost of supplies," she said and then immediately regretted it. Why did he even care? It was none of his business.

He was staring at her in horror now. "You're kidding me."

"She's a very sweet old lady," Caitlyn started to explain.

He cut her off. "I don't think she's sweet at all. The old crony is taking advantage of you."

Caitlyn gasped. Her students loved her. "She is not. She's—"

"How many hours would you say this project is going to take?"

She clamped her lips shut and focused on the row she was working on.

"I've watched you working on this for ten hours, at least, and it looks like you've got a long way to go."

Caitlyn ignored him, but her brain automatically started calculating how many more hours she would most likely spend on this project, and the number was disconcerting. Especially if you divided it by a hundred dollars.

Ben leaned back on the couch and crossed his arms. "Do you realize that taking into account the electricity you're using and that cup of tea you're sipping, you're actually taking a loss on this project?"

Caitlyn pressed her lips together, wishing she had some sort of comeback that would put this infuriating man in his place.

But he was right.

"Shut up and watch your show," she grumbled. She moved farther onto her side of the couch with a sniff.

Don't you have any friends? Don't you have a life? She wanted to ask. But she didn't, of course. That would be entirely too rude and more than a little hypocritical seeing that she was camped out on the couch right beside him.

Instead she settled on, "Have you found a permanent place to live yet?"

One side of his mouth turned up in a knowing grin. He knew exactly what she was hinting at. *You are not welcome here.* The day his month-long sublet contract ended, he would be out the door.

"I'm not looking for a place." He popped a handful of mixed nuts into his mouth.

Dread replaced annoyance. Oh my God, he was the guest who would never leave. Maybe that's what he did. He just hopped from one apartment to the next until he drove the tenant so crazy that they kicked him out. That was it! That explained why his references gave such glowing reviews. It was a conspiracy. It was—

"I already own a place," he said.

Caitlyn's mouth fell open as she stared at him, the shawl forgotten in her hands. "What?"

"I bought a condo on the Upper East Side, but it's undergoing renovations. I'm just waiting for them to finish. It was supposed to be done weeks ago, but you know how it goes."

Caitlyn nodded. Yeah, sure, she knew how it went. Oh the troubles of being a homeowner in New York City. His woes were right up there with the plight of the migrant worker.

"So why are you staying here?" she asked, looking around her tiny, old apartment with its drafty windows and peeling paint. "Shouldn't you be staying at a hotel or something? I know you make a lot of money and—"

He looked over at her in surprised amusement. "And just how do you know that I make a lot of money?"

"You told me." *That night*, went without saying. She shifted on the couch and turned back to her knitting.

"I said that?" His face was the picture of dismay. At her pointed look, he added, "I thought we agreed to forgive and forget. I know I have."

She laughed at that. "All is forgiven and forgotten, but you did tell me that you make a lot of money."

His look was comically chagrined. "I'm a right bastard."

"Agreed. But that doesn't answer the question of why someone who has so much money—"

"I may make a lot of money, but I also lose a lot of money."

She blinked in surprise at the candor in his tone. He shrugged. "It's the nature of the game. But that's what I like about high stakes finance—no risk, no reward."

"So it's like gambling then?"

He leaned back against the couch cushion. "It's not so much gambling as it is taking a risk on something you believe in—something you feel has potential, a diamond in the rough. What? What are you grinning about?"

She shook her head, smothering a laugh. "Nothing, I just—I didn't take you to be so…philosophical."

He threw a peanut at her head. "Ah, fuck off," he muttered as he turned back to the TV. But he was laughing too.

"So you're subletting because it's cheaper than a hotel?"

He hesitated in answering and she glanced over. Maybe he'd just been distracted by whatever was on the television because he cast her a charming grin. "That's me. Financially responsible."

Caitlyn went back to her knitting. It wasn't until she was brushing her teeth and getting ready for bed that it dawned on her. When she'd asked him why he was subletting—he hadn't actually answered her question.

* * * *

On day number five of Caitlyn's challenging week of being stuck in the apartment with Ben, she got a welcome call from Meg asking her to join them at the bar for some drinks.

The timing was perfect. Not only was she eager to escape her roommate, but the heat in her apartment had broken—again—and the idea of cozying up to a drink in front of a fireplace sounded like heaven.

She had just started to bundle up in the entranceway where she kept all her winter accessories when she heard Ben call out from the living room. He had started the nightly couch tradition without her.

"Hey, where are you headed off to?" He was in the doorway, hunched over with his arms wrapped around himself. Bundled up in a heavy sweater with a giant scarf wrapped around his neck, his voice was muffled.

He looked pretty cute, actually, but Caitlyn would never admit that. She could only imagine what would happen to his ego if she did. It was possible he would no longer be able to fit through any normal size doorway if it got any bigger.

"Meeting some friends at a bar," she said as she slipped into her thickest winter coat.

Ben's eyes widened and he stuck out his lower lip to give her a puppy dog look that was as pathetic as it was amusing. "Please take me with you."

Caitlyn laughed. "Aside from my friend's husband, it'll probably just be a bunch of women hanging around talking. You'd be bored out of your mind."

Ben looked offended. "It just so happens my favorite people to hang out with are women. Particularly large groups of attractive young women who are drinking their cares away on a frigid winter's eve."

Caitlyn rolled her eyes and started to protest, but he cut her off.

"As your tenant, you can't, in all good conscience, leave me alone here in this deathtrap and allow me to freeze to death. It wouldn't be right."

As though on cue, a draft blew through the ancient windowpanes, and Ben burrowed even further into his ridiculous scarf getup.

"Okay fine." Caitlyn laughed. "You can come along, but don't complain to me if you aren't having any fun."

Chapter 4

Ben couldn't remember the last time he'd had more fun.

Watching Caitlyn around her friends was like watching a sea monkey come to life. Gone was that polite but distant roommate he'd gotten used to annoying around the apartment. Her face was flushed from a mixture of warmth and liquor, and her eyes practically sparkled in the firelight as she regaled her friends with a funny story about one of the old ladies who frequents her morning class.

Caitlyn had been right that it was mostly women—out of the half dozen who'd gathered at the end of the bar, Ben was the only man aside from Meg's husband, Jake, who was tending bar, and the blonde woman's roommate, Marc.

Her friends' interest in him would have been flattering if he didn't have a sneaking suspicion they were interrogating him to make sure he wasn't a sociopath or an axe murderer. Their protectiveness toward Caitlyn was sweet, but their interrogation techniques were far from subtle.

They took turns, each rotating to sit next to him and pepper him with questions until it started to feel like he was speed dating her friends. He supposed he passed because by their second hour, he was fully integrated into the group's conversation and they seemed to go out of their way to make sure he was included, even when his views weren't exactly appreciated.

The blonde, Tamara, had given them all an update on her landlord's wicked desire to sell the old, rundown movie theater where she worked. Judging by the chorus of sighs and groans, everyone seemed pretty torn up about this, and it was possible he should have kept his mouth shut. In hindsight, he would have. Oh, who was he kidding? He would have opened his big fat mouth if just to watch Caitlyn's cheeks get all rosy with anger.

"It's easy to see where the owner is coming from, isn't it?" It was a rhetorical question, and it had all eyes on him…and not in a good way. He turned to his left to see Caitlyn staring up at him in wide-eyed horror like he'd just admitted to being a necrophiliac or something. "What? I'm just playing devil's advocate here."

"He's right," he heard Tamara mutter beneath her breath before taking a gulp of her drink.

Caitlyn ignored her and kept her eyes focused on him. "Why are you defending him?"

"I'm just saying, the owner has a point. It's his property and most people aren't in real estate for nostalgia's sake. They're in it for a profit. It's an investment." He would have continued because, for better or worse, investing was one of his favorite topics. But she cut him off with a hand in his face.

"So what, historical significance and neighborhood pride mean nothing? It's only about the money?"

He was dimly aware that her friends had stopped talking and were watching them. Something in their intensity told him he was treading on sacred ground.

"Of course not, but love of history can't be allowed to stand in the way of progress."

Caitlyn's eyes narrowed, and he was suddenly and intensely aware of the short distance that separated them. Their lips, more specifically. At that moment, he would have given just about anything to taste those lips. The chemistry between them was blinding. A sick form of torture in that tiny apartment, knowing she was near but untouchable. At night he'd lie awake imagining he could hear her breathing as she slept in her bed just down the hall. Naked. Well, probably not naked but a man could dream. But he'd kept his distance, despite the painful erection he'd been experiencing for the better part of a week. Aside from the fact that he'd royally offended her *that night*, she was so clearly not right for him.

First off, she was as straight-laced as they came. She practically screamed monogamy and children and all that crap—everything he'd sworn off ages ago. Maybe if she was up for a one-nighter…but no. He gave himself a mental shake. She wasn't that type of girl. Still, sitting there so close to her was killing him. Especially as the alcohol worked its magic, making the logical part of his brain quiet down so the primal section could be heard. And that primal section wanted relief.

Her lips were close. So close. The need to taste those lips was nearly overwhelming. He could lean in and close the distance so easily. For a moment he thought she felt it too. Her eyes darkened and her lips parted as the air between them grew thick with tension. But then she leaned back a bit and fixed him with a stern glare. "Stop talking before you make me hate you all over again."

Ben struggled not to laugh, and he saw her lips twitching as well. He loved tipsy Caitlyn. She was even more fun to tease than couchmate-Caitlyn. And couchmate-Caitlyn was ridiculously fun to tease. And hot. Holy hell, was his couchmate hot. Inexplicable, really, since he rarely saw her in anything other than her comfy, lounging around clothes and bereft of makeup. But somehow she still always looked hot. And touchable. Too damn touchable. The woman could wear a canvas sack and a mud mask on her face and he would be aroused.

He pulled his mind back before it could go any further. It was hard enough keeping his sanity when he was sitting next to her alone on the couch. He didn't need to have explicit images parading through his skull.

What were they talking about? Right. He slapped a hand over his heart as if her words had physically wounded him. "Caitlyn, my sweet, we've come so far from that first, dreadful date. I thought we were over all that."

A heavy silence hung in the air, and he watched Caitlyn's eyes widen with a mixture of amusement and—uh oh—horror.

"Wait a second, *this* is the date from hell?" For such a tiny woman, the pregnant one had a surprisingly loud voice.

Caitlyn kept eye contact with him as she winced. He gave her his best apologetic smile, and he caught a flicker of a smile in return. Thank God, she wasn't really angry.

Slowly turning to face the others, he stage whispered, "I didn't realize it was a secret."

"Obviously," Caitlyn whispered back, loudly enough for everyone to hear.

Her friends' astonished silence was broken by Marc and the blonde giggling. The pregnant one and the supermodel—her sister, he'd learned—were eying him with varying degrees of curiosity and animosity.

The knockout with the red hair and green eyes looked far more amused than her sister as she shot him a saucy wink. "I can't believe this is the guy you were complaining about. He could spill his drink on me any day of the week."

Ben had to laugh at her outrageously flirty tone as she eyed him like a piece of candy. She was gorgeous, there was no doubt, but there was something standoffish about her. She was the type of woman he would typically go for—the type that screamed worldly, sophisticated, and just out for a good time. But he hadn't given her more than a glance since the moment they'd arrived. He'd been too focused on his roommate.

Holy hell, what was wrong with him? Clearly Olivia had done more of a number on him than he'd thought. That train of thought was cut short as he found himself the topic of conversation, as though he wasn't sitting *right there*.

"You never mentioned how good looking he was," Marc said just before his roommate threw a hand over his mouth to stop him from talking any more. He caught her shooting Caitlyn a look of empathetic alarm.

"That's not true," the pregnant one said. "She *did* say he was hot."

He turned in his seat to face Caitlyn, whose face was bright red. "Really," he drawled. "She said that?"

The redhead rolled her eyes. "I wouldn't get too excited. She also said you were obnoxious, stuck up, and... What was it, Meg?" She looked to her sister.

"A buffoon," Meg said.

Ben tapped a finger to his chin, pretending to think that over. "All true, I'm afraid."

Marc had managed to unpeel the blonde's hand from his mouth and chimed in. "Even if he is all those things, he's still better than Robert."

Robert? Who the hell was Robert? The name brought on an irrational but primitive wave of possessiveness.

And apparently he wasn't the only one who had a reaction to the name. At the mention of Robert, he noticed that all four women turned to glare at Marc while his roommate swatted his shoulder roughly. Marc held his hands up in mock surrender. "Okay, okay, I'm just saying...."

"And on that note," Caitlyn said a little too loudly as she shot up out of her seat, "we're out of here."

Ben had to hustle to keep up with her as she gathered her belongings and made a hasty retreat. Whoever the hell Robert was, the mere mention of his name was enough to kill a party.

* * * *

Ben followed her out of the bar and into the cold, dark night—but when he stopped at the curb to hail a taxi, she took a sharp right and trudged through the snow toward the next intersection.

"Don't you want to cab it?" Ben called after her.

"No."

"Okay then, I guess we're walking." He jogged to catch up with her.

She looked over in surprise as he joined her. "You don't have to walk with me."

"Well I couldn't in all good conscience allow you to walk home alone when I'm heading to the same place."

He was struck dumb by the sudden smile she turned on him. Good God, she was gorgeous when she smiled.

"How very gentlemanly of you," she said. Her brown eyes were shining up at him in the glow of the streetlamps.

He pretended to tip his imaginary hat. "At your service, m'lady."

Her soft laughter hit him with a physical force. He loved that sound.

"Just call me Archie Leach," he joked.

She literally stopped in her tracks to gape at him. "I can't believe you just said that."

"Impressed I know Cary Grant's real name?" He shrugged. "I told you in our e-mails that I was a fan of old movies. That was the conversation starter, remember?"

She was looking at him as though he'd grown a second head. "So that was real?"

Of course it was real. He'd loved the e-mail exchanges they'd shared before *that night*. In the dark days following the breakup, those lighthearted e-mails about classic movies and other trivial topics had been a saving grace. What did she think, that he tasked his assistant with e-mailing the hot chicks on the dating site? Not a bad idea, really.

She shook her head and fell into step beside him. "Sometimes it's hard to reconcile all the different sides of you."

As someone who considered himself a pretty straightforward guy, he had no idea what to make of that statement, so he chose to ignore it.

"That's why I e-mailed you in the first place, you know."

She blinked her beautiful brown eyes up at him in confusion. A stray curl peeked out from beneath her hat, and he itched to tuck it back in. He shoved his gloved hand into his jacket pocket.

"Your reference to Cary Grant on your page," he explained. "That's what caught my eye. I read that and I thought... I'm your guy."

"Ha!" Her laugh was clearly mocking, but her smile was intoxicating. He would never tire of making her smile.

But he pretended to take offense at her laughter. "I'll have you know women are constantly comparing me to classic movie stars. I've gotten Clark Gable, Erroll Flynn..."

She paused for a moment to size him up, as though giving it serious thought. "Clark Gable, maybe. Definitely not Cary Grant."

"Fine, oh wise one. And what, pray tell, does Cary Grant have that I do not?"

She sighed wistfully and tilted her head to the side as she considered. "He's funny—"

"I'm funny."

"You're sarcastic."

"Cary Grant was totally sarcastic."

"He was sardonic," she corrected.

"Okay, what else?"

"He's modest, self-deprecating—"

Here he had to intervene. "And that's what you think you want in a man?" He shook his head. "Believe me, you have more than enough modesty for one couple. You could use someone with some bravado. Next."

"He needs to be charming, elegant. Classy."

He stopped to turn and face her, and pointed toward himself. "Check, check, and check."

Caitlyn gave him a deadpan look before turning to walk away.

He jogged a bit to catch up with her. "All right, what else do you need in your perfect man? This is interesting stuff."

She looked up at him and those brilliant, expressive eyes were dazzling in the light of the streetlamp. For a moment he couldn't breathe.

"How did this get to be about me and my perfect man?" she asked.

"You deserve to find him." When she gave him a questioning look, he hurried on. "Your Cary Grant, I mean. You deserve that."

He glanced over and saw her staring at him with an indefinable look in her eyes. Confusion mixed with something stronger, deeper. He looked away quickly and forced a lighter tone. "If it's Cary Grant you want, then that's what you'll get. Nothing is too good for my roomie."

"So you're going to help find my Mr. Right now?" she asked.

"Honey, I could be your Mr. Right Now," he said with an exaggerated wiggle of his eyebrows that had the desired effect of making her laugh. "But yes, that is exactly what I intend to do. Trust me, I am way better at picking online dates than you are."

"I've only gone out with you so far," she protested.

"My point exactly." He glanced at her out of the corner of his eye. "Just look how well that date turned out."

She pretended to think that over before giving him a serious look. "You're right. I need help."

They walked in silence for a moment before she spoke again. "Can I ask you something? Why did you really reach out to me on that dating site? I mean, aside from the Cary Grant reference."

"Easy. Your picture. I thought you were hot."

She rolled her eyes, and he wondered for the millionth time if she had any idea just how beautiful she was. They walked in companionable silence for a bit before she asked him with unexpected gravity. "Seriously, Ben, why did you pick me? Why did you e-mail me in the first place?"

Oh man, she really had no idea. The fact that she clearly didn't was equally adorable and heartbreaking.

"I *am* serious. You're gorgeous." He paused for a moment, and then the words came out of his mouth of their own volition. "And if I really wanted to overanalyze, I'd probably say it was because you seemed like the exact opposite of my ex."

She glanced over, her eyes filled with surprise that he was fairly sure matched his own. *Where had that come from?*

"How so?"

He shrugged, wishing he'd never brought up the topic in the first place. "Because you're so…*sweet*."

She recoiled as though he'd slapped her. "I hate that word."

He had to laugh at her vehement reaction. She was, after all, the walking definition of sweetness. A soft-spoken, kindhearted artistic soul who spent her free time painstakingly knitting a family heirloom for a little old lady? The woman was bloody Mother Theresa. "What's wrong with being called sweet?"

Her answer was a huffy sigh.

The streetlamp above cast her face in a warm glow and she was an open book. She was frustrated but trying not to admit it. Now he was really intrigued.

She shook her head with a laugh that sounded forced. "I guess I've got some ex baggage too."

He feigned shock. "The ex thought you were sweet? What a bastard."

Her laugh made him want to burst into song like he was a character in some goddamn musical. What the hell was it with her?

There was a hint of self-deprecating laughter in her voice when she said, "No, he thought I was boring."

Now it was his turn to flinch at the blasé way she said the words—as though she believed it.

He placed a hand on her arm to stop her, and she turned to face him, her eyes wide with a questioning look and her lips…oh Lord, her lips. He wanted to kiss her so badly his whole body ached. He would press her soft curves against him and kiss her until she was moaning with desire. *Get it together, man.*

He actually had to clear his throat to make words come out. "You do know you're not boring, right?"

Her smile was mocking and he hated it. "I sit around and knit all night so, you know…not exactly the life of the party over here."

Before he could protest, she continued on. "Anyway, I thought he was happy. Or content, at least."

"But he wasn't?"

One corner of her mouth turned up in a pale imitation of a smile. Her tone was flat. "He wasn't."

It was physically painful to see the joy drain from her expression, her eyes losing their spark. Her ex had done that to her. He'd clearly broken her heart. They continued walking before Ben asked, "Were *you* happy?"

For a moment he thought she wasn't going to answer, but then she said, "I was content."

He wanted to punch her ex in the throat for the sad look that crossed her face. He'd bet all his money the ex in question was the Robert whose mere name made Caitlyn deflate earlier at the bar.

He hated emotional moments, so for lack of anything better to say, he mumbled, "I'm sorry."

She glanced over quickly and then looked away. "It's okay. It was hard at first, but then I realized that he was probably doing me a favor. I mistook comfort for love."

"I did the exact opposite. I mistook passion for love." Did he really just say that out loud? She had some sort of Barbara Walters effect on him, apparently, because he was talking to her like she was his bloody psychiatrist.

She was looking up at him with an impish grin that made it nearly impossible to keep his hands to himself. "That sounds way more fun."

He let out a surprised laugh at that. "Maybe at first, but passion in the bedroom quickly turned into passionate fighting. We're talking plates thrown against the wall, waterworks in very public places, the works."

Her eyes widened. "That sounds awful."

"The worst part was, it was addictive. I got used to the drama and so did she. After a while, it felt like, if we got too comfortable, she got antsy. She couldn't just enjoy being together." Probably because they'd had nothing to talk about when they weren't fighting. God, that was depressing.

Caitlyn's quiet voice cut into his thoughts. "Did she end it?"

He took a deep breath. The memory of her betrayal still stung, but he forced a casual tone. "I guess technically I'm the one that ended it. Although sleeping with my friend from work had a good deal to do with it."

Caitlyn's gasp of outrage was sweet. No, not sweet, he corrected himself. It was heartening.

They'd reached the front door to her apartment building, and she turned to look up at him with such concern, it made his heart ache. When was the last time anyone had looked at him like that?

"I'm sorry she hurt you," she said. The words so simple and so natural coming out of that beautiful mouth. He thought she would turn to open the door, but her brows furrowed together and her eyes locked with his. "Are you okay?"

And there it was, the question that no one bothered to ask him—not even his friends and family. He deflected their concern with quips and sarcastic remarks and they rolled their eyes and dropped the subject. But here, now, this little beauty had asked the question that had the power to cripple him. *Are you okay?*

No. Not really.

Her hand slipped right through his chainmail armor and rested on his arm, and he lost all rational thought. The kind concern in her eyes was a drug, and he had the sudden and intense desire to spill his guts to her—to confess every sin and have her kiss away every pain. She was reaching behind her to open the door, but she still held his gaze, and those gorgeous, pouty lips were undeniable.

He leaned in slowly, giving her a chance to back away, but she continued to stare at him as though hypnotized. And then his lips covered hers and he was lost to the feel of those soft lips parting beneath his own with just the tiniest nudge on his part. Her sweet warm breath mingled with his as he deepened the kiss. The little moan she let out was more than he could bear. Any sense of decorum fled the building, and he pulled her against him with one arm while opening the door with his free hand.

They stumbled in through the doorway and he pressed her up against the closed door, kissing her jaw and nipping at her ear as he fumbled to remove her scarf and jacket. He wanted to kiss more of her, see more of her. Oh God, he wanted to feel all of her.

They were both panting for air when her hands cupped his face and drew his lips back to her own.

Chapter 5

Caitlyn lost any hope for coherent thought. She dragged his lips back to meet hers like she was drowning and needed his air to breathe. She *was* drowning. She couldn't get enough of his lips, his tongue, those hands, which were trying to touch her through the thick layers of winter bundling. She wanted to help him shed the clothes but couldn't do anything but kiss him. It was incredible. His lips were strong, almost possessive, as he pressed against her and his tongue teased hers, drawing her out, making her ache.

He pulled back briefly and she bit back a moan of disappointment.

"Want to fuck?"

The words were like ice water in her face. "What?"

His fingers were tugging at the zipper of her jacket, trying to free her from the thick layers of winter.

"Want to fuck?" he repeated, his breath hot and heavy.

He leaned back in to resume kissing, but she jerked away. When he tried again, she pushed him back and watched his eyes widen in surprise.

"What's wrong?"

Want to fuck?! Speechless, Caitlyn gaped at him before pushing him out of her way and heading toward her bedroom.

"Caitlyn, wait," he started. But she was halfway to her room and in the middle of a battle between desire and fury. Fury won out as she cut off his next protest with a gesture she had seen a million times but never actually done.

She flipped him the bird.

There was a brief moment of stunned silence, and Caitlyn experienced a surge of furious triumph. But then his loud guffaw of laughter followed her into her bedroom. She could still hear him laughing as she slammed the door behind her.

The nerve of that guy. She fumed over those words as she got ready for bed. *Want to fuck?* Like she was the kind of girl who just slept with whatever random guy was camping out in her spare bedroom.

Why not? You're a grown woman, you can sleep with whomever you like.

She scowled at her reflection in the mirror. Sure she'd thought he was hot from day one, but she'd never contemplated sleeping with the guy. Or fucking him, as he so charmingly put it.

Her traitorous brain flashed on a memory from the night before when his thigh had brushed up against hers. Despite the flannel of her pajamas and the completely unsexy reality TV show they were watching, she'd gotten so turned on she'd been thoroughly uncomfortable for the rest of the night.

But physical attraction aside, she hadn't seriously considered sleeping with him. And she couldn't really be considering his offer now. She was not that kind of girl. She'd only ever slept with two men, both of whom she was in a committed relationship with.

And look where that's gotten you—single, lonely, and painfully horny.

Not to mention heartbroken. Besides, what if she didn't *want* a relationship with the man, but that man happened to make her so turned on she could barely breathe? Because she most certainly did not want a relationship with Ben, even if he was interested. Which he clearly wasn't. But if he was…

He was still a rude, annoying bastard, Caitlyn concluded. Ex baggage aside, he was the living definition of the kind of macho alpha males she despised. He drank too much and cursed too much and always thought he knew what was best for everything and everyone around him.

They would be miserable together and probably end up killing each other if they ever went on a second date. She unclasped her necklace and took out her earrings, getting ready to go to bed. Alone. After inhaling deeply, she blew out the air forcefully, hoping to dispel some of the sexual tension that had her on edge.

It was decided. He was Mr. Wrong. No amount of perfect kisses would sway her opinion on the man.

But those kisses had been perfect. Just thinking about it made her heart race and the aching throb between her thighs deepen.

But if it was just sex… She could practically hear Alice's voice in her ear, the devil on her shoulder. *You need to get laid.* Maybe Alice had been right. Crap, maybe Ben had been right when he'd said the very same thing. She would be the first to admit that she'd been in something of a rut ever since Robert walked out on her.

And Ben wanted to sleep with her. It wasn't like hot guys were falling over themselves to proposition her. Would it really be so bad to have some fun before she gave up on dating and locked herself up in a nunnery?

Clearly there would be no strings attached, no big talks about where they were headed, no...*emotions*. Maybe it wasn't such a ludicrous idea after all.

It was those thoughts that kept her up half the night, tossing and turning as she battled with frustration and temptation. But while that line of reasoning was all fine and good in the dark quiet of her bedroom, in the cold light of day, Caitlyn was horrified anew.

How could she have even contemplated sleeping with her roommate? Temporary roommate but still, a roommate. Talk about asking for disaster. If one of her friends came to her asking for her advice on this same situation, she would tell them to run in the opposite direction and don't look back. It was bad enough that they'd already gone on a date from hell, but add sex into the equation and this little truce they had going would be over. She was still healing from a horrible break up and so was he.... The last thing either of them needed was another complication.

Besides, she had kind of gotten used to having him as a roommate—although his slobby tendencies hadn't gotten any better. But he was easy to be around other than that. Why mess with a good thing?

Still... That next morning, Caitlyn warily left her bedroom. Not that she thought Ben was going to pounce on her or anything but she had no idea how she was supposed to act. She'd never once made out with a roommate before, temporary or otherwise. She'd also never had one ask her if she wanted to fuck.

Maybe her life was pretty boring after all.

She had no idea how she was supposed to act, or what she was supposed to say. Alice would know what to do. Of course, Alice would have slept with the hottie roommate his first night in the apartment and not given it a second thought.

Why couldn't she be more like that? Embrace excitement and say to hell with the consequences. Because she was a dowdy old stick-in-the-mud, apparently.

She managed to make it through her morning routine without running into him. As she quietly slipped out the front door, she closed it behind her with a sigh. That wasn't so bad.

That was how she would deal with this. She wouldn't deal at all. There were only a few weeks left until he was out of her life for good. Until then, she'd avoid him—and avoid temptation.

* * * *

She was avoiding him and it drove Ben nuts. They hadn't been roommates for long but long enough to know that Caitlyn was a creature of habit—particularly when it came to eating and knitting, the two functions that were apparently critical for her survival.

First, she'd skipped her typical breakfast that morning—he'd heard her scramble to leave the apartment before he had a chance to leave his bedroom. Then she failed to come home for dinner between work and teaching, which she always did—she'd told him so herself. And then, when she finally came home, she'd scurried past the living room where he was camped out next to her giant basket of knitting supplies. She'd mumbled something about being exhausted after a long day. Yeah, right.

Had he offended her that badly? Or was she so turned off by his advances that she couldn't face him? He could still hear the sexy little noises she made while he was kissing her and feel her fingers holding him tight. No, she had definitely not been immune to the chemistry.

He shifted on the couch as his erection strained against his jeans. God, he really needed to stop thinking about that kiss or he would never be able to be seen in public.

It had been two days since he'd had more than just a glimpse of his sweet, curvy roomie, and he hated to admit how on edge he was. He'd offended her, that much was clear. But that had never been his intention. The fact that he could unknowingly hurt a woman like Caitlyn is exactly why he never dated women like her. He'd spent his childhood watching his asshole of a father wear down his kindhearted mother. Aside from the fact that he had a work ethic and didn't gamble all of his money away, he'd turned out just like the old man. But he'd be damned if he ruined everything and everyone good around him like his dad had done. And Caitlyn was good...too good. She was too sensitive, too emotional, too...good for him. He knew it, and she knew it. But good Lord what he wouldn't give for one night to finish what they'd started.

There was no doubt in his mind that a night with Caitlyn would be unforgettable. The way her pale skin would look as he peeled off her clothing, her brown wavy hair fanned out on his pillow, those wide eyes glazed over with desire as he brought her to climax—

He shifted in his seat again. Focus, for the love of God. She clearly wasn't interested in a cheap, casual affair—or anything more, as far as he could tell. But he hated to think that he had hurt her feelings...or worse, made her feel uncomfortable in her own home. Which meant they had to talk. He needed to clear the air.

His ex would laugh hysterically if she knew that he actually wanted to talk. How many times had he made lame excuses to avoid talking about their feelings, and now here he was plotting a touchy-feely intervention.

His new roommate would be the end of him.

When she returned home from the store that night, he was ready.

She was about to breeze right past him in the living room, but then she did a double take and came to a stop.

"What is that?"

"What does it look like?"

Her lips pulled to the side in a cute display of annoyance that he was becoming all too familiar with. What was it about Caitlyn that made teasing her so damn fun?

"It looks like a space heater," she said.

"Bingo, give the girl a prize."

She was outright scowling now. "Space heaters aren't allowed in this apartment."

"Why not?"

"Safety reasons, I guess. I don't know, I just know it's not allowed."

"I don't think landlords are allowed to freeze their tenants to death, so I'd say we're even. Besides, who's going to tell?"

She gnawed on her lip, clearly at a loss for an answer. He was right and she knew it. But she still wasn't taking the bait.

He leaned in even closer to the offensive object in question and made a show of warming his hands.

She wrapped her arms around herself and gazed at the heater with longing. "I was just going to, uh, read in my bedroom."

"Suit yourself, but if you find yourself getting too cold in there, you're welcome to share my heat."

There were so many dirty jokes that were dying to come out of his mouth, but he resisted the urge. He needed to be on his best behavior if he was going to put Caitlyn at ease. Her comfort mattered to him, though he couldn't exactly explain why he cared quite so much. But there it was. He didn't want to be the person who hurt her. And if he ever found out that someone else had hurt her… Well, he was fairly certain that person wouldn't stand a chance in a fight.

She held out for a millisecond longer, shifting from foot to foot as she eyed the heater with obvious longing. Finally caving, she came to sit beside him on the couch.

She leaned in next to him to get closer to the space heater, and he could smell the soft lavender of her shampoo and… Was that whisky?

"Oh, that feels so good," she breathed.

He had the sudden and intense desire to pull her into his arms and pick up where they'd left off the other night. Sitting back against the cushions, he tried to get a little distance.

"So about the other night," he started.

He could see her shoulders stiffen and her lips tighten into a thin line.

"I just wanted to apologize."

Her shoulders eased a tiny bit.

"I shouldn't have kissed you like that. I'd had too much to drink and didn't mean for that to happen. I'm sorry, it won't happen again."

She turned to look at him then and she looked...hurt? No, that couldn't be right. "You're sorry for kissing me?"

The pained look in her eyes was a punch in the gut. Ah shit, he'd said the wrong thing. "Look, I swear I won't kiss you again if that's—"

"I wasn't mad because you kissed me," she interrupted.

Well, okay then. Thoroughly confused, he tried to make sense of her answer. *Did that mean she'd liked the kiss?* At that hopeful thought, he found himself staring at her lips and fighting the urge to lean in to taste her. *Did that mean he could do it again?*

"I was angry because of what you said," she finished.

He blinked at her like an idiot. What he'd said? What had he said?

"You asked me if I wanted to...fuck." Her cheeks turned a neon shade of pink at the word, and it took everything in him not to laugh at her discomfort. Her eyes narrowed on him and it was clear she was not amused by his amusement.

He threw his hands up in surrender. "Look, I'm sorry, I really am. I didn't mean to offend you. I just got carried away in the moment, and I thought you wanted the same thing."

"I did." Her cheeks turned flaming red in a heartbeat.

They were both shocked into a momentary silence at that.

If Ben had been uncomfortable with desire before at the sight of her lips, hearing her confess that she'd wanted him just about put him over the edge. His fingers dug into the arm of the couch to keep from touching her.

"You did," he repeated. *What the hell?* "So what's the problem?"

"It wasn't the fact that you asked, it was the way you asked." Frustration laced her voice.

Ah, so that was it. His big, crude mouth had gotten him into trouble yet again.

She gave a little huff of annoyance that she had to spell it out. "No woman wants to be asked like that."

"So what should I have said?" He couldn't help it, winding her up was just too much fun.

She shifted uncomfortably on the couch. "I don't know, but you shouldn't have used the F-word."

"So what do you want me to call sex?"

She flinched a bit at the word. "I don't know…making love?"

He widened his eyes and backed away, pretending to be alarmed. "Love? Caitlyn, are you telling me that you *love* me?"

She shot him a look. "Don't be an idiot. I don't even like you."

He bit the corner of his mouth to keep from laughing aloud. It was almost too easy.

"Stop laughing at me."

"Who's laughing? Not me, definitely not me." She moved to turn away from him, but he caught her hand and they both stilled. Sweet Jesus, he'd never felt such instant electricity before. Just holding her hand was a turn on.

"Ben." His name came out on a sigh, and he wanted to hear her say it again. He was desperate to hear her say it in the throes of passion. He leaned in slowly, giving her every chance to pull away.

Her lips were tantalizingly close when she stopped him.

"Wait, I—"

Fighting against the overwhelming gravitational force that was pulling him toward her, he backed off enough to see her face.

She looked worried. Shit.

"It's just that—" she started and stopped.

What was he doing? He was supposed to be apologizing, making her feel safe and comfortable in her own home, and what does he do? He comes on to her *again*.

"I don't know if it's a good idea," she continued. Her hands were toying with the edge of her jacket, and her gaze wouldn't meet his.

Of course she didn't. This was not the kind of woman who casually slept around; everything about her screamed monogamy. She deserved to have a real relationship with a great guy. A much better guy than him. She was right to not settle for less.

Ben moved away from the siren and forced a grin. "Don't sweat it."

"If we were to do this…." Her mouth opened and closed as if words failed her. Putting her out of her misery, he reached to grab the remote and end the conversation. He didn't need her to spell out all the reasons why sleeping with your roommate was a bad idea. Of course it was a bad idea—that was his M.O. He was aching for a no-strings-attached affair to help get his mind off the traitorous bitch who'd betrayed him. But Caitlyn was most certainly not the one. She deserved far more than a quick roll in the hay with a guy who was slated to leave her life in a few weeks.

When it looked as though she'd given up on having *the talk* and settled back on the couch beside him, he glanced over and noticed that she was still bundled up in her winter jacket and accessories.

He plucked the bright red hat from her head and studied it. "This is gorgeous, did you make it?"

Her eyes lit up and all trace of awkward conversations went out the window. "I did. Actually, I designed it."

He studied the hat again, this time taking note of the intricate cable design. "Impressive."

She took it back from him and plopped it back on her head. "Hats are easy."

Her cheeks were still flushed from the cold, and her eyes were bright now that they were talking about a topic that excited her.

"What else have you designed?"

She shrugged and looked to the ceiling as she compiled a list. "A couple of sweaters, some shawls, a whole lot of hats. I'm working on a baby sweater at the moment."

"That's incredible."

She shot him a wary look, clearly worried he was teasing her.

"I mean it, that's really impressive. Do you sell these patterns?"

She rolled her eyes, but she was still smiling. "Why does it always come down to money for you?"

"Because that's my job," he said, a touch too defensive. He'd never felt the need to defend his deep-seated desire to make money until this woman. Growing up in a struggling household, he'd learned at an early age that financial security was what mattered most—it meant being independent, not having to rely on others. That kind of security was what his father had always strived for—but his failure to get ahead had fueled his resentment when it came to Ben's mother and their family. Thanks to Ben's drive and hard work, he would never end up like that.

Most people admired his tenacity in business. But somehow this one made money sound like a bad word. He tugged on her hat in a teasing gesture. "Besides, I'll be moving out at the end of the month, and someone has to pay for all this." He gestured around the small apartment as though it was a spacious home and she laughed.

He found himself grinning like an idiot at the sound.

"Don't worry, I'll find another subletter and will manage to make ends meet. I always do."

A nagging fear forced him to ask. "Another man?"

She gave him a questioning look. And rightfully so, the reptilian portion of his brain had apparently seized control, and it seriously impeded his speaking abilities. He cleared his throat and tried again. "I mean, you're going to get another strange man in here to share the apartment?" Not better, really.

Her brows drew together and the laughter fell from her tone. "I use a respectable site and I do reference checks."

He literally bit his tongue to keep from protesting further. He made a mental note to get the name of this next subletter and do his own background check. Especially if it was a man.

This particular brand of possessiveness was foreign to Ben, and he was not at all sure he liked it. He watched her profile and was momentarily overwhelmed with a feeling he couldn't quite describe. Tenderness, maybe.

What was wrong with him? If one thing was clear, it was that this woman was not his type. She deserved someone who would treat her right, someone who had a good heart, a stable job, and who believed in stuff like family and marriage and till-death-do-us-part. She deserved someone who would take care of her and be a gentleman.

Holy shit. She deserved Cary-bloody-Grant.

That thought made him choke on a laugh, and she turned to him with a suspicious look. "What are you laughing at?"

"You," he teased.

She raised her brows in a look he was becoming all too familiar with. It said, "You may be certifiable but at least you're amusing."

He loved that look.

* * * *

Caitlyn was beyond relieved that the tension had lifted. There was nothing worse than feeling anxious in your own home.

So why was she so utterly disappointed?

It was stupid. It was irrational. But she couldn't help it. She was truly bummed. And all because Ben had respected her wishes.

It's not like she really wanted to get involved in a casual fling with her roommate. That sounded like a bad decision in so many ways. But he could have at least *tried* to convince her. Irrational disappointment left a hollow pit in her stomach.

She tried to ignore it as she and Ben settled into their nightly routine, catching up on each other's workday while she knitted and he flipped through the channels incessantly like a child with ADD.

Typically she could drown out any anxious thoughts or inner monologue by zoning out with her latest knitting project. But, try as she might, she spent the entire evening stewing over Ben's words.

Don't sweat it. That's what he'd said. First of all, it sounded like a bad catch phrase from the 80s. She's propositioned for the first time in her life, and when she turns him down, she gets something that sounds like a freakin' Nike slogan?

What was she getting so worked up about? *She* was the one who'd said no.

But she hadn't said no. Not really. Not yet. And he could have tried to persuade her.

What was she thinking? Did she really want her roommate to be pushing her into sex? Of course not.

Maybe.

She watched him out of the corner of her eye as he laughed at the late night host's opening monologue. He was attractive. There was no denying it. And more, he was sexy as hell. That devil-may-care cocky attitude was annoying, but it definitely added to his roguish appeal. Obviously he wasn't long-term boyfriend material—he was so clearly not Mr. Right.

But he would make an excellent Mr. Right Now.

Caitlyn bit her lip to keep from laughing out loud. She had been spending far too much time with her roommate.

Pulling the yarn a little tighter than necessary, Caitlyn gave herself a stern lecture. She should be relieved that he let the topic go so easily. Sure, it had felt a little scandalous to be thought of as a sexual object for a couple days. All right, it had felt kind of awesome. It wasn't every day she was hit on by a hot guy. But she wasn't that kind of woman—she wasn't the femme fatale, she was the girl next door. And that was fine by her. She would meet a guy—someone like her ex—who shared her values and her lifestyle, and she would go back to being in a stable and safe relationship.

She yawned and Ben noticed. "You bored? I can change the channel."

She shook her head. "Just tired. I should head to bed, but this heater feels so good."

He looked at her like she was crazy. "What kind of asshole do you think I am? I got you a heater of your own—it's in your bedroom."

Her chest grew painfully tight at the unexpected thoughtfulness and she stared at him for a moment in surprise. For a self-declared bastard, Ben could be incredibly sweet. "Thank you."

His lip pulled up in a lopsided grin that made her breath catch in her throat. "You're welcome."

As she gathered her knitting supplies and wished him good night, it occurred to her that Ben may be a cad and a jerk, but he was also turning out to be a friend.

Chapter 6

The next day was Saturday, which meant Caitlyn was at The Ellen at the crack of dawn to meet her friends for their bi-monthly "Operation Petticoat" gathering.

Meg and Jake were already there and hard at work by the time she arrived. To be fair though, they lived above the bar, which was next door, so they just had to walk down some stairs to get there.

Tamara walked in after her, followed closely by Marc, who looked worse for the wear. "Rough night, buddy?" Jake called.

Marc muttered something about never drinking again before curling up with a coffee in the corner. Tamara, as usual, was ready for business. She grabbed a ladder and some tools and started on the molding above the theater entrance, which was sagging noticeably.

"Where's Alice?" Caitlyn asked.

"My baby sis is late. As usual," Meg grumbled. It was hard to take her annoyance too seriously when she looked like a pregnant elf. Her brown curls bobbed around her rosy cheeks as she scrubbed a particularly nasty bit of grime off the glass counter of the concession stand.

"So where's Ben today?" Meg asked.

Startled, Caitlyn looked up. How had Meg known she'd been thinking about him? She felt like she'd been caught with her hand in the cookie jar. She shrugged. "Sleeping, I presume."

"You didn't invite the hottie roommate?" Marc called from his hiding spot.

"To help clean an old theater at seven AM on a Saturday?" she answered.

"I bet he would have come." That came from Tamara who normally kept her opinions to herself. But now she was giving Caitlyn a knowing smile. That girl heard more than she let on, Caitlyn would swear to it.

Caitlyn could feel the telltale heat coming into her cheeks, and Meg did not miss it. "What's going on with the two of you?"

Caitlyn kept her gaze firmly focused on the spot of floor she was cleaning where someone had spilled a soda. "What do you mean?"

When she glanced up, Meg raised an eyebrow in her classic "oh please, don't even try to lie to me" face.

Caitlyn pursed her lips before spilling it with a heavy sigh. "We kissed."

Marc's propped up feet fell from the chair with a loud thud, and even Tamara stopped working long enough to stare at her with blatant curiosity.

Meg's look was so ecstatic anyone walking into the room would think she'd just won the lottery. "Get out!"

Jake had just walked back into the lobby and stopped at the sight of his wife's excitement. "What's going on?"

"Caitlyn and Ben are doing it," Marc answered.

Caitlyn gasped. "We are not!"

Jake's grin was as big as his wife's. "Well all right, Caitie-kins. Good for you."

Caitlyn's face couldn't get any hotter if she was burned alive. "We are not 'doing it.' It was a kiss. Just a kiss."

Just an amazingly hot, can't-stop-thinking-about-it, once-in-a-lifetime kiss.

"I knew it," a sultry voice said from the doorway. "He was totally into you."

Cold air blew in from behind Alice, giving her auburn curls a model-in-front-of-a-fan quality. *Alice.* Now there was a woman men fantasized about. She was the kind of sexy, experienced woman a guy like Ben wanted. It was just his bad luck that Alice lived alone in a studio and he was shacked up with the dried-up spinster of the group.

"I don't believe it was just a kiss," Meg said. "I saw the way he was looking at you the other night."

"Yeah, like you were a gourmet feast and he was gonna eat you up," Marc said.

Caitlyn rolled her eyes. God bless her friends—her well-intentioned, too kind friends. They were forever trying to boost her ego, particularly since the breakup.

"So what do you think, Caitlyn? Are you guys going to get hot and heavy?" Meg asked.

Caitlyn tried to ignore their fascinated stares. She supposed it was rather extraordinary that their plain, bookish friend had some romantic interest going on. They heard about Alice and Marc's adventures in love every other day but for Caitlyn, this was a phenomenon on par with snow in July.

"He's not my type," she ended up saying.

Marc made a sputtering noise as though he was too outraged to speak. "Not your type? Not your *type*?"

"He's too…" Caitlyn groped for the right word. "Manly."

Alice dropped her coat over a chair as she settled in next to Marc to watch the others work. "Oh no, not *manly*," she teased.

Caitlyn laughed as she tried to defend her logic. "I'm not saying he's not—"

"Hot," Marc provided.

"Sexy," Tamara called from her perch on a ladder.

"Fine, yes, he's…" She waved her hand in vague gesture. "He's all of those things. But you guys know me. That's not the kind of guy I'm looking for. I want someone who has long-term potential, someone who's—"

"Ugly?" Alice finished.

"Asexual," Jake offered.

"Boring!" Marc called out.

They were all laughing at that point and Caitlyn shut her mouth with weary resignation. What was the use?

"Speaking of boring," Meg said, fidgeting in her seat. "Robert came into the bar last night."

Caitlyn froze. The mood in the room shifted from lighthearted teasing to awkward silence as everyone waited to see Caitlyn's reaction to her ex's name. She had to admit that she'd overreacted just a tad when his name had come up the other night. Talking about Robert in front of Ben had seemed awkward. Besides, she'd been having fun and she hadn't wanted the memory of Robert to ruin it.

But now, Ben wasn't around, and the familiar curiosity that nagged at her whenever he was mentioned came rippling to the surface.

"Oh?" Caitlyn thought she did a fairly good job of looking nonplussed, but her friends were still acting like the room was carpeted with eggshells.

"Why would he come to Cagney's of all places?" Tamara said the words that Caitlyn was thinking.

Meg didn't answer. Caitlyn knew her friend well, however, and noticed that she was concentrating too hard on her grimy spot and her tone was forced casual. There was more to this story.

"And?" Caitlyn prompted.

Meg bit her lip before blurting it out. "He was with Becca."

"Becca," Caitlyn repeated. A lightbulb went off. "Becca, as in the bartender from Coppersmith's on Sixth Avenue?" It was one of the bars they frequented when Jake and Meg wanted a break from Cagney's.

At Meg's wary nod, Caitlyn did her best to hide her shock. "They were…together?" She had a picture of Becca with her cropped tank top and cleavage spilling out as she leaned over to refill their drinks. Surely not…

"They're engaged."

The blood drained from her head, making her lightheaded and nauseous at once. The words echoed off the walls, and the silence that followed was deafening. Until everyone started talking at once.

"I am so sorry to tell you like this. I just didn't know how you would react and—"

"It's fine," Caitlyn interrupted. The others stopped trash-talking Robert and Becca at the sound of her voice.

For her part, Caitlyn was surprised to hear her voice coming out so calm and collected when her insides were in the middle of rearranging themselves into a conga line.

"It is?" Marc asked. They were all looking at her like they didn't believe her.

"It is. It's fine," she said, with a bit more enthusiasm than was warranted. She forced a shrug. "It's been nearly a year since he—" *Since he walked out on me.* "Since we broke up. Of course he's moving on. Why shouldn't he?"

Silence.

"Yeah, but why take her to Cagney's?" Tamara's quiet voice asked.

Excellent question. But she didn't want to think about the possible answers so she forced a shrug. "Why not? He lives in the neighborhood, and he always liked the vibe there."

Why not? Because it's *my* bar and Meg and Jake are *my* friends. You can't break up with the girl and keep the perks, it didn't work like that. But apparently no one told Robert.

All eyes were on her, so Caitlyn grabbed the mop and bucket and continued to clean the floor with remarkable energy. When the others followed her lead and got back to cleaning a few seconds later, she turned to Meg. Of all the churning emotions, curiosity was taking the lead. "What did he say?"

Meg kept her voice low so the others couldn't hear. "Oh, he was his usual uptight self."

"Meg—" Her voice held a warning. She wanted honesty, not her friend's sugarcoated version of events.

"He asked about you."

"And? What did you say?"

Meg shrugged. "I told him you were good—the same."

The same. The words stung more than Meg would ever know. Caitlyn knew her friend hadn't intended to hurt her, but sometimes the truth hurt. She was the same. She was still working at the same dead-end job, living in the same apartment, watching the same old movies with the same group of friends. Nothing had changed in the past year.

Except for Ben.

Having a sexy bastard of a roommate was definitely new. And that kiss... Well, that had been a first in so many ways.

That thought eased the sting just a bit. Enough so she could say, with only a hint of sadness, "So, Becca, huh?"

Meg's snort was totally unladylike and completely at odds with her angelic face. "Yeah, can you believe it? I can't imagine what he sees in that skank."

Caitlyn could. Becca practically oozed sexuality and excitement. She had a loud laugh and a bawdy sense of humor. She was known to be a party girl, not exactly the type to sit at home on a Friday night knitting a shawl for an old lady.

Is that what Robert had wanted all along?

Of course he did. What man wouldn't? Robert had made comments about her lack of passion. She believed the word "cold fish" had been used on more than one occasion. Teasingly, of course, but there it was. For someone like Robert—someone who avoided conflict like the plague—the real truth could be found in the teasing.

Passive-aggressive piece of shit.

She wondered how Becca dealt with his veiled insults and criticisms. Or maybe she'd never seen that side of him because she was everything he wanted—everything Caitlyn was not.

* * * *

Ben had fallen into an Internet suckfest.

Like picking at a scab, Ben couldn't seem to stop. It had started innocently enough. He'd just wanted to catch up on some work e-mails, and one of his coworkers had posted a picture of an office happy hour. He used to be a staple member of those work outings, but now that he'd exiled himself to working from home pretty much full time, he was no longer part of the in-crowd. So he'd looked at the pictures to see who all was there.

And there she was, hanging off the arm of his partner and former friend, Alejandro. So it was official. They were a couple now. Fantastic.

He still wasn't quite sure how it happened, but soon he was looking at all of the pictures that his colleagues had sent from the past couple months' worth of work outings, scouring the photos for a glimpse of her like some sort of junkie. She was in seven pictures. Whenever he found a new one, he got a jolt of renewed anger. The bitch had taken over *his* happy hour crowd.

When he ran out of e-mails, he'd taken the ultimate plunge into hell. He'd followed a link to her Facebook page.

He was still there, on her page, obsessing over every post and status update since the day he'd moved out, as though he could find the meaning of life in her chipper blurbs about yoga class. When the front door opened and Caitlyn walked in, Ben slammed his laptop shut with the exaggerated haste of the truly guilty.

Caitlyn studied him for a moment, clearly surprised by his spastic reflex. "What are you doing?"

"Nothing." Perhaps he'd said that too quickly.

She looked from him to his laptop and her eyes widened to the size of saucers. "Oh my God, were you watching porn?"

"What? No!" Again, too quick and his voice actually broke like he was a prepubescent teen.

"Oh my God, you *were*." Caitlyn's face was the picture of horror. "Ugh, take it to your room, at least."

"I was not watching porn. I was—" Oh sweet Jesus, this was embarrassing.

She watched him expectantly.

"I was on Facebook."

There was a brief silence before she burst out laughing. At him. And somehow he didn't mind. His own lips were twitching up at the corners as the sound of her amusement. He really had become addicted to hearing her laugh.

"So glad you're entertained," he said.

She wiped a tear from her eye. "I'm sorry. You just looked so… *guilty*."

He shifted over so she could sit beside him on the couch. "Yeah, well, cyberstalking my ex is not exactly something I'm proud of."

She made an *ahh*ing noise that should have annoyed the hell out of him. He didn't want or need anyone's pity. But when he looked over at her, it wasn't pity in her eyes. It was understanding, and kindness, and… God, she was really hot. How was she single?

She gestured toward the computer that had been unceremoniously shut. "Can I see?"

He looked to her in surprise, but she was totally serious. Why not?

He opened to Olivia's photos and watched Caitlyn study his ex with the same small frown she wore when she was analyzing an intricate new pattern in her knitting.

"She's beautiful."

Ben gave a little grunt of agreement. It was funny how one's view of a person could change over time. He was aware of the fact that outwardly, his ex was considered beautiful. He remembered thinking that when they first met. But now, after so much time—so many fights and lies and manipulations—all he could see was the harshness in her sharp features and the vanity of a woman who wielded makeup like a weapon.

He pointed to one of the many pictures she'd posted of herself and Alejandro.

"That's the guy she cheated on me with."

Caitlyn's nose scrunched up in disgust. "Ew, he's a bloaty-faced, washed-up creep."

He let out a bark of unexpected laughter as he studied the picture of his partner. She had a point. He looked like the epitome of a Wall Street asshole.

He turned to her then. "Caitlyn, those may be the sexiest words to come out of your mouth. To come out of *anyone's* mouth."

She flashed him a small smile. "Glad I could help."

He shook his head. "I just—I can't believe they're actually dating," he said. "Screwing around is one thing but, I mean, look at them. They look happy."

He thought Caitlyn wouldn't respond, but when she did, her voice sounded strained. "At least they're not engaged."

Panic set in when he glanced over to see tears swimming in her eyes. Oh shit. He did not do tears. "You okay?"

She nodded and blinked back the tears before they had a chance to fall. She inhaled deeply. "I'm fine. Just surprised to find out my ex got engaged, that's all."

The pained look on her face cut him like a knife. He had no idea what to do to make her feel better. Well, he had one.

Shoving himself off the couch, he grabbed his jacket and headed for the door.

"Where are you going?"

He spun around at the door. "Go put on those comfy PJ's you're so fond of. I'll be back in a jiff."

He came back ten minutes later to find that Caitlyn had followed his orders and was now curled up on the couch in the pale blue flannel pajamas that were boxy, unflattering, and yet somehow incredibly sexy. They made him think of wrapping on a birthday present that's just waiting to be discovered.

She looked up in question when he walked into the room, and with a flourish he produced two bottles—a bottle of wine and a bottle of whisky. "What will it be, madam?"

"Whisky," she surprised him by saying. "This day definitely calls for whisky."

"As you wish." He gave a little bow before tossing a box in her direction.

"Chocolates?" She sounded so surprised, like no one ever gave her impromptu presents before. He really was starting to despise her ex-boyfriend.

He decided then and there that he would help her find her next boyfriend, someone worthy of her. They'd joked about it before, but now he was serious. It would give him something to focus on so he couldn't obsess over Olivia's Facebook statuses. He'd find her someone decent and caring….someone who treated her the way she deserved to be treated.

In the meantime, he supposed he would have to show her what she'd been missing out on.

* * * *

The whisky was good. Too good. The first glass had gone down slowly, but the second was disappearing before her eyes. As the drinks went down, the conversation went from the mundane to the silly to the absolute absurd.

"No, I'm serious. If you could have a superpower, what would it be?"

"Are we talking—flying? Becoming invisible, that sort of thing?" Caitlyn asked.

Ben shook his head and took a gulp of his drink. "No, I mean, what quality do you possess that would be your super strength if everything about you got amplified."

Caitlyn's gaze drifted to the ceiling as she contemplated her answer to a question that had stemmed from a lengthy conversation about the pros and cons of the recent rash of comic book movies.

"I don't know, I guess loyalty?"

Ben made a buzzer noise. "Too boring, try again."

Predictability? Steadfastness? Somehow everything she came up with sounded too boring to admit. She gave up with a shrug and reached for her glass. "It's official, all of my superpowers would be too boring for words. Maybe my superpower would be bore people to sleep—a superhero for insomniacs."

She gave a self-deprecating laugh at her own joke, but Ben was shaking his head in annoyance. "How can you say that? You are so far from boring it's ridiculous."

Her heart gave a leap of joy at the compliment, even though she knew very well he was determined to cheer her up this evening. He'd probably try to convince her she was as beautiful as a supermodel soon. Still, it was sweet of him to say.

"What about you? What's your superpower?" she asked.

He turned to face her with a surprisingly intense expression. "I'm serious, Cait, don't sell yourself short. You're the most interesting woman I know—you have interesting friends and interesting hobbies and interesting career goals and interesting…interests."

Caitlyn stared at him wide-eyed. "That's a lot of 'interestings,'" she mumbled.

His eyes moved down to her lips and the atmosphere in the room shifted. The air between them was thick with unspoken words.

"You're also passionate," he said.

The word hung between them—a word laced with meaning. Caitlyn reminded herself to breathe. He was just being nice. For a self-proclaimed asshole, he was really very kind.

"Not passionate," she heard herself saying. Why, oh why, couldn't she just accept the compliment?

"Says who?" he asked.

Caitlyn's mouth had the good sense to finally remain closed. It was bad enough that she'd admitted to being passionless, but it would be horrific to admit that her ex had proclaimed her to be frigid and bad in bed.

But the answer was obvious. Ben's eyes darkened, and his voice was close to a growl when he said, "That man is an idiot."

Caitlyn opened her mouth to reply. *Indeed* maybe, or, *amen to that.* But nothing came out of her mouth. She watched him stare at her lips, his eyes darkening dangerously, and it was the most intensely hot moment of her life.

He wanted her. There was nothing forced or kind about it. He was hot for her, and it was written all over his face. And, oh holy hell, she wanted him, too. Bad.

He moved toward her with a decidedly predatory look in his eyes. When there were mere inches separating them, he said, "I am going to kiss you now."

Yes, please. But she didn't say anything—she couldn't. Her mind and body were frozen in anticipation and longing for this kiss.

He waited for a half second, giving her time to back away or to cry out in protest, but nothing in the world could have made her pull away at that moment. Instead, she leaned in.

His lips were warm and hard as they crushed against hers. She couldn't stop the moan of pleasure as he pulled her into him so she was firmly pressed against his chest.

She wrapped her arms around his neck and tangled her fingers in his hair as she lost herself in the hot, deep kiss. One of his hands was pressing her to him while the other moved to her leg. He stroked her thigh, moving higher and higher as his lips continued their assault and the heat between her thighs grew to an unbearable pressure.

Oh God, it felt so good. She met his tongue with her own, and moaned in frustration when his hand stopped just shy of her aching center.

His lips left hers to trail kisses down her jaw to her neck, and Caitlyn's head dropped back to allow him full access. He slid his hand around from her back to her side so he was grazing the side of her breast, and Caitlyn froze.

She couldn't take the teasing caresses anymore. She thought she might explode if he didn't touch her where she needed to be touched.

"Please," she whispered.

His lips were against her ear; his tongue flickered out to lick her lobe. "Please what, beautiful?"

She knew he was teasing her, making her say it out loud. Somehow the intimacy of it, of whispering what she wanted as he kissed and stroked her, was unbearably hot.

"Touch me," she whispered.

A growling sound came out of Ben as his self-imposed restraint broke and the hand on the side of her breast cupped her full weight in his palm as he kissed her with a passion she'd never known.

His tongue took full possession of her lips and her tongue as his hands touched her everywhere, moving over her breasts, her stomach, and at last stroking the hot and pulsing area between her thighs.

She moaned with sheer, unadulterated pleasure at the sweet relief as his palm pressed against her. She bucked against him, long past a point where she had any control over her movements.

"You want that, gorgeous? You want me to fill you up?"

Her response was somewhere between a whimper and a moan, but the message was clear. *Yes, yes, oh God yes.*

Maggie Dallen

Keeping one hand firmly between her thighs, he used his other to unbutton the pajama top, slowly exposing her breasts to the dim light from the TV's glow.

She held her breath as the last button came undone and he pushed the cloth to the side. He had leaned back just far enough to take in her naked breasts, and the dark look of uncontrollable desire that crossed his face was nearly her undoing.

"You are fucking stunning," he said before dipping his head and pulling her against him so he could press his lips to each breast, dropping kisses until he reached her nipple, which he drew into his mouth and sucked. Hard.

She cried out at the sweet, torturous pleasure and her hands moved to his head, pressing him to her. She didn't want it to stop. He moved from one breast to the other, licking, lapping, and sucking until she was panting with desire.

When he came up for air, he surprised her by pulling away and standing up. Before she could protest, he leaned over and scooped her into his arms like she weighed no more than a pillow.

"I'm taking you to bed," he said.

It wasn't a question, but there was a pause, a moment, when she could have said no. Instead she leaned into him and kissed the side of his neck, causing him to groan. The sound gave her a jolt of feminine pleasure. She was suddenly desperate to make him feel as turned on as she was.

He took her to her bedroom and set her gently on the king-sized bed. He pulled his shirt over his head and unbuckled his belt, never taking his eyes off her.

Her skin was on fire under his stare. She could feel his gaze on her just as surely as his hands. Dimly conscious of the fact that she was still wearing her faded old pajamas, she made a move to slip out of the top.

She hadn't gotten far before he came to her side to help. Pulling her into a half sitting position, he deftly yanked off the top, all while showering her with kisses—her shoulders, her neck, and breasts—trailing all the way down her belly.

When he reached the top of her pants, he slipped two fingers beneath the elastic and tugged them off, leaving her lying there with only her panties to cover her.

Unexpectedly shy, she moved to cover herself, but he tossed her hand away and stood over her, devouring her with his eyes. "You are so fucking sexy."

Heady pleasure left her breathless. No one had ever called her sexy. Cute, yes. Sexy, never. A new boldness born from intense desire had her doing something she would never normally do. She allowed one of her hands to slide up her belly to cup her breast, fondling herself as he watched. His eyes narrowed, dark with desire, and for the first time in her life she actually *felt* sexy.

A guttural growl escaped him before he muttered a string of curse words and fell on top of her. His mouth claimed hers with a desperation that thrilled her. He had lost control and it was because of her. *She'd* had this effect on him—the thought was dizzying, empowering.

He kept whispering in her ear as he moved over her, telling her how hot she was, how sexy, how gorgeous. Every whisper only added to her heightening desire, his breath against her neck, the way his lips moved against her ear. The words themselves.

His hands were everywhere and her own struggled to keep up. Outrageously needy, her hands tried to touch him everywhere at once—his broad shoulders, his toned back, the hard contours of his chest and stomach.

"Jesus, Caitie, do you know what you're doing to me?" he whispered as he slid off his jeans.

She didn't need to answer because he'd moved back to cover her with his body, and the hard length of his cock pressed against her was the answer.

She moved to touch it. She wanted to touch it. But she hesitated. She'd never really known what she was doing down there.

Sensing her hesitancy, he took her hand in his in a surprisingly gentle grip and guided her. Following his lead, she stroked him gently through his boxers. He sucked in air and let it out with a groan. "You're a natural."

That made her grin, even through the desperate desire that had moved beyond aching to throbbing pain, begging to be eased.

He shifted on top of her, and she moved so that his hard length was nestled between her thighs, so close it was unbearable torture. She rocked her hips up, pressing herself against him, urging him to do it. To take her.

He stilled, his breath coming in pants. "Are you sure?"

She barely recognized the husky, sexy voice that answered, "I want you to *fuck* me."

In a heartbeat he'd shed their underwear, put on a condom, and was back between her thighs. He took her in one long, hard thrust that had her arching her back and crying out his name.

He paused for a moment, but she bucked against him. He felt so good inside her, so damn good. He moved then, slow thrusts as his mouth continued its assault on her lips and neck.

Her hands grasped at his shoulders, his neck, running over his back as the sweet tension built inside of her to an all-consuming fire. She moved beneath him, all form of thought lost in desire. "Please don't stop."

His lips returned to hers, and his tongue matched the thrusting intensity of his cock until the tension reached a breaking point and she came apart in his arms on wave after wave of pulsing, earthshattering pleasure.

He came immediately after and collapsed on top of her, a deliciously heavy weight that seemed like the only thing keeping her grounded to the earth.

He made to move but she gripped him tighter. "I'm crushing you," he said against her neck.

"I don't mind." That was an understatement. In that moment she was thoroughly content, her buzzing brain happily adrift on a sea of endorphins and her body a mass of luscious satisfaction. The solid pressure of his body on hers was delicious—a warm weighted blanket that made her feel like she was in a cocoon.

Cocoon. She smiled against his shoulder as the silly thought took hold. It was a fitting analogy. Whatever had just happened between them—it was so much more than sex. She felt different—desired, sexy, powerful. *Satiated.*

A few moments later, he shifted the bulk of his weight, but an arm and leg were still draped over her, keeping her warm and safe and grounded.

She sighed dreamily. *A girl could get used to this.*

Chapter 7

"That was fucking amazing."

Ben watched Caitlyn's lips curve into a lazy, contented smile as she sighed her agreement. He wasn't sure she understood so he said it again, "Fucking amazing."

"It really was," she mumbled.

He toyed with the brown locks that fanned across her pillow, watching in fascination as she came back to her senses.

This woman was sensual and passionate and undeniably sexy as hell. He wanted to kill the man who'd ever made her doubt that. He'd seen the hesitation in her eyes, felt the tentative hesitation in her touches, and seen the wary look that had flickered in her gaze when she lay naked before him. Someone had done that to her. Someone had told her lies and made her doubt her appearance and her sexual nature.

He had a brief but intense urge to slam a fist into that someone's face.

Unwelcome memories from his childhood filled him with a familiar frustration. He'd spent his entire childhood watching his sweet but fragile mother shrink before his very eyes. He and his brother found photos of her when she was younger—vibrant and beautiful—but as he'd grown older, she'd grown smaller thanks to the fact that she'd been saddled with a man who didn't appreciate her. His father may not have been physically abusive, but it wasn't just a strong hand that could crush a flower. Neglect and lack of appreciation and kindness had the same effect. It just took longer.

He'd watched his father destroy his mother slowly and painfully, day after day, until she was a shell of her former self when she died of cancer five years ago. He hadn't been more than thirteen when he'd vowed that he would never be as cruel as his dad. He and his brother may have inherited their father's gruff nature and crass language, but that was where the similarities ended.

He'd always stayed far the hell away from anyone vulnerable or delicate like his mother—anyone who he could potentially hurt. That meant not letting any woman too close—not unless she was just as hardened and jaded as he was. Olivia had fit the bill perfectly…at first. The woman was as fierce as they came. No man could hurt her, not with all the walls and pretenses she'd built for herself.

He forced his mind back to the present, and back to the sexy woman lying naked beside him. He'd won the jackpot tonight. After weeks of fantasizing about his tantalizing roommate, he'd finally gotten his chance to take her to bed. And it had been bloody fantastic. Better than his daydreams. She'd been a firecracker in bed, once she'd overcome her hesitations.

She still wore that sexy, satisfied smile, but her eyes had drifted shut. Her breathing evened out and he took the opportunity to get his fill. Beautiful. From head to toe, the woman was perfection. The kind of curves that men dreamed about and a feisty passion in bed that already had him dreaming about the next time.

Not that there would be a next time. Not necessarily. Although the night was still young, and they still had almost three weeks of sharing the same roof. Why not share the same bed, too?

He brushed a strand of hair out of her face and was rewarded when her smile widened in thanks. Her eyes remained shut. Maybe she wouldn't want this to be more than a one-night deal. Of course she wouldn't. Tonight, she'd been drunk. She was reeling from the latest news of her ex's engagement. But tomorrow? Tomorrow she'd remember that he was her jackass roommate who annoyed the hell out of her.

Thanks to that wretched first date, she'd already seen his true nature, and she was smart enough to steer clear of assholes with a charming smile. She deserved more, and she knew it. She deserved someone far nicer than him, someone who appreciated her more than that idiot ex. She deserved better. She deserved—

"We're going to find you your Cary Grant."

Her eyes shot open at that, and she turned to him with a questioning look. "Pardon me?"

He propped himself up on one arm so he could get his fill of the amazing view spread out before him. "I'm going to help you find a proper boyfriend. One who will appreciate you and treat you like you deserve. We're going to find you your bloody dream man."

Her laugh was enchanting. "And what brought on this sudden urge to find me a mate?"

"Because you deserve it, and it's time for you to move on with your life. Besides, I'll be moving out in a few weeks and you'll need to find some other hot body to take advantage of."

He wiggled a brow and she rewarded him with a shit-eating grin.

"And this?" She made a vague gesture toward their naked bodies. Her cheeks turned a pretty shade of pink, adorable really given what they'd just done.

"That's up to you, my lovely flatmate. Do you want to do this again?"

Please say yes. For the love of God, please say yes.

Her little nod made him happier than he was willing to admit. He resisted the urge to pump his fist in the air. *Keep it cool, jackass.* "Perfect. Then we'll be doing this again."

Her cheeks reddened even further, but she was smiling. "So we're like…" she trailed off.

"Fuck buddies," he finished. Her eyes widened meaningfully. He tried again. "Friends with benefits?"

"Better."

He laughed and leaned over to press one last kiss against those gorgeous, soft lips. "All right, friend. On that note, I'm off to my room."

She didn't protest and for that he was grateful. Everyone knew the first rule of keeping a sexual relationship solely about sex was that you didn't literally sleep together.

Still. That being said. Prying himself away from her soft, warm, naked body took every ounce of his will power.

* * * *

"You did what?" Meg's squeal was high-pitched and had several of the barflies looking in their direction.

"Keep your voice down," Caitlyn hissed.

Meg slapped a hand over her mouth, but her eyes were comically wide as she studied her best friend. Caitlyn took a sip of her drink, enjoying her friend's shock. She was still a bit shocked herself at the turn of events the night before—but no regret. All day at work she'd replayed the night before in her head, and each time it was just as delicious.

"So are you guys . . . dating now?" Meg asked.

Caitlyn shook her head with a bit more vehemence than necessary. "Of course not."

"Of course not," Meg echoed, in a teasing tone. "Why not?"

Caitlyn sighed. How could her friend not see it? "We're not into each other like that. You know me, I'm looking for someone who wants to settle down, someone stable and…predictable." God, she sounded like she was describing her accountant.

"Yeah, but—" Meg started to protest.

"And he's not into me like that," Caitlyn finished. She could see her friend's loyal shackles rise. Meg was about to launch into one of her patented pep talks about how she was the most beautiful, funny, talented, blah, blah, blah.

"Trust me, Meg. I've seen the kind of woman he goes for. He wants someone far more fun and worldly." She saw his ex's photo in her mind… *and glamorous and sexy and elegant.*

Her friend thankfully let it go. "Okay, fine. No dating. So what are you then?"

"Friends with benefits." Caitlyn bit her lip to hold back a goofy grin. *Fuck buddies.*

Meg was giving her a wary look. "Are you sure you can handle a no-strings-attached relationship?"

"It's not a relationship," Caitlyn corrected.

Meg rolled her eyes. "You know what I mean. I don't want to see you get hurt. You're not the type to…*not* get involved."

Caitlyn knew her friend meant well, but at that moment the words "you're not the type" stung. Maybe she *was* the type. Just because she hadn't yet didn't mean she never could. She tilted her chin up. "I'll be fine."

That confidence lasted precisely as long as it took to walk home from the bar. Now how exactly was this supposed to work? Nerves warred with excitement. How was she supposed to act?

Just be yourself. Be normal. Nothing has changed.

Ben was working on his laptop when she came into the living room. He barely glanced up as she passed by to drop her stuff off in her bedroom. "Hey," was all she got.

Good, that was normal.

When she came back in, he was already settling into their routine. He'd moved his work so she could join him on the couch and was starting the ritual channel changing when she sat beside him and picked up her knitting project. An hour later, he'd settled on an Alfred Hitchcock movie.

See? Normal. Nothing to be anxious about. They were two grownups who'd slept together. No big whoop.

"This requires popcorn," Caitlyn declared as the opening credits began to roll. She was in the kitchen on her tiptoes, reaching for the box on the highest shelf, when she heard him come in behind her.

"Now this looks appetizing." His voice was a growl, and she froze mid-grab as shivers ran up and down her spine. That was all it took. One absurdly overt come-on and she was horny as hell. Amazing.

She didn't know how to respond, but she didn't need to because a moment later he was directly behind her, her bottom firmly nestled against his hard cock, which was straining against his jeans, his hands wrapped around her waist, already slipping beneath her top to move up to her breasts.

Her head fell back against his shoulder, and he took the opportunity to nuzzle her neck and drop kisses along her jaw.

When his fingers reached the lace edge of her bra, she arched her back, silently begging for his touch. God, she was insatiable around this man.

And like that it dawned on her. She wasn't frigid. She wasn't passionless and cold. Clearly not if this man—this relative stranger—could make her wet and aching with a mere touch.

It wasn't her that was the problem. It was *him*.

All thoughts were lost at that point as Ben, who was breathing heavily in her ear with undisguised need, slipped a hand down the front of her jeans and found the sensitive nub.

She gasped for air as his fingers worked their magic down there. And then she was begging. All out begging for it.

Ben fumbled with the button and zipper of her jeans before shoving them down, followed quickly by his own.

They never made it to the bed. Or the couch. They never even made it to the kitchen floor. Ben eased her forward until she was leaning over the kitchen counter before slipping a hand between her thighs to part them for easier access.

"Jesus, Cait, you are so wet for me." The raw need in his voice was heady and had her arching her back so she could tease him even more, and she was rewarded with a growl as he gave her ass a little spank. "You are so fucking sexy."

He paused with his cock pressed against her, his breath hot against her neck. "Tell me what you want."

She couldn't take the aching any more. She needed it. She needed him. "Fuck me."

He slid inside, filling her completely until she was breathless and moaning and unable to use words. But he knew exactly what she wanted and how. He set a slow, torturous pace as he took her over the counter, bringing them both to the point of unbearable pleasure before driving them over the edge.

Okay, *that* was not normal. When they'd come back to their senses and cleaned themselves up a bit, they resumed with life as usual, which meant popcorn and chatting and old movies.

Maybe this was the *new* normal.

* * * *

The new routine lasted that whole week. Each night, she'd come home from work and a pleasant night of chilling out on the couch would escalate into heavy petting and then a passionate bout of lovemaking. Sometimes twice. And each night ended with Caitlyn in her bed and Ben in his—a perfect example of friends with benefits.

The fact that this epically awesome scenario had a time limit—there was only two weeks left until Ben was scheduled to move out—only added to the thrill. Granted, every once in a while, she experienced a pang of disappointment that this would come to an end, but that knowledge also took away any pressure. There were no questions about what came next for them or what the future held. They would have their fun and then go their own ways. No hurt feelings, no broken heart.

It wasn't until she received an SOS text from Meg that she realized she'd been so caught up in the new non-relationship, she'd let her other friendships fall to the wayside.

"Where are you?" Meg texted. "Are you alive?"

Oops. Caitlyn was at work, stocking the last of the new shipment when she got the text. "Sorry, M. Been busy."

"Clear your busy calendar for tonight. It's Tam's b-day so you better be there."

"There" was Cagney's. Obviously. It went without saying.

"I'll be there," she texted.

A couple hours later, the shop was dead and her coworker, Beth, was tallying up their totals for the day. "Do you mind locking up for me? I've got to head home to change before going out tonight."

Beth's ever-chipper smile was on in full force. "Of course."

"Great, thanks." Caitlyn grabbed her coat and hat and was heading toward the door when she paused, Ben's voice goading her in her head.

"Hey, Beth?"

The girl glanced up with a questioning look and Caitlyn almost lost her nerve.

"Uh, I've been thinking lately…about maybe typing up some of my patterns—"

"Oh my gosh, that is a fantastic idea," Beth gushed.

"You think so?"

Beth was looking at her like she was nuts. "Are you kidding me? People are always asking about your samples. Everyone wants to make them."

"Really?"

Beth's eyes lit up in excitement. "Can I be your test knitter?"

Caitlyn blinked in surprise. "Uh, sure. Yeah, that would be great."

"Cool." Beth was beaming at her as she walked out of the store, but Caitlyn's grin was impossible to match. She was really going to do this. And it was all thanks to Ben.

* * * *

Ben cradled the phone against his ear as he waited for his assistant to stop with the questions

"Why are you so…cheerful?" Natalie sounded distrustful. And maybe she had a right to. But he ignored her. They may be close, but he wasn't about to share the fact that he was "cheerful," as she put it, because his hottie of a roommate was a tigress in bed.

She was also sweetness personified and fun to hang out with. More than that, she was no-strings-attached and was just as happy as he was with that situation. He leaned back and grinned at the ceiling at the memory of the way she'd kicked him out of her bed the night before when he'd started to fall asleep.

In his defense, they'd done it several times and he'd been exhausted. He was still bone-tired, but it had been worth it.

She was exactly what he needed to get over Olivia. A light, carefree fling. They wouldn't even see each other again after this. The elated smile fell a bit at that.

He shook off the gloomy thought. There were still two weeks left of roomie sex time before he moved out. He'd have had his fill before then and they would be sick of each other by then, no doubt.

So instead of answering his assistant, he got down to business. "Any update from Darren?"

"He just sent over his new proposal this morning. His new project has some additional property investments he wants you to take a look at."

"Great, I'll take a look tonight."

He heard Natalie's long suffering sigh over the phone. "Why do you insist on working at night and on the weekends? Haven't you ever heard of a life?"

It was a constant complaint on her end, but now it struck a chord because for the first time in ages he nearly opened his mouth to argue that he didn't do that. He usually did, definitely, but since moving in with

Caitlyn, his nights had been spent relaxing on the couch with her rather than doing work as usual.

He frowned as his assistant finished the tirade. Once off the phone, he started to open the file she'd e-mailed, but was interrupted by Caitlyn's arrival.

After tossing her belongings in her bedroom, she came back into the living room to tell him that she was heading out for a birthday party.

Ben took one look at the file full of documents on his desktop before shutting the laptop and turning to face her.

"Can I come?" The moment the words came out of his mouth, Ben knew he had lost any coolness he may once have had.

But seriously, now that he could no longer socialize with his former work friends and he'd lost the rest in the breakup, his social life consisted pretty much of one woman. One incredibly sexy, beautiful, and intelligent woman. Who was leaving to go to a party without him.

"I mean, I don't want to crash a private party or anything," he added. *But please let me come.* He contemplated giving her puppy eyes but thought that may be pushing it. She was already giving him an adorably knowing look.

"Of course you can come, and you won't be crashing anything. A bunch of us are meeting up at Cagney's to celebrate Tamara's birthday."

"Cool, I like Tamara." For the life of him he couldn't remember which of her friends was named Tamara—the blonde, the supermodel, or the pregnant lady—but it didn't matter, since he'd liked them all.

As if reading his mind, she cocked a brow as she moved past him to get into the bathroom. "Do you even know which one Tamara is?"

He pulled his best offended look and scoffed. "Of course. She was the pretty one."

She gave him a skeptical look before shutting the door on him. He heard the shower turn on and had the overwhelming urge to join her. But then she would never make it to the party on time.

An image of her gloriously curvy body dripping wet under the shower's spray filled his mind until he thought he'd go mad with wanting. Dammit all to hell, he was going in there. Just as he neared the door, he heard the shower turn off.

Damn.

Later. They would definitely be taking a shower together at some point this evening. When she came out wrapped in a towel, her wet hair piled up on her head with only a few loose tendrils framing her heart-shaped face, all hope of being on time was lost.

She gave him a warning look as he moved toward her. He was positive that his intention was utterly obvious by the hungry look on his face and the erection that he made no effort to hide.

"I have to get out of here," she said, but he saw the change come over her, the transformation that he knew and loved. Each and every time they'd slept together, her cheeks flushed with arousal, her eyes grew heavy-lidded with desire, and she wet her lips in anticipation.

God he loved to see that transformation. Watching Caitlyn transform from the sexy librarian into the sexy sex goddess was quite possibly the best aphrodisiac in the world.

She was backing up into the bedroom, her hands teasing him as she slowly let the towel slip lower and lower until her nipples threatened to peek over the edge.

"We're going to be late," she said as he got so close he could smell the clean scent of her shampoo and body wash.

"Then we better be quick."

Her eyes closed and her lips parted as he leaned in to claim those sweet, soft lips. He tugged gently and the towel that clothed her slipped out of her fingers and dropped to the ground.

He pulled back to take in the full length of her, standing there in all her seductive glory. He couldn't stop the groan that escaped him. She was remarkable. He should be grateful time was of the essence—he was so turned on he wasn't sure he could hold out for more than a quickie.

He leaned down so he could draw one of her rosy nipples into his mouth while his hand toyed with her other breast. Her soft gasp almost made him lose control.

Easy, boy. Even if he was about to explode with wanting, he needed to make this good for her, too.

He slipped his free hand between her thighs to stroke her core. She was dripping wet and panting for air. She wanted this as much as he did. *Thank God.*

Moments later they tumbled into the bed, arms and legs intertwined as they ground against each other, lips and hands everywhere at once as they devoured one another until they came in a quick but thoroughly satisfying climax.

A little while later she emerged from the bedroom and stood in front of him in the kitchen. "What do you think? Do I look okay?"

"You look amazing."

It was true. She was wearing a simple black dress and black knee high boots, but it was the flushed cheeks and sparkling eyes that made her more of a knockout than ever.

But then, maybe it was because he knew what had brought on tonight's glow and that he had been an integral part of it.

She toyed with one of her brown curls, looking adorably soft and sweet and kissable and annoyingly self-conscious. He took her hand in his and leaned down to kiss her lightly. "You look fucking gorgeous. As always."

Her blush deepened and her smile made his heart expand at a frightening rate. "Grab your purse, we're already late."

Chapter 8

"You're late," the pregnant friend said the moment they arrived.

"Sorry, Meg." Caitlyn leaned over and kissed her friend on the cheek. Meg turned her radiant smile on him.

"Nice to see you again, Ben." The knowing look was subtle but it was there. Yup, this little ball of belly knew he was sleeping with her best friend. Well, at least she looked happy about it.

He had the sudden desire to pump this woman for information. What had Caitlyn said about them? About their extracurricular activities?

"You've met the others," she said as she led them over to a booth in the corner where he recognized Marc and the two women—the pretty blonde and the striking supermodel. Now if he could only figure out which one was Tamara and which one was Alice.

"So glad you could make it for Tam's birthday," the supermodel said with a grin.

Supermodel, Alice, and dainty little blonde was Tamara, check. He took Tamara's hand in his and gave it a kiss, which got a laugh from the crowd and an inscrutable look from his date.

No, not date. His roommate. Dammit.

The pregnant one's husband came over to greet him with a manly slap on the back—the ever-popular, not so subtle "don't you mess with my wife's best friend" gesture known the world over. "What can I get for you, man?"

And they were off. Ben was tagging along. Again. But he didn't care because he was also having fun again. The group of well-wishers grew and their little group extended across several booths and around the bar. At one point a three-man jazz band came in and started setting up in the corner— live music was a Friday night regular event at Cagney's, he discovered.

He was having fun talking to the birthday girl—surprisingly funny once she warmed up a bit—and her roommate, Marc, who was equally entertaining. Together, they had a Gracie and Burns quality to them. When he told them that, they got excited. Very excited. And judging by the looks exchanged between them, his off-hand comment had just earned the equivalent of street cred from this old movie crowd.

At some point while he was talking to Tamara and Marc, Caitlyn wandered off to mingle with some of the other guests. He spotted her at the end of the bar talking to a group of friends he hadn't met yet. For a second, his lungs dropped to his stomach. God, she was beautiful. She tipped her head back to laugh. How was it that every man in this place wasn't all over her? Were they blind?

Alice sat next to him with a fresh drink. "It's nice to see her so happy."

He looked over to see her watching him watching Caitlyn. Oh shit. She was giving him that knowing smirk. Here it comes. She thinks they're really a couple. She wants to see Caitlyn settle down. Of course her friends would want her to find a boyfriend, a real one, not a fling that happened to be crashing at her place.

"Relax, Romeo, Caitlyn made it clear you guys are just temporary."

"She did?" Of course she did.

"Of course she did." The supermodel's smirk grew to a grin. Oh great, he was entertaining her.

"What else did she say?" He instantly wished he could suck those words back in. But despite her evident amusement, Alice answered seriously. "Enough to know that you're one of the good ones."

Oh shit. Wait, what did that mean? Had *she* said that?

As though reading his mind, she added, "Don't worry, she doesn't think you're the one or anything."

He let out a breath. That was a relief. That should be a relief. So why did it feel like the supermodel had just stood on his chest with her high, spiky heels digging directly into his heart?

The amusement faded from her eyes and her tone dropped an octave. "If you hurt her, I'll kill you."

He maintained eye contact as one does with a crazy person. "I believe you." He really did. The woman was beautiful but intimidating.

She was clearly waiting for him to say more. "You said it yourself, she knows this isn't going anywhere. How could she get hurt?"

Alice was studying him with an intensity that was unnerving. He had the unpleasant feeling she was finding more there than he knew. "She's not like you...or me." Alice gave him a rueful grin. Whatever she'd seen in him, it was clear she recognized it. They were comrades. Birds of a feather.

They were bastards.

He tipped his glass back until there was nothing but ice left. "Meaning?"

She arched a brow at him.

She's too good for you, dumbass.

Alice used her straw to toy with the ice at the bottom of her glass. "I've known Caitlyn for a long time. She's not the type to just have a fling and walk away. I know she thinks she knows what she's doing but..."

He glanced over at Caitlyn, looking so alive and happy and confident. "Maybe you underestimate her."

He enjoyed the surprised look on her face before she responded. "Maybe. But if you hurt her—"

"You'll kill me," he finished. "Yeah, I got it."

He raised his glass. "And if I hurt her, you have my permission." She burst out in a laugh and raised her glass to cheers his.

At least they understood one another.

He looked back to Caitlyn and caught her looking at him. "You. Look. Beautiful," he mouthed.

A pink flush rose in her cheeks and she rolled her eyes. But she was grinning and that made him smile.

"Oh man, I got it all wrong," he heard Alice say beside him. "She's not the one I should be worried about, is she?"

Before he could muster up a proper response, he was distracted by the sudden and drastic change in Caitlyn. All the color drained from her face and her eyes widened to the size of saucers.

What the hell?

He followed her gaze toward the door where a lanky, nondescript man had just entered with a slinky blonde on his arm. He didn't need Alice's muttered curse to figure out who he was.

It was Tamara who actually said it. Her sweet, girly voice said, "Fucking shit, it's Cait's ex. Who invited that twat?"

* * * *

Caitlyn's hands were sweating. Why were her hands sweating?

Oh no, he'd spotted her. And so had Becca. They had spotted her and they were smiling a weird "we know this is uncomfortable but let's be adults" kind of smile that made her want to scream.

She found her lips forming a matching smile of their own as if of their own accord. "Yes," her lips seemed to be saying. "Let's do put all this breakup unpleasantness behind us and let bygones be bygones." Her lips had a decidedly prim and proper British accent.

Maggie Dallen

Meanwhile her brain, her heart, and every other organ in her body was screaming in agony. They stopped to greet Jake and Meg at the far side of the bar. That bought her a couple minutes at least to gather the scattered contents of her brain.

She did not want to deal with this. She did not want to see him. Especially not with her. The other woman. The woman he wanted to marry after being together for a matter of months. They'd lived together for five years when he'd hemmed and hawed over whether they should share a bank account to pay rent and bills.

"Caitie," Robert said. That was it. He said her name. And then he went in for a hug.

The smile on Caitlyn's face stiffened into a grimace at the familiar touch and feel of this man. Just the smell of him was an onslaught of memories and emotions. And not a single one was pleasant.

When he let her out of the awkward embrace, he moved to the side so Becca could smile at her in that condescending "poor loser, I've got your man" kind of way. "You remember Becca?"

"Of course." She forced a smile. "How are you, Becca?"

Before the other woman could answer, their stilted conversation was interrupted by an impossibly merry British man.

"There you are, love," Ben said as he burrowed his way between Caitlyn and the man seated next to her at the bar.

She looked up in surprise and was greeted by a sweet, lingering kiss. What the—

"Aren't you going to introduce us?" Ben asked, eyes wide with false innocence.

Caitlyn bit her lip to keep from laughing. Of course Ben knew. She glanced over and saw her friends in the booth watching the soap opera unfold. They were grinning like fools over Ben's timely kiss.

"Ben, this is Robert and Becca," she said.

She determined then and there that Ben had missed his calling as an actor. He launched into conversation with Robert and Becca, taking over the introductions and charming the pants off everyone in a one-mile radius.

All the while, he was making quite a show of touching Caitlyn. While asking Becca about business at her bar, he took one of Caitlyn's sweaty palms in his and interlaced their fingers, absently drawing it up to his mouth at one point to place a kiss on her knuckles, sending a jolt of electricity through her.

He wrapped an arm around her and pulled her in close so they were quite literally joined at the hip, and when Robert started boring them all with a story about his office Christmas party, he leaned over under the guise of asking her if she needed another drink and whispered something so dirty it made her laugh out loud.

They were saved from any further conversation when the band struck up its first song, a soft, slow oldies tune that had a number of people on the makeshift dance floor.

"If you'll excuse us," Ben said, looking only at Caitlyn as if no one else was in the room. "My gorgeous girlfriend promised me a dance. Isn't that right, Cait?"

She didn't have a chance to reply before he had tugged her out of her seat and away from the most unpleasant conversation of her life. Well, it had been until Ben showed up.

"You were incredible," she said with a sigh as he pulled her into his arms and they swayed to the music.

He was grinning down at her. "I have to ask you something, Caitie," he drawled her name with an over the top American accent to sound like Robert.

"What's that?"

"How the hell did you stand that boring prick for so many years?"

The ball of emotions that had threatened to turn into tears shattered into a million pieces as she burst out laughing. "I have no idea," she managed to say.

He was watching her with a smile, shaking his head in disbelief. "You deserve a medal of honor."

"I know." And she did. It had been so long since she'd seen her ex that she'd forgotten what a bore he was. Not just a bore—a self-absorbed, patronizing snoozefest. Next to Ben, he'd looked like a Pez dispenser—his mouth just kept flapping, but there was no passion or humor there, just utter crap.

The three-man band was playing a jazzy swingtime number, and Ben twirled her so quickly she gasped and then laughed.

"You've got an audience," Ben said when he pulled her back into his arms, nuzzling her neck and looking for all the world like an honest-to-God boyfriend.

He was right. Robert and Becca were watching them—no, staring. Her friends in the corner were outright gaping, and they were smiling. She would have to explain to them later that this was all a show. But in the meantime—Ben spun her around and she could no longer see any of them—in the meantime, she would enjoy the show.

Neither of them could be called professionals but they knew enough steps—and improvised the rest. Several songs later, she was gasping for air, partly from the dancing but mainly because Ben kept making her laugh.

She couldn't remember the last time she'd laughed like this. Or the last time she'd had *fun* like this.

Certainly never with Robert. Look at him sitting over there like a lump on a stump. Poor Becca.

Ben wrapped an arm around her as he led the way toward the bar and ordered them both another round of drinks. "How do you feel about a little PDA to really seal the deal?" he asked.

He was already leaning in for a kiss, and she met him halfway.

The bar ceased to exist.

That's how it was when he kissed her in her apartment, but she'd had no idea that magical ability could happen anywhere and at any time. But no, here she was, surrounded by friends—and Robert—and one kiss had her thoroughly addled.

"That was nice," she murmured when he lifted his head.

"Mmm," he agreed. He looked like he was going to dip his head again and come in for more. Yes, please.

An hour and several PDA's later, they were still cozied up at the bar talking when Meg came up to them.

"Well, if it isn't the happy couple," she teased.

Caitlyn blinked up at her friend as if in a daze.

How long had they been sitting there, talking by themselves? This was supposed to be her night out with friends. Shoot.

But Meg was grinning at her with a knowing look. She knew that look. Oh no, her friend was getting ideas about her and Ben.

She looked over at her group of friends at the end of the bar, all of whom were watching them. Yup, it was unanimous. She was going to have to explain that this was all for Robert's benefit.

Robert and Becca's—wait, where were they? She scanned the bar and they were nowhere to be found. Ben leaned over the bar to order them another round, and Meg leaned in so only she could hear. "They left ages ago."

So for the past hour, they'd been holding hands and whispering and kissing for the world to see. That had been just...

Heavenly.

Crap. She battled a rising tide of horror as the truth of it washed over her. She'd been having fun. No, she had been having *the time of her life*. With Ben. The man who she was absolutely not allowed to form feelings for. The man who would be out of her life in a little over a week, never to be seen again.

Meg was giving her a funny look, and she was grateful that Ben was distracted by the bartender. She had to get her thoughts in order. She had to get a grip.

"Are you okay?" Meg asked.

She nodded and took a deep breath. She could do this. Having fun and enjoying a man's company was not a crime. It would not necessarily end in heartbreak and misery. She just had to focus on all the reasons why they would never be a real couple. His open hatred of committed relationships, for one. And two... Her brain came up blank. There were reasons, she knew there were.

He was an asshole. Remember that first date?

When Ben had been rejected and in pain?

"I'm fine," she said to her friend. "Just having a little too much fun."

Meg's expression was way too knowing for Caitlyn's liking. "Sorry if I've been, uh...a little preoccupied."

Meg was laughing. "Are you kidding? That show you two put on has been all anyone is talking about. I wish I could have videotaped Robert's expression."

Caitlyn laughed. Right, Robert. That was who this had been for.

Meg headed toward their group of friends, and Caitlyn turned back to Ben. *Tomorrow.* Tomorrow she would get her head on straight. For now, she was going to enjoy herself.

It was one night. How much harm could one night do?

She'd enjoy it while she had it and deal with the repercussions later. But for now, why let pesky emotions spoil a perfect evening?

Chapter 9

Whatever whisky Jake was pouring, it was good stuff because Ben could feel the buzz throughout his entire body. Or maybe that was the effect of dancing with Caitlyn. She was a good dancer. Or maybe it was the laughing. He couldn't remember the last time he'd laughed so much.

But Robert was gone and their show was over. And Ben had every intention of taking his roommate home and making love to her. Fucking her. Dammit, she'd gotten into his head.

"You ready, beautiful?" He came up behind her and leaned down so he was talking directly into her ear. The vanilla scent of her perfume filled his senses as she turned her head to smile at him, her lips so close to his, all he would have to do is…

She beat him to it. Closing the distance to press her lips against the corner of his mouth, sending electricity racing through him. He stepped closer so she could feel the hard length of him against the small of her back. "Maybe it's time we got out of here."

He was gratified to see her pupils dilate and her breathing grow rapid. Her instant transformation from good girl next door to sex goddess would never cease to amaze him.

For the millionth time that night he wished he could shove it in Robert's face. What a dick. What a small-brained asshole. Let's face it, his prick was probably equally small. How else to explain the fact that he couldn't see the hot, sexy female he'd had right in front of him all those years.

And then he'd gone and ditched her for the obvious. The man had no taste.

Thank God it had ended when it had or she might still be with that loser, wasting her time with someone who didn't appreciate her or see her true beauty and sex appeal. Not like him.

She flashed him a quick, blinding smile before turning to say her good-byes, gathering her belongings as she did.

He licked suddenly dry lips. Shit... He was nervous. But that was stupid. Why should he be nervous to take home his flatmate, the woman he'd been sleeping with for a week? This was just another night for them.

Although it wasn't. Nothing about this night was like their usual routine. There had been dancing and drinking and laughing and...romance.

The air left his lungs in a rush, and for a moment his gaze flickered to Alice, who was watching him with an unreadable expression. Her words from earlier in the night came back to him. *It isn't Caitlyn I should be worried about....*

Bullocks. He had this under control. What they had was good. She turned back to him then, her eyes alight with humor and mischief—a sexy kind of mischief that had him so hard he could barely walk. See? This was fun and games. She knew that. He knew that. The supermodel knew nothing.

So he shoved those thoughts to the side and helped Caitlyn into her coat.

They barely made it through the front door before they were on top of one another, fumbling with buttons and zippers in a frantic race to strip down to nothing.

"I think I'm addicted to you," he growled against her neck as she straddled him on the couch. She was down to her underwear, and he could feel how wet she was through her panties.

It was the truth. He was addicted to sex with this woman. Hell, he was addicted to her smile, to her laugh, to the way she chewed on her lip when she was concentrating.

She moaned against his mouth when he stroked her. "More," she whispered.

"You want it fast, sweetheart? You want it now?"

He felt her nod. When she pulled her head back to look at him, her eyes were half closed. She looked as drugged as he felt.

He wanted to watch her come, despite the fact that he was desperately in need of release. Yanking her panties to the side, he slid a finger inside her, using his palm to press against her clit.

Her head fell back with a moan of pleasure. God, she was beautiful when she was turned on. He couldn't tear his eyes from her face as she rocked her hips against his hand, her breasts rubbing against his chest with the movement. He was so ready, but he needed to do this first. He needed to see this.

When she came apart in his arms, it was the most beautiful sight he'd ever seen. He loved to see her lose control, and he loved being the one who could make her let it all go.

He stroked her back as she caught her breath, her head buried in the crook of his neck. He turned so he could drop a kiss on the top of her head. She pulled back at that, her eyes glazed with satisfaction.

Leaning in, she whispered in his ear, "Now it's your turn."

It was a struggle to breath as her hands made their way over him, moving with a surety and deftness that was heady. She had him right where she wanted him. He was completely under her control. She'd come a long way from the girl who was too shy to touch his cock their first night together.

That was the last coherent thought in his brain as she positioned herself over him, taking him into her heat.

* * * *

Caitlyn watched Ben scoop up another dollop of whipped cream off the top of his breakfast. "Is there actual food under there or did you just order a pile of whipped cream for breakfast?"

He looked up from his plate with a haughty look—not easy to do with a dollop of whip cream poised in front of his face. "I'll have you know that French toast is widely regarded as a breakfast of champions."

"Mmmhmm."

The diner around the corner from her apartment was packed, since it was a Saturday morning. Hungover and miserable, they'd both agreed that it was a greasy spoon kind of morning.

Several cups of coffee and an omelet under her belt, Caitlyn was no longer miserable. In fact, she was grinning like an idiot at her roommate.

"What?" he asked. "Did I get whipped cream on my nose or something?"

"No," she said with a laugh. "I was just thinking about last night."

His wicked grin matched hers. "Which part? Making Robert squirm or the naughty bits that came after?"

"Shh." She glanced around to make sure the tables next to them hadn't heard, positive her cheeks had turned a flaming red.

Ben laughed. "How can someone so brilliantly seductive one moment be so prudish the next?"

Her blush deepened as her mind flashed back to some of the things they'd done the night before. She shrugged. "I'm complicated, I guess."

He was right in a way. There was this other side of her now. A part of herself she hardly recognized. And she owed it all to him.

She watched her crass, man-child of a roommate delve into his ridiculous breakfast with a silly grin. Who would have thought that this guy, who she'd despised at first sight, would be the one to open her up to her sensual side?

She definitely hadn't seen that coming.

A rush of gratitude toward this man and his influence had her leaning forward. "I want to help you."

His eyes shot up from his plate. "Excuse me?"

"You were amazing last night—"

He wiggled his brows like Groucho Marx. "Why, thank you."

Rolling her eyes, she laughed. "Not that. I mean, yes that was amazing too, but I was referring to your performance at the bar."

"Oh that." His satisfied smirk was oddly charming. "We did make that jackass ex of yours miserable, didn't we?"

The memory of Robert's stunned face when Ben leaned in to kiss her was enough to make her laugh all over again. "I don't know if he was miserable, but he was definitely surprised."

"Felt good, didn't it?"

"Mmmm." She allowed herself a brief moment to revel in the memory before getting back to her point. "That's why I want to help you."

He leaned over and lowered his voice. "You helped me quite a bit last night."

"How is your mind so thoroughly entrenched in the gutter this early in the morning?"

He shrugged. "It's a gift." He took another bite and then pointed his spoon at her like a sword. "Okay then, spill. How exactly do you think you can help me?"

"I can do the same for you," she said. At his blank look, she added, "I'm going to help you make your ex jealous."

The side of his mouth twitched up in amusement, and for a moment Caitlyn's excitement waned and her stomach fell. Oh crap. Of course he was amused. How conceited of her to think that she would be enough to make his ex jealous. The woman was a freakin' model. She'd probably laugh at the idea of him moving on with her—

"That is a fantastic idea." He cut off her downward spiral into self-esteem hell.

"Yeah?" She could hear the doubt in her voice.

"Are you kidding me?" His entire face was lit up with excitement. "It would drive her nuts to see me with someone like you."

Someone like you? What did that mean? Maybe she didn't want to know. "Okay then, so how do we do this?"

Ben leaned back in his chair, his eyes looking over her shoulder as he appeared to give it some thought. "The Christmas party," he finally said.

"The Christmas party?" she echoed.

"Our office Christmas party. It's in two weeks. If I know Olivia—and I do—she won't be able to resist going with Alejandro, if for no other reason than to make me furious."

He muttered something about the spawn of Satan under his breath, and Caitlyn waited for him to continue.

Ben took her hand in his and met her gaze. "Caitlyn, will you be my date to the party?"

A rush of excitement swept over her from the physical contact or the thought of resurrecting their roles from the night before or maybe it was a combination of the two. "I would love to."

He smiled back at her and the air rushed from her lungs. God, that smile was hot.

As if reading her mind, he leaned in once more. "Now that's settled, what do you say you and I pick up some whipped cream from the corner store and see what other uses we can find for it."

She pretended to think it over. As if she would turn down the chance to try out something new in bed with Ben. The clock was ticking on their little arrangement and she meant to make the most of it. "We'll have to be quick. I've got to help clean up the theater today."

His face fell. "On a Saturday?"

She rolled her eyes. "It's always on a Saturday, Mr. Perceptive."

He grumbled a bit under his breath. All she caught was the tail-end of "rather hang out at a dilapidated old scrap heap than with me."

"Hey, what are you calling an old scrap heap?"

He leaned back in his seat and raised one brow in challenge. "What is your deal with that place? I mean, I get that you love old movies and all, but movies can be viewed anywhere these days, you do realize that, right?" Before she could respond, he leaned over and lowered his voice as if he was letting her in on a secret. "There's even this thing called streaming movies. You can watch them from the comfort of your own home."

"Very funny." Caitlyn held up a finger to list her reasons. "One, it's so much better to watch old movies on the big screen the way they were intended. You said so yourself the other night when I took you there to see *On the Waterfront.*"

"I was just trying to make you happy to get into your pants when we got home." Ben took another bite of his French toast and ignored her hand that smacked his shoulder from across the table.

"I don't believe you. Anyways, whether you're a classics fan or not, no one can deny the rich history of that building. The architecture, the memories—"

"Yeah, yeah." Ben waved away the rest of her speech. "I've heard this spiel from your friend Tamara. What I want to know is, why is this place so important to *you*?"

Caitlyn toyed with the remainder of her meal. "It's home."

She glanced up, ready to find Ben smirking at her or focused on his food, at the very least. Instead she found herself the center of his attention, waiting for her to continue.

It still took her by surprise that he was so interested in her. Robert had never even pretended to take such an active interest in her hobbies, her interests, figuring out what made her tick. And he was supposed to be in it for the long haul. The milk in her fridge had a longer expiration date than she and Ben, yet he never ceased asking her questions, challenging her, making her look at her life from a different point of view. Like now. She'd never really given her attachment to the theater too much thought, but now she took the time to sort through the emotions that always surfaced when she thought about the theater and its possible demise.

"When I moved here, I didn't have anyone." She kept her gaze on her plate, not wanting to see his pity. "My parents died in a car accident when I was in high school and I didn't have any siblings. I wasn't terribly close with my extended family who let me live with them while I finished school."

She shrugged, as if the memory of those painful years after their death didn't still hurt. When she glanced up, it wasn't pity in his eyes but a warmth that eased some of the pain.

After clearing her throat, she finished her story. "I met Meg freshman year of college and we became good friends. We both loved old movies so we went to The Ellen all the time and found a home for ourselves there. That's where we met Tamara."

Heat flooded her cheeks. That must sound ridiculous, but it was true. "I fit in there, with Meg and Tamara and the rest of the crew."

When she looked up again, she saw...not pity...but something dangerously close. Sympathy, or empathy maybe. Either way, that wasn't what she wanted from this guy. What she wanted was to enjoy the rest of the time that they had together. She leaned over across the table and narrowed her eyes. "Are we going to sit in this diner all morning or are you going to pay the check so we can go have some fun with whipped cream?"

Ben's hand shot into the air. "Check please!"

* * * *

"What are you so happy about?" Marc grumbled.

"Seriously," Tamara added. She pushed back a long lock of blond hair and scowled up at Caitlyn. "I know you were drinking just as much as the rest of us, so what are you so chipper about?"

By a unanimous vote the night before, the crew had decided to push the cleanup efforts to the afternoon. The owner had canceled the Saturday afternoon children's movie matinee anyways, so there was no rush anymore.

The fact that the owner was slowly but surely eliminating movie showings—which equaled money in his pocket—was definitely not a good sign. It only enforced the rumors that he was planning to sell. If that was the case, one would think he'd invest in an actual cleaning crew, Caitlyn thought as she pushed the mop around.

She could feel Meg's eyes on her. The others had lost interest in Caitlyn's unexpected—and apparently annoying—perkiness in light of their own hungover misery. But Meg, who hadn't touched a drop for obvious reasons, was clearheaded and frighteningly observant. "You are too happy."

Caitlyn glanced over at her, where she was perched on a stool. "Too happy? Is that even a thing?"

Meg nodded. "It is and you are. What's up?"

Caitlyn shrugged. How could she explain? It wasn't just Robert's shock last night or the awesome post-breakfast sex this morning. Although both of those were factors. But more than that, it was this sense of freedom.

Last night had reminded her of something, which she couldn't put her finger on. For the first time in ages she felt light and carefree. A younger version of herself, not like the old woman who worried too much and was too scared to leave her apartment.

Meg was still watching her with suspicion, so she shrugged. "I don't know, just in a good mood, I guess."

Meg's answering murmur sounded skeptical. "It wouldn't have anything to do with that sexy roommate of yours, would it?"

Here we go. "For someone who's been urging me to get a sex life for so long, you're awfully judgmental of my current situation."

Caitlyn kept her tone light, but she saw Meg's flinch and a stab of guilt hit her in her gut. Her friend was only trying to look out for her. She knew that, but it was still frustrating. How could Meg not see that this was a good thing? Ben was helping her—not just with her ex but with moving on. Even better, he was helping her to see that she wasn't a cold fish after all. It hadn't been her that was the problem; it had been them—her and Robert. They hadn't had passion. Not the kind that she and Ben had at least.

"I'm happy that you're having fun," Meg said, her eyes studiously fixed on the to-do list in her hand. The bigger her stomach had gotten, the more she'd morphed into the role of team leader, assigning tasks to those without a giant belly handicap.

Caitlyn waited for her friend to continue. That wasn't everything Meg wanted to say. She was just glad Tamara, Marc, and Jake were chatting amongst themselves. One friend's unsolicited advice was one thing, but hearing opinions from the group at large? No thanks.

"I'm just worried," Meg continued. "I don't want to see you get hurt."

Caitlyn sighed. "I know. But please don't worry, okay? It's not like that between us. It's just sex." She flashed back to the way he'd had her laughing so hard this morning that tears were streaming down her face as she tried to escape his wrestling moves to take a shower. "And friendship," she added. "But that's it."

Meg's head tilted to the side as she studied her. "And just what do you think relationships are based on?"

Caitlyn resisted the urge to roll her eyes. Setting the mop to the side, she walked over to stand in front of Meg. "Neither of us wants a relationship right now." Meg opened her mouth but Caitlyn cut her off. "And even if I did, believe me, I wouldn't want it with Ben. We are complete opposites. It obviously wouldn't work. Not in the long run, at least."

It was the truth. Even if they both wanted more, they wouldn't make it as a couple. They were too different. It was something she'd known from that first night and what she'd been saying to herself ever since. But this time, saying the words out loud, they didn't exactly ring true. They sounded like a mantra she'd repeated so many times she'd forgotten the meaning.

If Meg was going to protest again, she was mercifully cut off by Alice's noisy arrival.

"Well, I did it," she said as she strolled in, looking for all the world like she'd been in hair and makeup all morning, compared to the rest of them.

"Did what?" Meg asked.

"Made it here on time?" Tamara asked, glancing at a nonexistent watch on her wrist. "Oh wait, no, that's still a feat yet to happen."

Alice ignored the teasing as she waltzed into the center of the lobby. Once all eyes were trained on her, she grinned. "I got my company to back a fundraiser for us."

Caitlyn looked to Tamara and Meg, both of whom were blinking up at Alice in surprise. "What does that mean?"

Alice had clearly been waiting for that because she whipped out a rolled up poster from behind her back—it was a professionally done poster, advertising for a costume party fundraiser at the theater itself.

"Costume party? Awesome!" Marc said.

Alice nodded, her wide grin full of excitement. "Right? I was thinking we could go with an old Hollywood theme. What do you think?"

She was looking at Tamara, as were the rest of them. It was really her decision.

Tamara bit her lip as she studied the poster. "It sounds wonderful but... I can't imagine the owner will go for it."

"Didn't he give you free reign over special events?" Jake pointed out.

Tamara's eyes widened and a hint of excitement lit up her face. "He did. And he doesn't pay much attention to what goes on around here, anyway."

"And he's never owned up to the fact that he's selling," Marc added. "So you can play dumb."

She looked to Caitlyn, as if needing to hear approval from all her friends before saying yes. "It's true," she added. "If the owner is going to be underhanded about putting the theater on the market, why not take advantage? I think it's a great idea."

After that, it was just a matter of finalizing the details and making sure the logistics would work. When Tamara took out the theater's calendar to check what date would work, the answer had Caitlyn frowning.

"What is it?" Meg asked.

"Oh nothing, I'm just supposed to go to Ben's office Christmas party that night. But it's fine, we can come here afterward."

Now Meg was scowling and Caitlyn hurried on. "It'll be fine, I promise. We'll get here by nine at the latest."

Meg raised one brow and Caitlyn sighed. Here it comes.

"You are going to be Ben's date for his office party?"

Caitlyn mentally kicked herself. She should never have said anything. Of course her friend would read into this. "It's not like that. I'm not going to be his date-date. Well, I am, but only like he was my date at last night's party. It's just to make his ex jealous."

Meg looked unconvinced.

"I swear!"

Some of the worry on Meg's face melted away to be replaced by resignation. "Just promise me you'll be careful, okay?"

Caitlyn nodded. "Of course I will."

Chapter 10

Gregory was glowering at Ben over his beer. "What are you so happy about?"

They were in a back booth at one of Gregory's favorite dive bars. An odd choice for lunch, perhaps, and an even odder choice for a billionaire like Gregory. For a rich guy, his friend had pedestrian tastes. That afternoon he even looked the part of a starving artist. His normally slicked-back black hair was falling over his forehead and his typically clean-shaven face was covered in stubble. He looked…disheveled.

"I'm having a good day," Ben said. Leaning back in the booth, he couldn't help the self-satisfied grin as he thought about Caitlyn's startling offer that morning. And the amazing sex that had followed once they'd returned home.

"Happiness doesn't suit you," Gregory said.

Ben let out a bark of laughter. "Don't worry, old friend, I'm only happy because Caitlyn and I have hatched a revenge plot against my ex. I haven't gone and become optimistic or anything."

Gregory's brows rose in a cynical, questioning look. "Are you sure your roommate isn't the cause of this sudden—and *annoying*—upbeat mood?"

Ben sighed. He should never have told his friend about this arrangement. "It's not like that. We're just friends."

"And roommates, and lovers, and apparently partners in crime now," Gregory added.

Ben took another sip of his beer. The more he denied it, the more his friend would leap to the wrong conclusions. Instead, he changed the topic. "What's the matter with you?"

Gregory didn't even flinch at the abrupt shift or the rude question. "I don't know what you're talking about."

"Don't you?" He pointedly looked his friend up and down, pausing meaningfully at the empty shot glasses that sat in front of him.

Gregory exhaled loudly and thrust a hand through his already disheveled hair. "Vanessa moved out."

Ben froze. "Oh."

What else could he say? *Sorry?* He wasn't really. He'd known Gregory for a long time, well before Vanessa had come on the scene, and he knew from firsthand experience that she was no good for him. He'd watched her manipulate him and tie him up in knots. Not unlike his ex, actually. Maybe bad relationships were contagious.

But despite the fact that he was relieved by this sudden turn of events, it was never fun to watch one's friends in their misery. Caitlyn would know the right thing to say. What would she say?

"That's tough, mate." Well, she wouldn't use the British slang, but she would find a way to empathize without judgment. She was good like that.

Gregory's jerky nod was his only response. Then he took another long swig of his drink. "Yeah, well. I know it's for the best, it just…"

"Sucks," Ben finished. "Yeah, I know. Been there, done that, remember?"

Gregory's lips twisted up in a pale imitation of his usual lopsided grin. "Speaking of your twisted ex, what's this scheme you and your *friend* concocted?"

Ben chose to ignore his friend's sarcastic tone when he said "friend." Instead he told him about their act at the bar the night before, doing his best to make it entertaining and light to keep his friend distracted. It was the least he could do.

"Sounds like you two had fun." Gregory's face was unreadable, but Ben heard the unspoken judgment.

"I'm telling you, it's not like that."

"Whatever you say. So what's the plan now? You two are going to pretend that you're a real couple at the Christmas party?"

Ben couldn't help but smirk at the thought of Olivia's face when she saw them together. "Seeing me move on…and with someone like Caitlyn? It's going to kill her."

Gregory laughed, most likely at the sheer evil in Ben's voice. But his friend's next question threw him. "Someone like Caitlyn?"

Ben's head shot up. "What?"

"You said 'someone like Caitlyn'—what does that mean?"

Ben shrugged. Why would his friend not let this go? He seemed intent to make something out of this that wasn't there. He knew Gregory long enough to know that he was no prude. He had nothing against casual flings and one-night stands. But apparently he drew the line at sleeping with one's roommate because he couldn't seem to get it through his thick skull that it was just about sex.

He thought of their nights on the couch. Sex and friendship. But that was it.

Gregory was watching him, waiting for his answer.

Someone like Caitlyn... What *had* he meant? He made a few vague gestures with his hands as he struggled to find the right words. "You know, someone who's..." What? Sweet, caring, intelligent, funny? "Classy."

Gregory gave a little snort of laughter. "What is she, a dame or something?"

Ben gave a long suffering sigh. "I don't know how to explain it. But trust me, Olivia will hate her. Caitlyn is everything Olivia is not. She's not manipulative or bitchy, and she's not trying to claw her way to the top."

Gregory kept silent and Ben found himself babbling. "She's the type of woman you take home to meet your parents, you know? She screams out long-term, mother of your children." He took a quick sip of his beer, excruciatingly aware of Gregory's eyes on him. "Plus, she's hot," he added with a shrug.

"Hmm." It wasn't much of a response after that odd little diatribe. Ben thought perhaps Gregory had moved on, but a few moments later, he said, "And you're sure she's not *your* long-term, mother of your children type of woman."

Ben recoiled into the cushioned booth in horror. "Of course not! How long have you known me? How many women have you seen me with? Do you really think she sounds like my type?"

Gregory shrugged. "Sometimes tastes change."

Ben deflated a bit as his defensive anger dissipated. His friend was angry and hurt. Besides, Gregory had never met Caitlyn. If he met her he'd see that she was so not his type. Except in bed, obviously. In bed, she was his perfect match. But anywhere else and the idea of them as a couple was laughable. Even Gregory, who was his biggest supporter, would be able to see how incompatible they would be. Even Gregory would admit that she deserved better.

Gregory had always had his back, but there was no way in hell he'd ever let Ben date his sister. Why? Because he knew him—he knew that when push came to shove, he was a selfish bastard. One who'd chosen to pursue money rather than love. And one who was capable of hurting anyone stupid enough to love him.

"So," Gregory said, a little too loudly. "Have you and Darren signed the deal? Are you backing his latest real estate venture?"

A twinge of guilt had Ben reaching for his beer again. He never had gotten around to reviewing the new docs thanks to Caitlyn's interruption. For a self-professed workaholic, this slip was akin to playing hookie or taking an actual vacation.

"Haven't reviewed it yet," he admitted.

Gregory grabbed a fry off Ben's plate. "Darren ran it past me and it looks good. He's got a solid plan, especially for that block downtown. You know the one with that old movie theater that's practically falling down? Seems the owner is finally willing to sell."

Ben's blood ran cold. His stomach made a move to flee. *Oh fuck.*

"Something wrong?"

Ben cleared his throat. "No, no. Not really. It's just... There might be a bit of a conflict of interest there."

Gregory's forehead furrowed in confusion. "Since when? Are you working with another real estate company that's got its eye on that block?"

"Uh, no, not exactly."

Gregory's look of confusion turned to unabashed curiosity, most likely at Ben's awkwardness. "Not exactly?"

Oh fuck it. He told Gregory everything—about the little crew that was determined to keep The Ellen open and, more importantly, Caitlyn's involvement.

"This would kill her," he said. "And she'd kill me in turn."

Gregory's obvious amusement would have made him furious if he wasn't so relieved to see his friend back from the brink of depression. "Don't tell me you—you, 'Ben-the-ruthless-asshole'—would actually tank a solid investment rather than hurt the feelings of your new girlfriend?"

Ben shook his head. "She's *not* my girlfriend." Noting the looks from the patrons around them, he lowered his voice. "But she is my friend. And her friends are kind of my friends, too."

Which was true, he realized with a start. He'd gone from one friend to a slew of them, thanks to Caitlyn.

"But I'm not tanking anything," he added.

"So you're going to back his plan and ruin Caitlyn's little pet project?"

Ben paused. He couldn't say yes. Physically, he couldn't form the word. Every time he went to say it, he had an image of Caitlyn's face if she found out, and it just about crushed him. "I don't know yet."

When Gregory smirked, he added, "I haven't even reviewed the new numbers. It may not even be worth the risk."

Gregory just shook his head in amusement. "I may not have seen the numbers, but I know a good project when I see one. This one has serious potential. I'm kind of pissed I didn't think of it myself."

Shit. He'd have to tell her, that much was clear. Either way, she should know that the owner was moving forward with his plan to sell. She and Tamara and the others deserved to know that much, at least.

He'd tell her when he got home. When he got to *her* home, he mentally corrected.

Crap. This was not going to be fun.

He was temporarily distracted by Gregory's flailing hand as he attempted to get the waitress's attention, though with a quick glance Ben could see she was far more interested in flirting with the bartender than in serving her customers.

"You want another round, too?" Gregory asked.

Ben looked at the clock on his phone. "A bit early to get sauced, no?"

He ignored Gregory's scowl. Right. Who was he to judge when he'd spent the better part of two weeks in a drunken coma in Gregory's spare bedroom after his split. Still, he hated to see his friend in such a sorry state.

"Can't have another, I'm afraid. Caitlyn and I have plans—" He ignored Gregory's look of cynical amusement and drained the last of his beer. "We're heading uptown for a screening of *Vertigo*."

When Gregory started to laugh, he added with more defensiveness than absolutely necessary, "It's just a movie. Jesus, grow up."

His friend eventually stopped laughing at him and let his hand drop. Ben saw the brief glimpse of desolation in his friend's eyes and forgave him for the mockery.

"Come with us."

He started to shake his head but Ben cut him off. "Come on, you can't keep drinking like this. You need to get out of the house. Be around people."

Gregory's eyes narrowed on him. "Are you sure I won't be intruding?"

Ben rolled his eyes and slapped down some money on the table. "We'll see you there at eight."

* * * *

Caitlyn practically pounced on Ben the moment he walked through the door. She couldn't help it; her good mood had made her a crazy person. "Guess what?"

He dropped his jacket onto the couch and flopped down beside it, a tolerant smile on his face. He hadn't shaved yet and a five o'clock shadow gave him a sexy, disheveled look that had her itching to climb into his lap.

Oh, why not? They'd long since broken the unspoken rule of only having close physical contact at night or in the bedroom. She'd come to crave his cuddles almost as much as his body. Almost.

He laughed as she made herself comfortable on his lap and he pulled her against him so she was nicely nestled. "What are you so excited about?" She started to tell him all about the fundraiser that Alice was planning. A marketing professional, any event Alice planned was sure to be a success. She had the connections and the know-how to bring in lots of money, enough to garner the kind of attention they needed to get the theater on the list of protected properties.

Ben's hands were rubbing her arms, her shoulders, her thighs—but they stilled as she was talking. Even his lips stopped their exploration on her neck and were frozen against the side of her head.

Pulling back, her voice trailed off and she half turned so she could face him. "What's wrong?"

The unusual tightness around his mouth set off alarm bells. "What is it?"

"Caitlyn, uh…" He thrust a hand through his hair, his eyes not meeting hers but rather fixed on the doorway as if contemplating escape.

What the hell? Caitlyn's mind raced to think of what could have changed between that morning, when he'd been laughing and happy, and now? The only topic that ever made him this uncomfortable was Olivia.

So that was it. He must have seen the date on the poster. Caitlyn eased back against him, the tension melting as quickly as it had formed. Of course that's what he was worried about. "Don't worry," she said, reaching up a hand to lightly stroke his jaw. "I know it's the same night as the Christmas party, but I have no intention of leaving you high and dry."

He blinked at her as though not comprehending and she hurried on. "Your Christmas party is a dinner, right? Which is perfect because the party won't start until later, and it will go on until late in the night so we can show up late."

A heavy silence hung between them as she waited for Ben to return to normal. She hated seeing him so tense.

His deep inhale had her rising up and down against him. "Caitlyn, we need to talk."

Her eyes widened as she looked up at him. What else could be bothering him about a party? With a small smile, she said, "Are you dreading the idea of dressing up? So is Jake! God, why are guys so weird about costumes?"

His answering smile was strained. "I, uh, I have to tell you something…."

She waited patiently for him to continue, that uneasy tension starting to return as the pause lengthened. Finally, she prodded, "What is it?"

She felt his heavy exhale as he pulled her even closer. "I invited my friend Gregory to join us for the movie tonight."

Surprise had her stilling in his arms. That was what he wanted to talk about?

Before she could respond, he continued. "He's one of my oldest friends and his girlfriend left him. For good this time, God willing. He's a bit of a wreck and I just thought it would be good for him to—"

She cut him off with a kiss. She couldn't help herself. He was just too cute when he was being thoughtful. She pulled back long enough to say, "I think that's a great idea." Then he pulled her back in for another, far more thorough kiss.

Chapter 11

"Are you actually telling me you prefer musicals to non-musicals?" Caitlyn couldn't help but laugh. Ben's friend Gregory looked like such an alpha male, she would never have expected that little revelation to come from him. After seeing *Vertigo* at an uptown theater that showed old movies once in a blue moon, their conversation had revolved around Jimmy Stewart. As the threesome walked farther uptown to a bar Ben wanted to check out, she and Gregory had gone back and forth on their favorite Jimmy Stewart movies. The shocking revelation had come when she'd said her favorite was *The Philadelphia Story*, because it co-starred Cary Grant, obviously, and he had claimed that he preferred the musical adaptation, *High Society*.

She turned as if to study him further. "I would never have taken you for a musical man."

He lifted one brow and feigned a condescending tone. "I'm a Sinatra man."

She burst out laughing at that one. She'd been wary of Gregory at first—he'd seemed too stiff, too stuck up. But the more he talked and joked with her and Ben the more she liked him. He was charming in an old-school debonair kind of way. Ben had told her he came from money and it showed. He was confident and classy, but not entitled. This Gregory was a nice change from the sullen man they'd met before the movie.

Ben had told her all about his friend's breakup before they arrived and her heart went out to him. But he was in good company. If there were ever two people who understood how awful breakups were, it was her and Ben.

"I definitely like the classic movies better than modern," Gregory was saying as they sat down at a booth in the back. "I just don't think there's a market for them. They're never going to be as popular, and a theater needs to diversify if they want to stay open in this day and age."

She shared a look with Ben and he muttered, "Don't tell Tamara that."

"Who?" Gregory asked.

Caitlyn turned to Gregory. "Oh, my friend who runs a classic movie theater downtown. She's a purist. She thinks there should be a place in the city devoted entirely to old movies."

Gregory and Ben exchanged a look that made Caitlyn wary. "What?"

Ben shook his head quickly, but she could have sworn he gave Gregory a warning look before flashing that sexy grin her way. "Nothing. Gregory's just a cynic, that's all."

"I prefer realist." Gregory stuck his nose in the air and sniffed, making Caitlyn laugh.

Leaning over as if to tell Gregory a secret, she said, "I've got to know. How did someone like you"—she waved her hand to take in his clean-cut, well-groomed appearance—"ever become friends with someone like him?"

"Hey!" Ben pretended to be outraged as he reached for his beer. The men did look like polar opposites, though, there was no denying it. Ben's face was scruffy and unshaven, his hair was mussed as always, and he sported jeans and an untucked button down that had seen one too many washings.

She and Gregory ignored his protest and Gregory leaned toward her, so they were both pretending that Ben wasn't there and couldn't hear every word.

"We met in college, actually. He's a Neanderthal, obviously, but he has a tendency to grow on you." He took a sip of his beer. "Like a weed."

Caitlyn matched his serious expression and added, "Or a fungus."

"You two are hysterical." Ben shifted so his arm brushed hers and when she instinctively leaned in toward him, Ben's arm moved to wrap around her shoulders.

She caught the flicker of surprise on Gregory's face before he covered it. For a moment she wondered just how much Ben had told his friend about their relationship. In her mind's eye she could see how they must look from his point of view.

Like a couple.

But of course they weren't. She shifted beneath his arm, wriggling a bit to adjust. Amazing how comfortable she'd become around this man in such a short period of time. And that's what this was—short-term. An uncomfortable nagging feeling made her lungs feel heavy, like she had to fight for air.

She shook her head at her own overreaction. So it was short-term, that was the point. She'd never been good with good-byes and separation—probably half the reason her relationship with Robert lasted as long as it did.

The air she'd been struggling to breath came in a rush at that heady realization. Like a lens had been removed from her glasses, she had a glimpse of what her relationship with Robert had really been. What it would have looked like to an outsider. And it wasn't pretty.

Images of their day-to-day life together passed before her like she was watching a movie of her life. They never laughed. She couldn't remember ever laughing till she cried, not even in the early days. Not like her and Ben.

And when had he ever taken an interest in her knitting? Oh, she'd always accepted his lack of interest as his male prerogative, but it was important to her. Shouldn't it have been important to him?

And when had he ever challenged her? To get her out of her comfort zone or to meet new people or to turn her passion into a lucrative business? Never.

She was dimly aware of Gregory and Ben carrying on a conversation without her, but she couldn't focus long enough to contribute. Now that she'd seen the truth, she couldn't deny it. She and Robert hadn't been good together.

Not like her and Ben. She shook her head quickly at that thought. They might make a great couple for the moment, but they were certainly not long-term. That was the deal. Besides, they made great friends-with-benefits, they'd never even tried to be a couple, and they never would. But still, this time with Ben had been exactly what she'd needed to see the truth about her relationship with Robert.

Thank God he'd broken up with her.

Ben shot her a questioning look as she choked on her drink. "You okay?"

She nodded quickly, unable to stop the wide, possibly crazy-looking smile that spread across her face as a new lightness filled her. For the first time since the breakup, she could honestly say she was happy it had happened. Not only that, it was for the best. She was better off for it.

Her breath was coming in short, excited gasps. She needed a moment alone to compose herself. Ben must have noticed her odd behavior because he turned to her with narrowed eyes. "What's up?"

She couldn't help it. Overwhelmed with gratitude and appreciation for her temporary roommate, she leaned in and planted a quick kiss on his scruffy cheek.

That earned her a cute, boyish grin as he turned toward her. "What was that for?"

She shook her head. "Nothing. I don't know, just in a good mood, I guess."

Ben and Gregory were both staring at her like she'd lost her mind, so she cleared her throat and scooted toward Ben, gently nudging him out of the way so she could exit the booth. "Excuse me, I've got to run to the bathroom."

Once alone in the bathroom she threw a hand over her mouth to stifle the sound of her laughter. She was over him. After a year of grieving, she was over him...just like that. Well, it had probably been happening for a while but the realization was so sudden, so startling, it felt like an instantaneous event.

And she owed it all to Ben. Without him, she would never have gotten this new perspective. She wouldn't have had the comparison to draw on or the boosted confidence to see that Ben had been right this whole time. She deserved better. She deserved love—real love—and a relationship that made her happy.

* * * *

The moment Caitlyn disappeared from view, Gregory's carefree demeanor slipped and he leaned toward Ben with an urgency that was alarming.

"What are you doing with that girl?" his friend demanded.

Ben's mouth fell open but nothing came out. Finally, he said, "What do you mean?"

But he knew exactly what Gregory meant. And he didn't want to hear it.

"You know what I mean," Gregory said, his voice dangerously close to a growl. "Whatever you two have going on... She's going to get hurt."

A stab of pain in his gut had him shifting in his seat. He hated the overprotective way Gregory was talking, as if he knew Caitlyn better than he did.

"She's an adult," Ben started.

"She's naïve." Gregory didn't say it in a mean way but there was no doubt in his voice. "She's a sweet kid. Too sweet."

Too sweet for you. His friend may not have said the "for you" part, but he didn't have to. He was right, and they both knew it. He avoided a response by taking a large gulp of his beer. He couldn't bullshit Gregory. His friend was one of the few people who knew his track record with women and the vow he'd made to avoid getting into a relationship with someone like Caitlyn. But this wasn't a relationship, dammit. He had it under control.

Gregory's glare didn't let up, and Ben felt compelled to defend himself. "Look, we're just having fun. We both needed that after…everything."

His friend flinched a bit and he knew he was thinking about his own breakup hell. If anyone would understand, it should be him.

"We're helping each other," he continued.

Gregory made a grunting noise in disbelief. "I can see how she's helping *you*. But how exactly are you helping her?"

A nagging guilt gnawed at his insides at the insinuation that he was taking advantage of her. He wasn't. *So what was with the guilt then?*

"Does she know this isn't real?" Gregory crossed his arms in front of his chest, and Ben had a fleeting glimpse of what his friend would be like if he ever had a daughter.

"Of course she knows," Ben said. It came out sounding more defensive than he'd intended. Relaxing back into the booth, he struggled for nonchalance. "Look, I know she seems all sweet and innocent—"

Gregory raised a brow.

"And okay, yeah, she is," Ben added. "But she's a grown-up and she knows what the deal is. Believe me, she doesn't want a relationship with me any more than I want one with her."

Greg's eyes rounded. "You don't?"

"Don't what?" Ben took another swig.

"Don't play dumb." Gregory's disbelief morphed into a smirk. "Are you honestly trying to tell me that you wouldn't date that girl?"

"Woman," Ben corrected. "And no. She's not my type. You know that." Irritation laced his voice. He wasn't even trying to hide his frustration. Because Gregory *knew*. He knew Ben too well to think that was a good idea.

Gregory let out a snort. "Oh yeah, because your type has been working out for you really well so far."

"Like you're one to judge," Ben shot back.

A silence fell between them and Ben instantly wished he could take it back. Gregory was obviously still in the first stages of suck, and it was too soon to be using his bad taste in women against him. "Sorry," he muttered.

One corner of Gregory's mouth lifted in a poor attempt at a grin. "Don't apologize, you're right."

The silence was even more awkward after that, so Ben threw back the rest of his drink and slammed his bottle down against the table. "We're a poor excuse for two single gents out on the town."

Gregory gave a half laugh, but his gaze was focused on something over Ben's shoulder. Ben turned to see Caitlyn sashaying her way back to their table, an enchanting, smug little smile giving her a glow that left him breathless.

He could hear Gregory shifting in the seat across from him, but he couldn't tear his eyes away from Caitlyn. What had happened to make her so happy? He couldn't wait to find out.

Gregory's amused voice cut into his thoughts. "We're a poor excuse for two single men because one of us isn't single."

Ben's eyes shot to his friend. "What the hell does that mean?"

But Caitlyn had almost reached them so Gregory just said, "I think you know. Just promise me one thing. Be honest with the poor girl before she gets hurt."

Ben opened his mouth to retort—*I would never hurt her*, maybe, or *you have no clue what you're talking about*, but then Caitlyn plopped down next to him with a knockout smile. "So, what did I miss?"

"Nothing," Ben said a bit too quickly. He could practically feel Greg smirking across the table from him but he ignored it, keeping his focus on Caitlyn for the remainder of their drink. Caitlyn, who was glowing for some reason, which made him unbelievably curious. And turned on.

They left shortly after that. In fact, Ben probably was a tad rude trying to hustle Caitlyn into finishing her drink so they could get out the door.

She greeted every attempt on his part to rush her with a quizzical smile. "What's your hurry?" she asked as she took a bigger sip at his request.

"Yeah, Ben, what's the rush?" Gregory echoed. But Ben could hear the judgment in his friend's voice and see it in his eyes every time Caitlyn cuddled up against him or referenced an inside joke.

It wasn't like that! They weren't a couple and that was what they both wanted. Wasn't it?

Oh God, now Gregory's paranoia was contagious. Of course she didn't want a relationship with him. Hadn't they already established that he was not her type? She deserved someone who would treat her right, who knew how to be a proper boyfriend, and—most importantly—who wanted the things that she did. A future, and a family, and…well, love. Everything he avoided like the plague.

That was why he and Olivia worked together, because they'd had no future.

He paused with his drink poised just in front of his lips. Huh. He'd never thought of it that way before. He'd never had any reason to overanalyze or doubt his motives for being with Olivia or hers for being with him.

They were having fun—that was what he'd always told himself about their relationship. They were lucky because they had someone to sleep with every night but none of the headaches of a typical relationship. But now that he'd gotten some distance, it seemed utterly and stupidly clear.

He'd been with her because there was no future. And she'd probably felt the same way about him. They'd been drawn to each other because it wasn't real—there was no hope of letting one another down or being tied down for the long haul. They'd never once talked about the future. Her ambivalence about that particular topic was one thing he'd always liked about her. It made being together easy when there were no expectations. No one so invested that their hearts were at stake. No chance that he could hurt someone when she didn't truly care. And there was no way he could be hurt by someone he didn't love.

Sure being cheated on sucked, but it had been a blow to his ego, not his heart.

The realization had a funny effect. While on one hand he felt free, finally seeing the relationship for what it really, he also had a sick feeling in the pit of his stomach. God, he really was messed up. What kind of person sought out toxic, go-nowhere relationships?

Someone who didn't know how to love or someone who didn't want love. Either way, someone who was too messed up to be part of a proper couple.

In short, him.

It was no wonder Gregory wanted him far, far away from Caitlyn. He barely knew her but even he could see that she was too good for Ben. That she deserved so much more.

"You okay?" she asked, her nose wrinkled up in concern. She and Gregory were both watching him with interest, and he realized he must have not heard something they'd said.

"Oh yeah, just lost in thought I guess."

Neither of them seemed to buy it but they let it go. Before long Caitlyn had finished her drink, and he ushered her out of the booth and into a waiting taxi as quickly as he could, willfully ignoring Gregory's knowing smirk all the while.

Once home, they settled into their usual routine in front of the TV, but he realized they were both too caught up in their thoughts to pay much attention or to hold a conversation.

She'd stopped drinking for the night, but Ben needed another whisky to dull the thoughts that were racing through his brain thanks to Gregory's little lecture. It wasn't that he thought he was right, but still his friend's criticism unnerved him nearly as much as his own realizations about his last relationship. It wasn't until he had two more that the mental game of ping-pong subsided.

When he finally switched the set off, they were both yawning. Without thinking, he drew her into his arms, where she nestled up against him, her head nodding against his chest.

"I'm sorry," she said. "I'm too sleepy for..."

"Yeah, I know." He kissed the top of her head. "Me, too."

Chapter 12

Ben woke slowly the next morning. He felt good. Well, there was a bit of a hangover brewing but still, he felt amazing. He shifted so he could bury his face against Caitlyn's warm, sweet neck.

Oh holy shit.

He was cuddling. Worse, he was spooning. He was the big spoon—when had he become a spoon, for chrissakes?

He slowly pulled away, trying to disengage his intertwined limbs, but she mumbled something in protest in her sleep.

She was fucking adorable when she slept. So peaceful and soft and beautiful and—holy crap, he was watching her sleep.

This was bad. This was very bad. This broke every fuck buddy rule ever created. And last night? No sex, just cuddles. Cuddles until they'd fallen asleep in one another's arms. Ben let out a quiet moan. They had broken the agreement, which meant they were in unchartered territory.

He looked back to where Caitlyn lay, looking sweet and innocent as ever. Gregory's words came back to him with a vengeance. *You're going to hurt that girl.*

That was the last thing he wanted. But maybe Gregory had a point. Clearly the boundaries between them were blurring. He flashed back to the way she'd snuggled up against him the night before. How he'd been perfectly content to sit there and cuddle. Cuddle, for God's sake!

Shoving a hand through his hair, he got out of bed and started pacing. He wasn't ready for anything more than fuck buddies. He'd made that clear. Hell, he was certain he couldn't handle more. He'd always known that about himself, which was why up until Olivia he'd avoided anything other than one-night stands.

Even if he could handle some sort of relationship, it would never be with this woman. Not that kind of relationship. He wasn't the type. Not for someone like her. She deserved a good man, not one who attracted drama, who always said and did the wrong things, who slept around too much, and drank too much, and made a mess of every so-called relationship he'd ever been in. Olivia had been the closest thing to a true girlfriend he'd ever had and just look how that turned out.

No, he wasn't ready for another relationship even if he could be better for her. Because, let's face it, he might get his act together for a little while but then he would always go back to his old ways. That's the way it always worked for him. He bored easily. That was why Olivia had lasted as long as she had. She'd gotten that about him because she was the same way. That was why there had always been so much drama. They couldn't stay together without it. They would have flamed out and died months earlier if the heat of anger and makeup sex hadn't fueled the fire.

Sure this was fun now, but it wouldn't last. That was a certainty. Walking away from Caitlyn made his chest ache, but he reminded himself of the alternative. If Gregory was right, she would get attached. It was no secret that being fuck buddies was a new thing for her. She wasn't used to getting close physically without an emotional connection as well. He stifled a groan at the memory of her rushing into his arms when he'd arrived home the night before, of the way her eyes had grown all soft and dreamy when they'd danced together at the bar...

Oh no. Gregory was right. He was going to hurt her. He was going to hurt the one woman who'd been nothing but kind, supportive, and sweet to him. She'd opened herself up to him and he'd ruin it, just like he ruined every relationship—real or not.

There was only one thing to be done. The realization sucked the air from his lungs with a whoosh. He had to put an end to this if he was going to avoid hurting her.

He knew what he had to do. But even as he opened her laptop and got to work, his chest ached. Even more reason to pull the plug on this thing. Clearly he was forming an attachment here and that was unacceptable. He had to put an end to whatever this was for both their sakes. Besides, he was supposed to leave in another week, anyways. His fingers paused over the keyboard. Maybe he could wait. Have one more week with Caitlyn.

No. One more week of sleeping together and talking well into the night, not to mention cuddling... He was already in too deep. Caitlyn was already too close to getting hurt. But if he ended it now, he could minimize any damage. He'd help her to move on to someone new and then he would slip out of her life once and for all.

* * * *

When Caitlyn woke, he was on the far side of the room.

"What are you doing?" she mumbled.

She was half awake and had a bad case of bedhead. And she looked adorable. Shit. This was bad.

He focused on the laptop before him and ordered himself to stay strong. "I'm finding you a date."

That woke her up. "What?" She was on her elbows and staring at him as though he'd just sprouted horns.

Good. That was the point. This was for her own good.

"Why are you on my laptop?" She still sounded half awake, her voice scratchy and husky…and unbelievably sexy.

"I needed to get into your account and your laptop was just sitting here." He ignored the cute wrinkle of her nose that he took to mean she didn't know whether to ask more questions or yell at him for invading her privacy.

"You really should update your passwords," he pointed out, nodding toward her laptop. "It was stupidly easy to get in here."

He turned his attention back to the laptop and resisted the urge to look up. There was too much temptation there, and he was determined to do right by her. She was kind and loving and, yes, sweet, and she deserved her Cary Grant. Not some bastard who was incapable of being in a healthy, committed relationship, who had an unstable job and no plans for a future. She deserved better than him.

"Why?" she asked. He glanced over to see her shaking her head and rubbing her eyes, trying to wake up and make sense of this conversation. He looked away again.

"Look here, this guy looks perfect." He brought the laptop to the side of the bed where he sat just far enough away that he couldn't touch her even if he wanted to. He handed over the laptop where a handsome man beamed back at them.

"What do you think?" he prompted.

She was studying the profile with a bemused look on her face. He supposed it was a bit of an odd way to wake up.

"He looks…nice," she said.

"I'm glad you think so because you and this fella are going on a date."

"We're *what*?"

He ignored her shock. She would thank him in the end. "I knew it would take you weeks of e-mailing and texting to sort out whether or not you wanted to meet up in person but really, love, it's just a date. How are you ever going to meet the right guy in this century at the rate you're going?"

She stared at him with an open mouth. Good, if she was speechless, he had a moment to sell his top draft for boyfriend material.

"He's a doctor."

Caitlyn's gaze dropped from his face to the screen. "I see that."

"And he's looking for a woman who wants to settle down and have a family," he continued. Good God, was that him talking? He sounded like a used car dealer. Maybe he should dial it down a bit.

"I told you I'd find you your Cary Grant," he reminded her.

Her smile was rueful and it was so beautiful it hurt. "You did say that, didn't you?"

He nodded. "I always keep my promises."

"What about that promise to do your dishes immediately after meals?"

"Well, I always keep the promises I want to keep."

She looked away from him then and her smile looked strained. Shit. Had he done that?

"Right," she said. "So when am I supposed to meet the good doctor?"

He let out a breath he hadn't realized he'd been holding. Thank the Lord, this was working. "Tonight."

"Ben!"

"Oh, I'm sorry, did you have other plans? Because I'm fairly certain you were in for a night of telly on the couch."

And hot, amazing sex, but that could wait until she returned from her date. Unless the date went well. Jesus, what if she brought him home? What if she wanted to sleep with the guy? What a nightmare. Maybe he should have thought this plan through. He could have set her up for a hundred dates…right after he moved out.

But that would defeat the purpose. Ben steeled himself against the jealousy that was making it difficult to breathe. The point was to get her sorted with another man—a proper man—before she grew too attached.

"I don't want to go on a date tonight," she said. She moved so she was sitting upright and the blanket slipped down, revealing her scrap of a nightie that was just barely covering her breasts.

His cock hardened instantly at the sight. All it would take was one little tug on that strap and the nightie would slip off her shoulder, revealing her beautiful breasts.

"Ben?"

He forced his eyes back to her face. What had she been saying? The date. Right. Focus.

"I thought you said you were ready to move on from that asshat Robert," he said.

"I am ready, but—"

"If you're ever going to truly move on, you need to start dating. You need to find a rebound guy. Take it from me. Why do you think I was on that date with you in the first place?"

At the mention of "that date," her eyes narrowed. "I was your rebound date?" She didn't sound offended. She sounded…pleased.

He had the uncomfortable feeling that he'd let on more than intended. "Of course, you knew that."

"Because you thought I was hot." It wasn't a question. She was looking at him with a little smile of pure, female satisfaction that drove him wild.

Of course he'd thought she was hot. What sane man wouldn't? Hadn't he told her that a thousand times? God, this woman was thick headed.

But she was his woman.

Nope. Not acceptable. That was exactly why he had to find her someone like—he glanced down at the dapper man on the screen—Nicholas. The good doctor Nick, who was looking for a sweet woman to settle down with and pop out some babies. He even liked old movies. Granted, he'd named *Casablanca* as his favorite move so he wasn't exactly winning any awards for originality, but knowing Caitlyn, she'd like that he was a romantic.

This guy was perfect. He would make Caitlyn happy and give her all the things that he could not. He looked down at the smiling photo. Bloody hell, this guy really was perfect.

* * * *

Caitlyn stared at the picture on her phone as she waited for her date to arrive. He looked perfect. Too perfect.

Ben had set her up with a Ken doll.

What if he had Ken's doll parts below the belt? She smothered a laugh that bordered on hysterical by taking a sip of her water.

Nicholas had left the location of their date up to her so she'd chosen a little café near Cagney's. If the date went well, she might take him there for a drink. If it was a miserable failure, Meg was on standby to lend a sympathetic ear. Win-win.

Lose-lose.

One hour later Caitlyn was certain her jaw would fall off from the effort it took to keep from yawning. She had never been so bored in all her life.

"I'm really glad you found me on that site, Caitlyn," he said between bites of a piece of cake they shared.

She smiled. *Actually, the man I've been sleeping with on a regular basis found you.*

How would he react to that? Perfectly, no doubt. The man sitting before her was perfect. So perfect. Too perfect. And he was humble to top it all off.

She smiled politely over his sweet story about working with young children in the pediatrics unit. How was he boring her with a story about cute kids? Cute kid stories were always...well, *cute*.

Her face hurt from polite smiling. Do not look at your watch. Do not look at your watch. Do not look at your—

"So what about you?"

Caitlyn blinked at the Ken doll. "Excuse me?"

"Do you want kids some day?" Dr. Nick took a sip of his coffee and looked at her expectantly.

Really? Were they really having the kid conversation on a first get-to-know-you date? Apparently they were.

"No," Caitlyn heard the lie come out of her mouth and saw Dr. Nick's brief frown of disappointment.

"I don't believe in marriage and family." Caitlyn didn't know where the lies were coming from, but they came out easily and they had the desired effect. Nicholas was practically chugging his coffee.

"But your profile said—"

Caitlyn gave him a rueful look. "My roommate created my page." She added a shrug that said "roommates, what are you gonna do?" for good measure. She saw him give the waiter a nod to signal for the check.

Good. Time's a ticking. Caitlyn had an image of the Manhattan that was awaiting her at Cagney's—an oasis in the desert. Let's get a move on, mister.

* * * *

It was hard to say who was in a worse mood, Ben or Gregory.

Unable to sit in the apartment alone to wait and wonder just what was going on between Caitlyn and Mr. Perfect, he'd opted to keep Gregory company. Lord knew the poor sucker needed the distraction. But Gregory seemed determined to bring up every topic Ben did not want to discuss.

"So you didn't tell her about Darren's plans for the theater, huh?" Gregory was sprawled across the opposite couch, looking worse for the wear.

Ben debated ignoring his friend's comment but decided that would only make Gregory latch on like a dog with a bone.

"No. I didn't tell her." His tone left no room for arguments. Also, he was seriously starting to doubt his decision to comfort his friend. He didn't want to discuss Caitlyn, or her friends, or their pet project. He was here to distract himself from thoughts of her—particularly what she was doing at that precise moment on a date with someone else. Someone who probably wouldn't spill his beer all over her lap or insult her life choices.

A little smile tugged at the corner of his lips at the memory of her indignation every time he called her out on being too accommodating with her knitting students. She really was adorable when she was angry.

"What are you sighing about over there?" Gregory was all but growling at him now. Oh, this was not good. And wait? Had he sighed? Oh this really was not good at all.

"I wasn't sighing," he lied. "Just wanted to get back to the topic at hand." He held up a manila folder as if in evidence of his sincere desire to work.

Gregory rolled his eyes and reached for his whisky. "The theater. Right. That's what I was talking about, too."

No. He'd been talking about Caitlyn and the theater. Big difference. He was here to get a little perspective on the whole situation. That was what Gregory was good for—he was nothing if not rational and level-headed. Ben eyed the rapidly disappearing whisky in his friend's glass. Well, usually he was.

Gregory waved a hand in the general direction of the folder. "All right then, what do you want to discuss about the theater?"

"Darren's proposal—"

"Is good." Gregory's short response was not helpful. This time Ben did sigh, but it was with a weariness that he didn't even pretend to hide.

"Look, I'm trying to look at this from all angles, okay? I want to see what all the options are before I—"

"Hurt Caitlyn's feelings?" Gregory had a dangerous look in his eyes that had Ben shifting in his seat.

"What are you getting at?"

Gregory leaned forward, set the glass on the table, and rested his elbows on his knees. "Darren's plan is a good one. You know it, I know it. The owner will know it as soon as you give Darren the go-ahead to approach him with an offer."

Ben opened his mouth and then shut it again.

"So, what are you waiting for?" Gregory leaned back against the sofa, looking as if he didn't have a care in the world.

"It is a good plan," Ben agreed. "But I have to take all options into account. The profit margin isn't the only item to consider here."

Gregory's eyes grew so wide that it would have been amusing if Ben wasn't the butt of the joke.

"Excuse me?" Gregory didn't even try to hide his laugh. "Is this Ben I'm speaking with?" He narrowed his eyes and feigned suspicion. "Who are you and what have you done with my friend?"

Ben rolled his eyes and made a show of flipping through the documents in the file. There was some truth to what Gregory said. It was a good plan and one that would almost guarantee a sizeable return, for Darren and for Ben. So why was he hesitating?

Okay, he wasn't going to lie to himself. Yes, the thought of the hurt look in Caitlyn's eyes if she knew he was helping the effort to tear down the theater, well…. That look would kill him. Just imagining it did weird things to his lower intestines. But it was more than that. Now he knew just how much that place meant to her. He would be taking away her safe place, her home. And it didn't take a genius to see that they all felt that way about the old building. Seeing how much she and her friends cared about the old place was sweet, but it also gave him some perspective. True, he was typically not one to care about historical preservation. He was more of a progressive capitalist kind of guy. But even he could see the value in a building like that. There had to be other options other than just tearing it down.

"This is about Caitlyn, isn't it?"

Ben's teeth clenched together. He really didn't want to think about her right now but it would be useless to deny her connection to all this. "Caitlyn made a good point," he finally said. "If you want to make any progress in that neighborhood, you have to show some respect for its residents and its history."

At Gregory's look of disbelief, he added, "Besides, she and her friends are trying to push this through the landmarks commission. If it's approved, this plan would be dead in the water."

Gregory gave a snort of disbelief. "There's no way that will go through in time. Not without some influence."

Ben fell back into his seat. If there was one person who had influence, it was Gregory. "That works both ways. It's stuck in red tape purgatory at the moment, which means it's fair game. But one word from the right person could either push it through or keep it mired in red tape long enough for a deal to be made and construction to be underway."

Gregory took a sip of his drink. He wasn't offering up his assistance, but they'd been friends long enough to know that Gregory wouldn't have brought it up if he hadn't been willing to help. Although it would probably be for a price—a cut of the action, no doubt.

Gregory leaned forward then and reached out for the file that Ben had been studying. "So are you telling me you really think there's a way that property could make some real money in its current state?"

Ben shook his head. "It would need a new owner, obviously. One with the means and interest. But yeah, I think it could work."

Gregory's smirk was really starting to irritate him. "But it wouldn't bring in as much as this." He waved the file folder.

Ben let out a lough exhale. "No." No matter how many times they'd crunched the numbers or gone over the options, this was the solid winner.

They sat in silence for a while, and Ben was dimly aware of the fact that Gregory was studying him as he made a point of checking his e-mails and replying to his assistant.

"You should have told her right off the bat," Gregory said.

Ben stiffened. He'd thought they'd moved on from that topic of Caitlyn. He was certainly ready to move on. Granted, he'd been sitting there stewing about what was going on right now. Had they kissed? Had they done more than kiss? What if the guy was being too forceful?

He checked his phone for the tenth time. She would have reached out if she needed help.

Okay, so maybe he'd been thinking about her all evening. That didn't change the fact that he didn't want to talk about her. But Gregory did not get the hint.

"The longer you wait to tell her, the harder it will be."

Ben frowned at his phone. "I know that. Which is why I meant to tell her yesterday. There just was never a good time. I'll tell her soon."

"Tonight?"

Ben tossed his phone down. "What is with you? Why are you so obsessed with this?"

Gregory grinned. "Just because my own love life is in shambles doesn't mean I want you to experience the same."

Oh for the love of... "How many times do I have to tell you that it's not like that between us?"

And he'd made sure that it would stay that way.

Gregory looked nonplussed by his angry reaction. "So you'll tell her tonight?" he asked mildly.

Ben's fingers clenched against the couch. "I can't tonight. She's...on a date."

Gregory's hand paused with his drink halfway to his lips. "She's what?"

Ben licked his lips and rubbed his hands against his jeans. "She's on a date."

"Why would she be dating someone else?"

Ben couldn't even let himself think about what Gregory meant by that. Clearly his friend was hoping to find something between them that just didn't exist. Why was she dating someone else? He cleared his throat. "Because I set it up."

Chapter 13

"It could not have been that bad." Meg was frowning at her over the counter, her big baby belly making her task of wiping down the bar an awkward event to watch.

"Are you even allowed to be back there in your state?" Alice asked. She was watching her sister work with a frown of disapproval as she and Caitlyn sipped their drinks on the other side of the bar.

"I'm pregnant, not an invalid," Meg said.

Caitlyn and Alice watched her try to reach a glass at the far end of the bar, her belly blocking the way so the glass was just out of reach. Meg looked like she was about to pop at any moment. "Surely you have people here who can clean for you," Caitlyn suggested.

Meg tossed aside the rag with a heavy sigh and gave up on trying to reach the errant glass. "Stop looking at me like that, Alice. It's not like pregnancy is contagious."

"Thank God for that," Alice muttered into her drink.

Caitlyn hid her laugh by taking a sip. Meg was glaring at them both and an angry, hormonal Meg was a bit frightening.

"Stop changing the topic," she ordered. "I want to hear what was so horribly wrong with the handsome doctor who saves the lives of small children."

"Well when you put it like that," Caitlyn said, causing Alice to give a snort of laughter and Meg to scowl at the two of them like disobedient children.

"He wasn't *bad*," Caitlyn clarified, "he just wasn't…" She struggled to find the right word. He just wasn't…

"Ben," Alice finished. She emptied her glass and set it down loudly, cheersing her own statement.

Caitlyn gaped at Alice, ignoring the frown that Meg was directing at her.

"Is that true?" Meg asked. "Have you gone and fallen for the fuck buddy?"

"No." *Yes.*

The air rushed from her lungs with a whoosh. Oh God, had she fallen for Ben? No, that was ridiculous. Then why was she comparing the doctor to him? And why did she miss him when she wasn't with him? Like right now. There was no denying the fact that she'd suffered several pangs of something scarily close to homesickness in the short time she'd been away from him.

Staring into her drink, Caitlyn had to face the fact—she'd gone and fallen for her fuck buddy. Her mind came to a crashing halt with that realization. Some form of nerves or fear or excitement—or maybe it was a combination of all three—had her breathing a little too quickly, her hands clutching at the edge of the bar as if that could help her find solid ground. Because this feeling, whatever it was—this was not stable, consistent, or safe. This was *not* what she'd been looking for. This…*whatever* it was she was feeling—it was terrifying. And exciting. Like a new world just opened up in front of her—breathtaking but risky.

Meg and Alice were sisters who looked absolutely nothing alike—except for this moment when they shared the same exact look of disbelief mixed with pity.

"Oh crap," Meg muttered.

"This is not good," Alice agreed.

Caitlyn could feel telltale heat creeping into her cheeks. Their words brought her crashing back to reality. There was no new world opening in front of her like a scene from *The Lion, the Witch, and the Wardrobe.* She was sitting at a bar on planet Earth. And they were right. This was not good.

They had an agreement. He didn't want anything more than sex. He couldn't have made that any clearer. And she hadn't, either. When had that changed? Frustration and fear had her stomach twisting into knots. This wasn't what was supposed to happen. They were wrong for each other. They were opposites in every way. This was just supposed to be about sex, for the love of God. Why did she have to go and fall for a guy who didn't want to be with her…again? Unless maybe he did want to be with her, too. A flicker of hope raced through her but it wavered and died in the face of logic. True they'd been having fun together, but they'd agreed that they could never be more than friends. Besides, hadn't he just set her up on a date? Not exactly the act of a man in love. Her next words came out on a wail. "What am I going to do?"

"Tell him how you feel," Meg said.

"Don't tell Ben," Alice said at the same time.

"Thanks, you guys are a big help."

The sisters shared a look, and Caitlyn had the funny feeling they were communicating silently. Great, her friends were telepathically gossiping about her.

"And what have the two of you decided?" she asked when they turned back to her once more.

"Tell him," they said in synch. Their talking in unison would have made Caitlyn laugh—or be slightly creeped out, perhaps—if she wasn't so disturbed by the verdict.

Tell him. Could she really do that? *Should* she do that?

What if she was wrong? What if they were terrible for one another and this was just an emotional hangover left over from the intimacy of sex? "How do I know if what I'm feeling is real?"

Her friends stared at her in amazement. For a brief moment, Caitlyn thought perhaps she'd stunned them with her incredible emotional insight. But then Meg said, "Are you kidding me?" She and Alice shared a look and shook their heads at her apparent idiocy.

"If you're feeling it, it's for real," Alice explained to her as though she was a child.

"Besides, we saw the two of you together," Meg added. "It's for real."

"But—" What if it didn't last? What if he broke her heart? What if he rejected her? She couldn't put those fears into words just yet. Instead, she settled for, "We don't want the same things."

"No offense, hon, but I'm not sure you know what you want," Alice said in a surprisingly gentle tone.

Meg nodded her agreement. "You can't go for what sounds good in life. You should be going after things that feel good—that feel *right*."

"Things that excite you," Alice added for extra measure.

Caitlyn stared at her friends in amazement. Were they right? Was she one of those people who had no idea what they really wanted? Maybe she'd been chasing the wrong things this whole time.

Mind blown.

At what point had she decided that the man of her dreams had to be a predictable snooze? She almost laughed out loud at that. This realization was more earth shattering than realizing that Robert had done her a favor by breaking up with her. The anxiety she'd been feeling was replaced by a lightness that made her dizzy. She'd been acting like her perfect man had to fit a certain mold. He had to be Cary Grant. But the Cary Grant she knew was fictional… He was an amalgam of roles. Perfect, charming, wonderful roles. Even Cary Grant wasn't perfect. What was that famous quote Cary Grant had said? "Everyone wants to be Cary Grant. Even I want to be Cary Grant." Her dream man wasn't reality. Ben was reality.

And their reality was perfect.

She said good-bye to her friends and dove into the snowy night. Adrenaline coursed through her veins as she asked herself over and over what she really wanted. What felt good. What felt right.

Ben. Nights at home with Ben felt right. Nights out with Ben felt amazing. Sex with Ben was better than anything she had ever experienced before. Why was she letting it go without a fight? Or without even admitting that she wanted it, at the very least.

She was a fool. Trying to figure out what she was going to say was too nerve-wracking, so instead she continued to play the game "what feels good?" Knitting, obviously. Publishing her patterns. It was a challenge and it could be a huge flop—but it felt right. It felt like she was moving forward in life and not just settling.

And it was Ben's idea. For all his talk about how bad he was for her, he was the one who'd encouraged her to take the next step with her knitting—and she'd never even thanked him. She smiled as she rounded the corner to her apartment. She could think of an excellent way to say thank you.

But first, they had to talk. Her hand hovered over the doorknob to the apartment. He was home, she was sure of it.

* * * *

Ben jumped out of his chair the moment she walked through the door. "You're home early."

He looked anxious. Was he worried? Jealous?

Now he was peering at her, studying her face as she peeled off layers of winter wear. "What's wrong?"

"Nothing's wrong."

"Did he make a move too soon? Fucking doctors." Ben looked ready to strangle the Ken doll.

"No, he was fine. He was nice."

Ben's scowl deepened. *Please say he's jealous.* Ben made a point of looking at the clock over the kitchen counter. "So you had a good time then."

He did not sound pleased. Caitlyn's heart warmed and her smile grew. This was good. This was very good. He was jealous and she had psyched herself up. It was now or never. "We need to talk."

Panic gave Ben a slightly dazed look. Oh crap, maybe she shouldn't have started the conversation with that particular phrase.

But he was already recovering. "Yeah, sure. What's up?" He moved past her to grab a wineglass and pour her a drink.

Good. Wine. Yes, wine would be very helpful right about now.

She spoke to his back as he opened the bottle. "I think maybe we should give us a try." Oh God, was that her voice? The words had come out on a rush of air, and it sounded like she'd just inhaled helium.

His back was still to her. She craned her head a bit trying to catch a glimpse of his reflection. His hands never faltered as he opened the bottle, but several seconds had passed and the only sound in the kitchen was the wine opener working its magic.

Turn around, please turn around.

When he spoke, his tone was joking. "The date was that bad, huh?"

Caitlyn's heart fell. There was her answer—but the masochist in her couldn't let go. She started it; she had to see it through. "I'm serious, Ben."

He turned around then to face her, the open wine bottle in one hand and a sad, almost pitying smile on his face. "Caitlyn." Her name sounded like a gentle warning.

He was turning her down without even giving her a chance to make her case. Unshed tears made her chest ache. He wouldn't even consider that maybe, just maybe, they could be good for each other.

"We talked about this," he said. "We agreed—"

"Yeah, I know." She hated how defensive she sounded, like an angsty teen. "I'm just saying—I just thought…" Her voice gave way to a shrug. Was she really going to explain to this man the reason they should be together? She hadn't even believed it herself until her friends had forced her to face what was really going on between them. But just because she now knew what she wanted—him—that didn't mean he had to feel the same way. She couldn't force him to want something he clearly didn't want. Her voice was small when she finally finished her sentence. "We have fun together."

He rubbed a hand over his stubbled jaw in a gesture she was coming to know well. "Cait, we agreed this would be just sex, remember? No emotions, no strings attached. We agreed, right?" He sounded like he was on the verge of begging her to agree with him.

He was going to leave her. That thought rang out above all the others that were racing through her brain. She had ruined everything. She had been having the most fun she'd ever had in her whole life and now she'd gone and destroyed everything. She forced herself to respond. "Yeah, we agreed."

He seemed slightly relieved now that she acknowledged that they had, in fact, agreed.

But I've changed my mind.

"You wouldn't want to be stuck with a jackass like me. Not when you can have a guy like Dr. Nick." The forced joking tone was almost too awful to bear. As if that wasn't bad enough, he quite literally nudged her in the ribs as he edged past her toward the living room.

Self-preservation seemed to kick in as anger temporarily overtook heartbreak. "Why won't you even consider it?" she asked as she followed him into the other room. "We're having fun together, right? And the sex is awesome, right?"

He looked like a deer in headlights as he rushed to reassure her. "Of course the sex is awesome. And yeah, we're having fun, of course we are."

"Then what's the problem?"

He gave her a look that told her she was being crazy. "The problem is—" He stopped with a bit of a huff.

The problem is, you don't want me. Don't make him say it.

He raked a hand through his hair and the look in his eyes was pleading. "We agreed it wouldn't work, that it would be a bad idea." He was looking for confirmation, for her to tell him it was all right, that he hadn't broken her heart.

She gave a little nod. "Yeah, I know. It's just that—" He was looking around the room, looking at anything but her. He was about to run away and the moment his condo became available, he would be out of her life.

Anything she needed to say, she had to say it now. It was now or never. Pride be damned, this could be her one and only chance to speak the words that had been clamoring to get out ever since she'd fallen asleep in his arms the night before. If she was being honest with herself, she'd known last night that he was the one responsible for this change in her. He had brought out the best in her. It may have taken her friends to wake her up to the fact, but deep down, this feeling had been growing for weeks. Now it was time to put it into words.

"I thought I was falling in love with you."

Her heart broke even as the words slipped out. This was not the way it was supposed to go. The next time she fell in love, it was supposed to be perfect. It was supposed to be reciprocated, at the very least.

How had she hoped he would respond? With a kiss, maybe. Or that he would draw her into his arms and gaze in her eyes and admit that, despite his best intentions, he'd gone and fallen for his fuck buddy roommate.

Instead he looked like he'd been slapped across the face. "Oh shit."

Yup, she was an idiot.

* * * *

Ben was living his worst nightmare. His worst fear come true—he'd gone and hurt Caitlyn, the one person he never wanted to see in pain.

But she was standing before him now and pain was clearly written all over her pretty features. He'd done that. *Way to go, asshole.*

She was waiting for him to say something. Anything. But for the life of him, he couldn't think of anything to say. Nothing sounded right. His brain had temporarily shut down along with the rest of his body, and he stood there in the center of the kitchen like he was shell-shocked. Because he was!

The L-word. She'd used the L-word. That was all he could think, over and over, as the paralysis spread. Why would she do that? They weren't supposed to feel anything for one another. Friendship, maybe, but not this. And why the hell would she want a relationship with him?

Because she loves you.

No, because she thinks this is love. Could she really not see how wrong he was for her? She couldn't have forgotten about their first date, not to mention all the other times he'd managed to drive her insane over the past few weeks.

He didn't do real relationships. Not with her, not with anyone. She *knew* that. Or he'd thought she'd known that. It was obvious. They'd spelled out the rules.

A groan escaped his frozen chest, and he saw Caitlyn flinch as though he'd struck her. Gregory was right; she was too naïve and too sweet for this kind of relationship. He should have known she would read more into it than was there. She was a woman who screamed commitment and destiny, not fuck buddy and short-lived fling. Of course she would confuse intimacy with emotions. And that's all this was. It explained his own confusion, too—why he was so confused over what should be a simple business deal. Why he was jealous of Mr. Perfect tonight. They'd both let themselves get carried away. But he at least knew the difference between this short-term connection and the type of relationship that Caitlyn wanted and deserved.

He would destroy her in the long run. How could she not see that?

This was his fault. He should have seen this coming. He should have listened to Gregory and put a stop to it earlier. Hell, he shouldn't have started anything in the first place.

But none of that mattered now. It was too late to turn back the clock and do the right thing. He had to make the best of the situation. Caitlyn was still staring at him with impossibly wide eyes, tears threatening to spill.

He couldn't think of any way to make this right. What would Gregory do? Oh hell, what would Cary Grant do? They would never have gotten themselves into this situation. He was on his own.

"Look, Cait, I—" he started. She continued to watch him in eerie silence. He wished for a phone to ring or the TV to miraculously turn on. Anything to save him from this stifling silence.

"I just don't think it's a good idea." The words sounded lame, even to him.

"Why not?"

His heart broke in half at the sound of her voice choked by tears. God, had he done this? Of course he had. This was exactly why he was no good for her and why she'd be better off without him. He would hurt her, over and over again. He couldn't give her what she wanted.

"It's not you," he started.

"Oh please, don't say it's not you it's me." She rolled her eyes and then swiped at them with the back of her hands to wipe away the tears that spilled over. She did it quickly but not quickly enough. He saw the telltale tears and they destroyed him.

"But it's true." Forcing aside the paralysis, he reached his hands out toward her, but she backed away. "Cait, I don't do relationships, you know that. At least, not real ones. It's not what I want, it's not who I am."

She was shaking her head but she didn't protest.

"My company comes first," he continued, knowing that his words were hurtful but also knowing that he had to go on…for her sake. He had to end this now before she got hurt even more. "And you're not the type of woman I typically go for." When her eyes rounded with offense, he quickly added, "Not that you're not hot and smart and sexy—"

"But?"

He let out the pent up breath in one long exhale. "But we want different things. You want, and deserve, something long-term, but I don't do long-term. I do flings and affairs. I have no interest in marriage and kids and a house in the suburbs. I like to party and I like a woman who knows how to have a good time. I'm not the type to stay at home and watch a woman knit."

It was official—he was a bastard. He was being hurtful and cruel, but he needed to get through to her. It was for the best, like ripping off a Band-Aid. She obviously wasn't seeing him clearly, and she needed to be reminded of who he truly was. A bastard. An asshole. He was the jerk

Maggie Dallen

she'd met on her first date. Oh, he might do a good job disguising it now and again, but ultimately that was who she'd be stuck with and she deserved more, so much more.

She crossed her arms in front of her chest and met his gaze. He was relieved to see the tears were gone, replaced by a steely anger. "You need to get out of my apartment."

He blinked once. Twice. He gave a jerky nod. "I'll be out of here tonight."

She was right to kick him out. And it was for the best, for her and for him. Because he wasn't sure he could spend the night without taking it all back and begging her forgiveness and taking her into his arms.

Space, that's what they both needed. She needed to get her head on straight and remember what it was she wanted out of life. It certainly wasn't him. And he needed space to remember who he was before this beauty came into his life and crept under his skin.

Chapter 14

Caitlyn was well aware of Meg's gaze on her across the bar, but she chose to ignore her.

"You've been nursing that drink for an hour," her friend said.

Caitlyn swirled the remaining sips in her glass. She didn't need any more drinks and the bar was about to close up, anyway. So why was she stalling? Because her home was completely uninviting.

She'd been puttering around the empty apartment for the past few days, trying to readjust to being alone. She used to love having the apartment to herself but now it just seemed depressingly empty. The silence was unbearable.

But Meg was trying to finish closing up and even Alice was packing up her belongings and getting ready to go. More and more lately, Alice had been hanging out at the bar, not just to drink but to help out her sister. She and Jake took turns forcing Meg to sit and rest while they took over whatever task she'd set herself to.

How Alice was managing to help out at the bar at night while still holding down her fast-paced job at the PR company was beyond her. Caitlyn was having a hard enough time balancing her work at the store with her new foray into selling patterns online. And moping. She somehow managed to find plenty of time for that.

Alice came over and sank into the stool next to her. "You can't avoid your home forever."

Caitlyn studied her friend, who somehow still managed to look chic even with her hair tossed up in a messy bun and wearing an apron. "How do you do it?" she asked.

Alice's brows drew together. "How do I do what?"

Caitlyn considered her next words. It was no secret that Alice was a fan of the casual fling. For the nearly ten years that she'd known her best friend's younger sister, the woman had never had a serious relationship, and not for a lack of suitors. She seemed to be content to have meaningless, short-term flings and never got hurt. At least not that Caitlyn had seen.

"How do you not get attached?" Caitlyn asked.

She thought she saw a flicker of something in Alice's eyes…something she couldn't name but that looked suspiciously like pain. Caitlyn instantly regretted her words. "I didn't mean," she started. "I mean, that came out wrong, I just meant—"

But whatever emotion she'd thought she'd seen in Alice's eyes was quickly replaced by laughter as her friend waved away her concerns. "Don't worry about it. I know what you meant."

Caitlyn waited for her to continue. She honestly wanted to know how to do it. Maybe keeping distance was a learned skill. Lord knew she failed miserably with Ben.

Instead of answering, though, Alice grew unusually serious. "I'm sorry."

Caitlyn blinked in surprise. "For what?"

She shrugged and cast a look over her shoulder to Meg, who was watching them both with concern. Turning back, she said, "Maybe we gave you bad advice. Maybe you shouldn't have told him how you feel."

Caitlyn mulled that over. "No," she said finally. "There's a lot of things I regret about the way things ended between us, but I don't regret being honest with him."

Now it was Alice's turn to blink at her in surprise. "Really? Even after…everything?"

Caitlyn gave a definitive nod. "I don't regret sleeping with Ben. And I don't regret telling him how I feel." She turned to her friend, hoping Alice might understand. "Being with him changed me, you know? I'm different, in a good way. I'm braver and more confident and willing to take chances…."

"You didn't need a guy to do that for you," Alice said.

Caitlyn grinned. "Maybe not. Maybe I would have gotten there on my own eventually. But I can't deny that he helped. He saw that part of me when I couldn't and he challenged me, pushed me to be that person. The person I want to be."

Alice's expression grew thoughtful. "Then maybe that's all he's meant to be. Maybe he was sent into your life for exactly that reason. Maybe you should be grateful for that and move on."

Caitlyn was stunned by Alice's words. And Meg, who'd been listening from where she stood washing dishes, looked just as surprised. Alice was not one to talk about destiny or relationships being meant to be.

Tamara's arrival just as the last customers left jarred them from their shocked silence, and Meg came over to join them. "Or maybe," she said, giving Caitlyn a long, searching look. "Maybe you need to give him time. It took you a while to realize how you felt about him, but once you did you acted on it."

"Yeah, but Caitlyn is brave," Alice interjected. "I don't know if Ben will have the balls to own up to his feelings."

Brave? That was definitely not how she'd describe herself. Caitlyn shook her head. She didn't even know where to begin. They were assuming that Ben must feel the same way, but he'd made it abundantly clear that he didn't.

Meg wrung out the dishrag in her hand. "Yeah, but…isn't it possible he just needs time?"

A surge of irritation made it hard to keep her temper. "Time for what? He's gone, Meg, and he's not coming back."

Meg ignored her.

Alice looked from Meg to Caitlyn and back again. "He did seem to really care about her."

She sighed. Now they were talking about her like she wasn't even there. Finally throwing back the last of her drink, she set it down with a little too much force and said it again, as a reminder to herself more than anything. "He's gone," she said again. "And he's not coming back."

The silence that followed her grim statement was broken by Tamara's soft voice. "Maybe that's for the best."

All three of them whipped around to face their quiet, sweet friend to find that she looked outright tortured.

"What's going on?" Meg asked.

"Tam, are you okay?" Alice asked.

Tamara ignored them, keeping her focus on Caitlyn as she told her story. "I was in the owner's office tonight, working on the books, and I saw something…."

A pit settled in Caitlyn's gut. Somehow whatever bad news was coming, it had something to do with her and Ben. "And?" she prodded.

Tamara tucked a strand of long blond hair behind her ear. "I saw a proposal on his desk. It looks like it's from a developer who wants to buy the property and tear it down."

This was met by groans of despair all around—their worst fears were coming true. But Caitlyn kept her gaze fixed on Tamara, who looked far too nervous. "And?" she said again.

Tamara swallowed visibly. "Ben's name was on the plans."

Caitlyn felt ice wash through her veins. What were the odds that Ben—her Ben—was behind this plan? "Are you sure?"

Tamara nodded. "It was his firm's name. He works for Lewis and Hurley, right?"

Caitlyn gave a jerky nod. "That's the name of Ben's firm." Her mind started to race. Ben wasn't the only employee in the firm, maybe he hadn't even known about it. Maybe it was one of his partners.

But that hopeful thought was cut short as Tamara continued. "I looked through the developer's letter to the owner and he named the investor. Ben is working with him on the plan to tear down the theater."

She was keenly aware of all the eyes that were on her, waiting for her response. Her first instinct was to deny it, to insist that there was some sort of mistake, but Tamara looked so certain. And it's not like Tamara had any reason to lie.

If it was true…if this wasn't a misunderstanding…

She took one look at the grim set of Tamara's lips and knew that this was no misunderstanding.

Oh, she was going to kill him.

* * * *

Ben was going to kill Darren. "What do you mean you approached the owner? I told you to wait."

Darren was a hothead, he'd known that from the beginning. But now, sitting across from the twentysomething trust fund kid with his slicked back, blond hair and that cocky little smirk—he was seriously starting to doubt his own judgment for getting into bed with this guy in the first place.

"What are you so upset about?" Darren asked. His arms were flung wide, draped over the back of the sofa in Ben's office.

Ben turned his back on the younger man and looked out the corner window to the Hudson River. He'd had this office for two years, but he felt like he was seeing it for the first time after working from home for so many weeks.

Home. That thought brought up an image of Caitlyn's small but cozy flat. *That was home.* Certainly not Gregory's penthouse or the new condo he'd be moving into in a couple weeks.

But he couldn't think about Caitlyn now. He had to focus on business and this deal, and his reaction to Darren's latest move had nothing to do with her.

Liar.

Okay, so maybe it had a little to do with her. But putting her anger and pain aside if she ever found out about this deal and his involvement,

Darren's move had still been rash. Rubbing his eyes with his palms, he struggled with how to make his new partner understand.

"Look, I know you're excited to get this moving, but there is red tape surrounding that property that will make it a landmine to deal with if you don't do it properly."

"You mean the historical preservation?"

Ben hated the knowing smirk on the younger man's face. "What did you do?"

Darren leaned forward so his elbows were resting on his knees. "It's not what I've done but what you'll do. I've done my research. I know you have friends in high places who can make sure the right people rule in our favor."

He wasn't wrong; that was the worst part. If Ben really wanted to make this deal happen, he could.

"We've been through this," Ben said. Pacing in front of the other man, he spelled it out yet again. "That block isn't the only location in the city where you can build your new hotel. I told you, my people have found other alternatives, better options."

Darren shrugged. "But this one is available now and the owner is eager to sell."

And you would be crushing the dreams of a small group of volunteers who are fighting to preserve the neighborhood's history.

But of course he couldn't say that aloud. He did not do emotion in the workplace. Hell, he didn't do emotion, period. One mention of the L-word and he'd bolted.

Nope. He would not relive that night. Not again. Or at least, not right now when he was in the middle of a business meeting. Lord knew he'd be replaying it over and over all night when he should be sleeping.

For now, he had to focus. "Even if this development isn't in danger from the historical preservation commission, you could still have lost our negotiating power if the owner has gotten wind of how eager you are."

Darren's smug smirk fell a bit at that. Good, the young developer was too arrogant for his own good.

"So what do we do now?" he asked.

Ben pulled his mind back from where it had strayed—where it always strayed—to Caitlyn. Turning to the other man, he said, "Let me handle it from here. In the meantime, check out the other proposals I put together for you. I think you'll find some even more appealing than the old theater's space."

Darren looked doubtful but he agreed, leaving Ben alone in the office. One thought had been nagging at him since he'd told him how he'd gone and approached the owner of the theater without his consent.

He had to tell Caitlyn.

She would find out eventually, especially if this deal went through, and it was best if she found out about his involvement from him. The thought of telling her was not pleasant, but he couldn't deny the surge of adrenaline that pulsed through him. He would be lying if he told himself that excitement had nothing to do with seeing Caitlyn again. Even if it was to give her news that she'd hate, that could make her hate him. He'd still get to see her.

This past week had been torture, sheer and simple. He missed her laugh, he missed her sense of humor, and he missed talking to her at the end of the day. He missed talking to her first thing in the morning. Not to mention her kisses and her body and making love...

Making love? Was that what he was calling it now? Holy hell, she really did have an influence on him, for better or worse.

"Am I interrupting?" Natalie was in the doorway, watching him. She'd been hovering like a nursemaid since he'd shown up in the office, probably afraid that he was going to lose his shit if he ran into Alejandro by the water cooler. There was still no love lost there, but he couldn't bring himself to get too riled up over a woman and relationship that had been a toxic waste of time.

Besides, he would have to face Alejandro and Olivia at the Christmas party that weekend. Alone.

Natalie took a step toward him. "You all right? You look like someone killed your cat."

Ben let out a weary laugh. "I don't have a cat."

"So then what are you moping about?" Natalie's mouth was pursed in that know-it-all way of hers, which he was certain drove her real children nuts. As one of the many people she treated like her child, he could only imagine their pain.

"I'm not moping." He turned to take his seat behind his desk in the hopes that it would make him look busy and important—too busy to answer any of his assistant's prying questions, at least.

"Whatever it is you've done, I suggest you apologize."

He looked up from his computer to see her still standing there, arms crossed in front of her chest. "Excuse me?"

Natalie shook her head. "You don't tell me anything but you don't have to. I heard how happy you were when you were staying with that roommate of yours. You even took time off work for a change."

"Yeah, and look what happened," he muttered. Maybe he wouldn't be in this mess if he'd been keeping an eye on Darren instead of having fun with Caitlyn.

He continued to ignore Natalie until she apparently tired of watching him in silence. "Whatever you did, say you're sorry. Go back to whatever was making you so happy."

What was making him so happy? Easy. Caitlyn. But he wouldn't make her happy. That was the point that everyone seemed to be missing. Natalie, Gregory, and even Caitlyn. Did no one care that she would get hurt if he went back to her? Well, he cared and he would be strong for her sake. For both their sakes. Because if things continued as they had, he knew without a doubt that he would be hurt, too. Because it would end, one way or the other. And when it did, she would be crushed and he would be worse off than he was after the breakup with Olivia. At least when he'd split with Olivia, he hadn't been plagued with what ifs and if onlys.

But maybe Natalie was right—not about going back to her, but about apologizing. He owed her that much at the very least. The way they'd left things… His heart still ached to think of the pain in her expression when he'd walked out. Maybe if he apologized, his conscience would give it a rest.

And he should tell her about the deal with the movie theater owner. She deserved that.

That adrenaline rush was back at the thought of seeing her. He glanced at the clock. Tonight. He would see her tonight. Grabbing his coat off the back of his chair, he called out a good-bye to Natalie as he headed out to meet her.

Chapter 15

He knew where she would be. It was a Tuesday night and Caitlyn was nothing if not a creature of habit. Tuesday nights were her nights to teach beginners knitting at the store. Which meant she would be arriving home at around nine-thirty.

It felt odd to be perched on the front stoop of her apartment building, the apartment he'd come to think of as home, so close but so locked. Right on schedule, she turned the corner, her head buried in the scarf that covered half her face. She didn't see him immediately.

Which gave him a chance to get his fill. His eyes drank in every feature, every stray lock of hair. He took note of the new hat she was wearing—one of her own creation, no doubt. Her mouth and nose were covered by the scarf, but he could see her eyes, which were pinched thanks to the wind buffeting her face.

God, she was lovely. How had he ever walked away from a woman like her?

Because it was the best for Caitlyn. And he couldn't forget that. He was here to apologize for his past actions and explain his involvement with the new development project so she wasn't sidelined. That was it. End of story. After this he would have no need to see her anymore, no reason to be a part of her life.

He sucked in air as if he'd been sucker punched. This would most likely be the last time he saw Caitlyn.

She looked up, and he knew the moment she spotted him because she came to a stop mid-step halfway down the block. He wasn't close enough to see the expression in her eyes and for that he should probably be grateful. He wouldn't be surprised if there was some hatred there.

When she resumed walking toward him at a slightly slower pace, he let out the breath he'd been holding and stood. He could do this. He could face her one more time. She deserved an apology.

When she was two feet away, she came to a stop again and she crossed her arms in front of her body, whether to shield herself from the cold or from him, he couldn't tell.

"What are you doing here?"

Her sweet voice drifted over him. Would it be too lame to think her words were music to his ears? Probably. "Hi, Cait."

"What are you doing here?" she repeated. Her tone wasn't angry. She sounded exhausted more than anything.

He cleared his throat and tried again. "How've you been?"

She shrugged. He took a step closer so he could see her beneath the glow of the streetlamps. She was close enough now that if he reached out, he could touch her.

The moment he caught a glimpse of her eyes, he wished he hadn't. There was a pain, a sadness, and he knew it was his fault.

Because she loved him.

No, she only thought she loved him. She was too naïve to know the difference between intimacy and love. That's why he had to be strong for both of them. To keep her from making a mistake that neither of them could fix.

"What are you doing here?" she asked once again.

Shit. What was he doing here? He shouldn't be here. It had been hard enough to walk away the first time, and coming back here was playing with fire. She was waiting for a response, shifting from foot to foot, most likely to keep warm in this bitter cold.

He jerked his head toward the front door. "Can we go in?"

"No."

His head reared back as if he'd been smacked. Yeah, sure, he should have expected that. He wished he could move the scarf so he could read her expression, but maybe it was better that he couldn't. It would make what he had to say that much easier if he couldn't read every emotion that crossed her face.

"I just, uh… I wanted to say I'm sorry."

She stopped shifting. In fact, she grew so still he thought perhaps time stood still. There was no traffic on her street, no other pedestrians, and the snowfall dampened all sound, leaving them in a bubble.

"You're *sorry*?" Her tone was biting and loud enough to shatter the bizarre illusion that they were living in a snow globe. "For what?" she demanded.

He opened his mouth to answer but she cut him off. "Are you sorry for being a blind, insensitive jackass or for going behind my back to tear down the theater?"

Oh Christ, she knew. It was official, he was going to murder Darren the moment their dealings were done. "Look, I wanted to tell you about that, but…"

Her eyes widened with impatience as she waited for him to continue.

"Ummm." Words. He needed words. But all he could do was watch in fascination as Caitlyn's mitten-covered hands moved her scarf and he finally got a glimpse of her full face.

And it was beautiful, even in all its righteous anger. Or maybe because of the anger, she had a glow he'd never seen before, a confidence he'd only caught glimpses of in the past.

"That's what you have to say for yourself? *Ummm*?" Her imitation of his dimwitted response was so spot-on he nearly laughed. Nearly. He wasn't that stupid that he would risk angering her even further at the moment.

Besides, she wasn't done. Not by a long shot. "How long did you know?" she demanded. She crossed her arms in front of her chest and didn't wait for him to answer. "Have you been spying on us while pretending to be our friend? Were you laughing at us this whole time?"

He heard the real question she was asking. *Were you pretending to be my friend? Were you pretending to care?* The silent accusation pierced him to his core. She stopped abruptly, and Ben realized with horror that she was choked up. Ben's mouth opened but no words came out. Dammit, of all the times to lose his ability to speak. "I was going to tell you, Cait. I wanted to tell you."

She started shaking her head before he even finished. "I don't want to hear it. I don't believe you."

And why should she? The first time they'd met, he'd lied about his name. From that point on he'd done nothing but take advantage of her sweet nature. Cursing under his breath, he ran a hand over his face. He blamed exhaustion for his inability to articulate. He hadn't had a good night's sleep since he'd moved out. Since that night. Since those words…

You're not my type. Business comes first. I'm not the type to sit around and watch a woman knit.

Who the hell was that guy? He'd relived the hurt expression on her face every second since walking out of that apartment. He would give anything to make things right. To help her move on, forget about him, and live the life she deserved.

"I was going to tell you," he said. "I didn't know the proposal included the theater. Not at first, not for a while."

Caitlyn studied him. "Not until after we became fuck buddies then?"

Ben flinched at the term. Sure, he used the phrase all the time… But she didn't. "Friends with benefits," he automatically corrected. What was happening here? It was like *Freaky Friday*.

Caitlyn's answering smirk spoke volumes. She didn't consider him a friend. Not anymore. Ben couldn't help but wonder if she would have felt the same way if the theater wasn't an issue and she wasn't doubting his loyalty. What if he'd had a chance to tell her himself? If it was just a matter of the way they'd ended things, would she still be staring at him with that cold, hard glare?

He shifted, his head tilting as he tried to see past the ice in Caitlyn's eyes to the sweet, kind woman he'd spent so much time with. "I hate the way we ended things."

"The way *you* ended things," she corrected.

Her words were another slap in the face. She was right. He'd ended it. It was his fault. But even as he told himself that, a voice in the back of his head resisted. No. He hadn't wanted this. He hadn't wanted anything to change. They'd been good together. What they'd had—a beautiful friendship mixed with mind-blowing chemistry—that was what he'd always wanted. It was perfect.

"I didn't want things to change." Even he could hear how defensive he sounded. But dammit, he hadn't wanted to change. She was the one who'd ruined what they'd had. "We could have kept going," he said, taking a step closer. He was so close now he could pull her into his arms.

Her cynical raised brow added fuel to his fire. "For how long?"

"What?" Her sweet vanilla scent was distracting him. "What are you talking about?"

She leaned in a bit so her face was inches from his, which did nothing to help with his focus issue.

"How long do you think we could have kept going like we were?" she asked. "Another couple of weeks until your new apartment was ready? Or maybe it would have had to end sooner if your attempts at playing matchmaker proved to be a success."

He tried to focus, he really did. But she was there. So close. Good God, how had he lived with her and not touched her every second of every day? She was a magnet and his body was incapable of resisting.

She saw it, the temptation in his eyes. He could tell by the way her eyes darkened and her pupils dilated. She felt it, too. He could have thrown his head back and howled with happiness. But he couldn't tear his eyes away from hers.

She gave her head a little shake, and he could practically see her brain scrambling to remember what she was so angry about. "No." She practically shouted the word, and a pedestrian walking past them on the sidewalk turned to stare.

She inhaled deeply and paused until the gawker was out of hearing distance. "Don't try to turn any of this around." She jabbed a finger into his chest. "You kept secrets from me. You are working against something you know I care about." Her eyes were starting to get suspiciously shiny, and Ben's throat grew constricted.

Don't cry. Please don't cry. There was no way he could take seeing her cry again.

She swallowed thickly before adding through clenched teeth, "You are the one who rejected me. You ended us."

"Because you deserve better." Ben closed the distance between them and grabbed her arms, willing her to understand. Their eyes met and he saw the same emotions reflected in hers. Pain, hurt, anger. How could he make her see? It *wasn't* her and it *was* him, but any attempt to explain that was waved away as a cliché.

He lowered his head so they were inches apart. The proximity was killing him. He was so close to tasting those lips and holding her in his arms, but he couldn't. He was here for one reason—to make her understand.

"You deserve better," he said again. "I'm sorry for the hurtful things I said that night but the truth is still the same. I'm not the guy you want. I'm not the man you need."

There was a deathly silence when he stopped talking. Caitlyn's eyes were so huge he thought he might drown in them. *Please tell me you understand. Please say you'll be okay.* He didn't want to hurt her. That was never what he'd wanted. He'd only ever wanted to help her, make her laugh, build her confidence. He'd only ever wanted to see her strong.

Whatever she saw in his eyes, her expression shifted. She'd come to some sort of conclusion, and Ben held his breath to see what it was.

"You're right," she breathed.

The words were a relief and a stab of searing, blinding pain. He was right. She deserved better. She finally realized the truth.

"You're right," she said again. "But not in the way you think."

Ben searched her face, looking for her meaning. Where was this going?

She backed away slightly, just enough so his hands fell to his sides. There was an emptiness where their physical contact had been.

"You know, when I first met you—not the blind date night but when you first moved in—I thought you were so confident." She shook her head, her eyes never leaving his.

A pit formed in his stomach as he realized she wasn't looking at him, she was seeing through him. He was more exposed than he'd ever been, but he couldn't move or look away from those big, brown eyes.

"This whole time, I thought you were so strong and I was the weak one. I saw myself as timid."

Ben reached out a hand to her but let it drop. His heart was aching in his chest. "You were never timid."

"I know." Her chin tilted up as she met his gaze, her eyes hard and her mouth set in a firm line. "I know that now. I'm not the weak one. You are."

Her words were a blow, a sucker punch to his gut, but he struggled to keep his face neutral. Much as he hated to hear it, he needed to and, more than that, she needed to say it.

Her cheeks were pink from the cold. Or maybe it was her anger, because her voice took on a hard edge. "All this time you've talked about taking what you want and being honest with yourself and others, but you haven't been. You haven't been honest with yourself or me."

Ben flinched. The combination of her words, her tone, and the cold anger in her eyes were making it impossible for him to block out what she was saying, and their effect was visceral, entering into his bloodstream like a virus and spreading throughout his body.

"You keep saying that you're not cut out for commitments and that business is your first priority, but that's bull. You're just too scared to commit."

He didn't want to hear anymore. Everything in him itched to walk away. Or pull her into his arms and kiss her until she stopped talking. But she was on a roll and her glare had him rooted in place, unable to escape.

"You said we want different things, that you're not the type of guy to sit around and watch me knit."

She spit out the words, and Ben flinched again as if she'd smacked him by throwing his words back in his face. He'd been regretting everything he'd done and said that night since it happened, but hearing her say it was heartbreaking.

"But that's a load of crap. Every word out of your mouth that night was bullshit. You want a relationship, you're just too scared to let yourself admit it. And you love sitting around watching me knit."

She took a step closer to him and jabbed another finger in his chest. Her jab was nothing compared to the stabbing pain where his heart should be.

"You love sitting on the couch with me." Jab. "You love going out with friends with me." Jab. "You love cuddling with me." The last was said through gritted teeth and with such menace it might have been funny... Except that it wasn't.

It was so far from funny. The nerves beneath Ben's skin were frayed. He was on edge and his hands clenched and unclenched against his sides. He wanted to reach out to her but he didn't dare. He couldn't hear any more, not without losing it. And there was more; he could see it in her eyes.

Her voice grew shaky. "And do you know what I think? I think you love doing all of those things because...because you love me."

He could hear her breathing in the heavy silence that followed. Something snapped for Ben. Her words echoed in his skull and vibrated in his body. This was not happening. He was supposed to be here to apologize. To make her feel better.

And she was slaying him.

He took a deep breath, and then another, and then opened his mouth to deny it. Instead his body took over and did what it had been begging to do from the moment she'd stepped into view.

In one quick move he reached out and pulled her toward him so she was pressed against his chest. *Where she belonged.* He shoved the thought aside as quickly as it popped into his brain.

Her breathing was ragged, and her gaze fell to his lips. She wanted this too, just as much as he did. That was all he needed. He lowered his head and his lips crushed hers. He was being too forceful, but he couldn't hold back. He wanted to stop her words, block out their meaning. But even more than that, he wanted her in his arms.

He let out a groan when her lips met his urgency with a matching passion. His hands cupped her face, moved into her hair so he could hold her closer. Bloody hell, he'd missed her kiss. He'd missed *her.*

The spark that was always there between them, a constant flickering force field, burst into flames. All thoughts, all reason, flew out of Ben's brain as his body took command of the situation.

She edged in closer so the full length of her was pressed up against him, and Ben's body ached to get closer. He ran his hands over her hair, her neck, her back, until he was cupping her bottom and pressing her up against him.

Her whimpering moan at the contact brought a flicker of sanity. He pulled back, their breath mingling as he struggled to make sense of the situation. What was he doing?

She loved him.

No. She didn't know what she wanted.

She thinks I love her.

No. He couldn't let her go on believing that. She would get hurt. This was a mistake. Her mistake because she was naïve and believed in things like fairy tales and happily-ever-afters. But he knew better and he had to protect her.

He would never hurt her with promises he couldn't keep.

Most likely sensing his hesitation, Caitlyn's eyes opened and met his, their faces still so close all it would take was a slight tip of his head and they could be kissing again.

And there it was. A flicker of hope gleamed in her eyes and gave her face a radiant glow. She thought this kiss meant…oh holy hell.

He'd come here to make things right and he'd managed to make them even worse. He was doing it again, leading her on.

She must have seen some of the panic on his face because she pushed back a little farther and her brows drew down in concern. "Ben? What is it?"

A panicky sensation made his throat tighten. What did she expect from him? She should know better. She deserved better than this…than him.

"I can't."

Her forehead furrowed in something akin to anger. "What? What do you mean?"

"I'm sorry, Cait." He took another step back, ignoring the sharp burst of pain the movement caused in his chest. "I'm sorry, but I can't do this."

Chapter 16

Caitlyn's heart ached every time she thought about Ben. *I'm sorry, but I can't do this.* A week had passed but Caitlyn couldn't stop hearing Ben's parting words. The words he'd spoken just seconds before bolting like a spooked cat.

"Did you hear a single word I said?"

Caitlyn turned to see Meg glaring at her from across the lobby. Tamara and Alice gave her a knowing, pitying look. Oh God, she'd become *that* girl.

"Sorry, Meg, what did you want me to do?"

Meg pointed toward the refreshment stand. "Double check the catering staff."

Alice rolled her eyes as Caitlyn trudged past her to do her job. "Don't worry about it. I hired the best caterers in the city. I'm sure it's fine."

Even though Alice had arranged all this—all of this being the costume party fundraiser for the theater—Meg had taken over as de facto leader of the prep team. Caitlyn and the others were fairly certain it was to keep herself distracted from the looming birth, which Meg was not so secretly terrified of.

She gave Alice a reassuring smile. All her friends had been worried about her this week—even Meg, though she'd seemed to have forgotten that she was supposed to be pitying Caitlyn, which was just fine by Caitlyn. She knew her friends meant well but she didn't want to mope over Ben anymore. She didn't want to talk about him or her feelings.

So manual labor was exactly what she needed. Then she could forget all about the fact that Ben was most likely at his office's Christmas dinner, gloating over his latest real estate deal, which would just be one more stab in the heart, as far as she was concerned.

Tamara was already behind the concession stand, where the catering company had set up a makeshift bar. She looked absorbed by her task, her little frame looking far too frail to be handling the large crates she was trying to move.

"Here, let me help you with that."

Tamara flashed her a smile, and Caitlyn asked the question she'd been pondering for the last few days. "Is this fundraiser going to do any good?"

Tamara's head shot up. "What do you mean?"

"I mean"—Caitlyn paused to shift the wait of the crate in her hands—"given the proposal that's on the owner's desk, do we even stand a chance of saving this place?"

Tamara's big blue eyes blinked at her in surprise. "I thought you knew...."

"Knew what?"

Alice drew near, risking the wrath of Meg to join their conversation. "What's up?"

Tamara looked from Caitlyn to Alice and then back again. "I'm sorry, I thought you knew. I thought Meg told you."

She looked to Alice for an explanation, but Alice was still focused on Tamara. "Meg thought Ben was going to tell her."

The sound of Ben's name had her chest tightening all over again, but she shoved aside the pain when they both turned to look at her. "We haven't spoken since...that night." She waved off their concerned looks. They all knew what night "that night" referred to. The night she'd been shattered into a million pieces.

Tamara gave a quick nod. "I know, I just mean, we thought he'd done it for you. Or, maybe... I don't know."

Caitlyn's patience was wearing thin but she took a deep breath. "What did *he* not tell me?"

"The deal is off."

Caitlyn's jaw dropped. She was aware that her mouth was open but she couldn't seem to close it. Too many questions were trying to come out at once. "What? When?"

But most importantly, *why?*

Tamara gave Alice a slightly panicked look and Alice stepped in. "Sorry, Caitlyn, we should have told you sooner. The developer, and Ben's company, took the offer off the table. They said they were going with a property farther downtown. One that's abandoned and not in danger of being named a historical landmark."

Caitlyn blinked at Alice. "Why didn't you tell me?"

Alice and Tamara shared a look of chagrin. "We thought he'd done it for you. Because of you," Alice explained. "Meg wanted to give him

a chance to tell you. She thought this was his attempt to…you know…
make things right."

A glimmer of hope pierced her thick wall of detachment. Dammit. She
had finally gotten to a numb state. This was not what she wanted to hear.

Alice was studying her closely. "Whatever you said to him that
night… It worked."

Caitlyn shook her head quickly. "This wasn't for me. They probably
just found a better location, that's all. Maybe they found out that the
landmark status will be moving forward."

Or maybe he did it for you. She couldn't think of that possibility.
Besides, if she was a factor at all, it was because he felt guilty for breaking
her heart. Again. For the last time.

Alice interrupted her internal pep talk. "How do you know that you
weren't a factor?" She looked to Tamara as if for backup. "We all know
that he cares about you."

"Yeah, as a friend." She saw her friends flinch in the face of her
cynical statement. She hadn't even bothered to hide the disgust and
disappointment. What would be the use? Her friends all knew the truth.
That she'd poured her heart out to Ben, then tried to convince him that he
felt the same way.

"He cares about you as more than a friend," Tamara said. "Anyone
with eyes could see that."

Caitlyn felt the telltale burning of tears behind her eyelids and blinked.
"Try telling him that."

"You were brave and he is being an idiot," Alice said. The resolute
look on her face said she wouldn't hear any words to the contrary, so
Caitlyn settled for rolling her eyes. That's what she'd told herself, that she
was the brave one for confronting her feelings and owning up to them.
But maybe it was time to face the truth. Maybe he really didn't love her
as anything more than a friend. Maybe what she'd thought was bravery
was just denial.

She blinked rapidly again and cursed under her breath. In less than an
hour she was supposed to be dressed, hair and makeup done, to be part
of the team who would welcome the donors who were attending. She
would not sabotage herself with tears. She'd wasted way too many of
those as it was.

* * * *

Bloody hell, he was a bastard. Ben was dimly aware of the party going
on around him as he wallowed in his self-hatred.

I'm no good for her. It would end in heartbreak. This was for the best.
The words had been running on a loop in his brain for a week—ever since he'd walked away, leaving her standing there looking forlorn and hurt in the snow.

He was no good for her. It would end in heartbreak. This was for the best. The never-ending mantra reminded him yet again. And he needed the reminder if he was going to resist the mad temptation to call her. He just wanted to hear her voice one more time. Make things right.

But isn't that exactly what he'd told himself when he'd gone off to see her last time? And look how that had turned out. He'd made everything worse. That kiss had been a disaster. An epically wonderful, soul-jarring disaster.

Perhaps if he just saw her one more time, though....

Dammit, he had to get these urges under control. No more of this "one more time" crap. Isn't that what drug addicts said? And that was exactly what this was. He was addicted to Caitlyn and he needed to kick the habit for both their sakes. Ben slammed his beer down, causing all eyes at the table to temporarily flicker his way.

He forced a smile and conversations resumed, though Ben was content to sit at the end, drowning in his misery as he studied his colleagues celebrating the holidays.

Well, he'd done it. He'd faced his greatest fear. Give the man a cigar; he was actually sitting at the same table as his ex and his former friend. And he was being civil—they all were.

Ben nursed his drink. He still had hours to go at the office holiday party and he refused to be *that* guy—the drunken mess everyone talked about on Monday morning. He tipped the glass back and drained the last few drops. Ah fuck it, what did he care? He was rarely ever in the office anymore, anyway.

His ex's laugh cut through the low murmur of voices at his table. All eyes turned to her. As usual. She looked more stunning than ever in a low-cut, red dress that clung to her curves. Her lips were a matching shade of red that he'd had to scrub off his cheek when she'd greeted him with a friendly kiss.

He watched her light up over something one of his coworkers said and he waited to feel something. Anything.

Nothing. All he felt was the empty pit that had taken up residency in his gut the moment he'd walked away from Caitlyn. It had only been a week, but it felt like a year.

There was a big part of him that wished it had never happened. But it had and it was all Ben could think about. Even now, sitting across from his ex and ex-friend, the image of Caitlyn's crestfallen face was all he could think about. The look of disappointment in her eyes and gut-twisting sadness—he'd done that. Dammit, that was the whole reason they'd agreed to keep it light. He hadn't wanted to hurt her.

He should have known she wasn't the type to keep feelings out of it. She was too caring, too open-hearted, too…Caitlyn.

And he missed the shit out of her.

He hadn't wanted to come to the party tonight, but he'd told himself he had to. He had to show up to be strong, to be brave. He had to prove to himself and to everyone else that he was over his ex.

Well here he was. He'd proved it. And who the hell cared? Of course he was over her. He'd been over her for so long he hadn't even known how over it he was. You can't have a broken heart when your heart was never in it.

How had he never realized that? What he'd experienced during his breakup with Olivia… That was nothing compared to the way he felt now. That had been wounded pride, but this? His heart literally ached. Up until this disastrous break-up—if that's what you could call ending a friends-with-benefits relationship—he'd never realized that the phrase *heartache* was anything more than metaphorical.

His ex laughed again and Ben once again wished to feel something. If for no other reason than to validate his presence in the room. He'd shown up tonight to prove that he was strong, that he could face his ex and his former friend and that they held no power over him. Of course they didn't. They were two self-absorbed workaholics who wouldn't know a real relationship if it punched them in the face. Just like him. So what was he trying to prove by being here?

"Ben?" The ex's voice cut into his thoughts. She and everyone else at the table were staring at him.

"What?"

She turned an amused look to the rest of their tablemates. "I'm sorry, are we boring you?"

He cleared his throat and shoved aside all thoughts of Caitlyn and the stabbing pain in his chest. "Sorry, what were we talking about?"

Natalie, who was sitting across from him, shot him a questioning look. She'd been watching him with that mix of pity and curiosity for the past week whenever he showed up at the office, but he avoided it now.

Alejandro spoke. His former friend, or bloaty-faced washed-up creep, as Caitlyn had so aptly described him, had been trying to get back into Ben's good graces ever since Ben started working out of the office again. Now, it seemed, he was looking for a chance to publicly earn brownie points.

"I was telling everyone what a great job you did with Darren's new property deal."

Ben shifted uncomfortably in his seat. This was one topic he didn't want to delve into, in public or anywhere else.

"Sounds like you helped him divert a disaster." Turning to the others, he explained, "Darren had his heart set on tearing down a theater in the Lower East Side to make way for a new hotel. But rumor has it the city is going to be fast-tracking the theater for landmark status."

Alejandro and the others were smiling at him as if they were all celebrating his success. "Can you imagine if he'd gone through with the deal before that happened? He'd be stuck with a run-down relic on his hands."

Ben swallowed back the automatic defensive response. *It was not run-down. It had character.* How many times had he heard Caitlyn and the others say that? It had history and class and, more than that, it had a hell of a lot of good memories for Ben. He and Caitlyn had gone there several times, once to help the so-called "Operation Petticoat" with their cleanup efforts and two other times to see classic movies. All memories that he would cherish.

But now was not the time to wander down memory lane. The entire table of coworkers was waiting for him to reply. "All part of the job," he muttered. Before anyone could ask more questions, he avoided further conversation by turning in his seat to hail the waiter for another drink.

He couldn't answer any more questions because he knew what they would be, and he didn't want to have to lie.

Well that was something new. Since when had he grown an aversion to lying? The waiter caught his eye and he held up his empty glass. Once he turned back, he found the others had resumed their conversation and it thankfully had nothing to do with Darren or the theater.

He could only imagine how the conversation would go if he'd tried to be honest. *How did you know the landmark commission would fast-track the theater through the process, Ben?*

Because I asked them to. Or, more like, in a fit of insanity and desperation he'd told Darren that was the case. He hadn't been able to help himself; the little brat was gung-ho about moving forward with the project, despite Ben's hesitation. And the entire time Darren was talking, all Ben could see in his mind's eye was Caitlyn's face when she'd accused him of using her and her friends. The look on her face if she ever found out that the theater was a goner...and all thanks to him.

So yes, he'd lied and said that the landmark commission was moving forward. The moment that meeting had ended, he'd raced to Gregory's penthouse and called in a favor. His friend hadn't asked questions, just made some calls. Amazing what a few phone calls from a billionaire of a legendary family could accomplish. Before Ben could say "ethical violation," the deed had been done. The movie theater would be saved.

Did Caitlyn and the others know yet? He wished he could be there when they found out. They were hosting a costume party fundraiser at the theater tonight—everyone was supposed to dress up as a classic movie star—they would all be there. There was no way Caitlyn would miss it. She'd probably been there all day helping to set up.

Caitlyn would be there. Bloody hell, he wished he didn't know that. It made staying away that much harder when he knew the exact course he could take to get to her. Like right now, for example. The theater wasn't far. Ten minutes in a taxi, maybe five if there was no crosstown traffic.

Not that she'd want to see him. Or would she? Ben toyed with the collar of his shirt, which felt too tight. No, he'd ruined things for good this time.

It was for the best. I would hurt her. She deserved better.

He repeated the words but this time, they didn't ring true. Oh, Caitlyn most certainly deserved better, but not necessarily for the reasons he'd been telling himself.

Looking at Alejandro and Olivia schmoozing it up for the crowd, sharing the occasional kiss for the audience around them—Lord knew Olivia loved an audience—all he could think was... I'm not like that anymore.

He didn't know when it had happened or how, but he had changed since the breakup. Since meeting Caitlyn. The old Ben would never have ruined a perfectly good business deal to spare a woman's feelings.

Not just any woman. His woman. Caitlyn.

And the old Ben wouldn't have sat here in silence, taking Olivia's pointed barbs and Alejandro's smirks. He would have fallen right back into Olivia's drama, no doubt. But he couldn't even bring himself to frown at the fake-happy couple. Why? Because he couldn't care less. He could see now how shallow those relationships were... They had to have been for that kind of betrayal to have occurred. True friendship and true love meant being loyal. It meant being trustworthy and thinking about the other person's feelings.

Which is exactly what he'd done for Caitlyn with the now-defunct proposal.

A swell of pride had him sitting a little taller. He'd changed. Or maybe, this new Ben had been there all along and he'd just needed a little help to see it. He'd needed Caitlyn.

He wasn't like them, not anymore. And he wasn't like his father. He stared at the drink in his hand, temporarily stunned by that realization. His father would never have put a woman's interests ahead of his own. He wouldn't have cared if his actions hurt his mother. But he was not like his father. Maybe he never had been. Maybe just knowing that he didn't want to be like that had made him different from the very beginning.

No, he was no longer like Alejandro and Olivia and he wasn't doomed to repeat his father's mistakes. He'd grown, changed. He now knew a real relationship when it came his way, and it was what he'd had with Caitlyn.

Some of the pride rushed out of him as the memory of Caitlyn's pained expression once more bombarded him. His groan earned him some curious stares, none more intense than Natalie's. He forced a laugh at the story Alejandro was telling but inside his brain was reeling. But that was nothing to the flip flops his heart was doing. It sank into the pit of his stomach before twisting with a stabbing pain.

Either he was having a heart attack or an epiphany because he was almost certain he saw a light—and the light sucked. She had been right. Caitlyn was spot on when she'd called him a coward.

He'd come to this dinner thinking he was being strong. Thinking he was proving something to himself and his ex. But that wasn't strength. He was a coward.

And in walking away from Caitlyn... It wasn't just because he was afraid she would be hurt; he was afraid of getting hurt himself. He'd never once risked his heart. In fact, looking back, he could see clearly that he'd gone to great measures to ensure that he never got too close. He kept his distance from women who could potentially love him, not just to protect them but to protect himself. He never let himself experience love because he was so afraid of heartbreak.

Until Caitlyn. Just thinking of her name brought the image of her wide brown eyes, angelic features, and those luscious curves. In his mind's eye she was laughing and it nearly killed him. *He loved her.*

There was no use denying it—to himself, or to her. Why had he tried? He'd known when she was in his arms that he never wanted to let her go. Hell, he'd known that night when she'd told him she was falling for him. His heart had nearly leaped out of his chest, and deep down he'd known then and there that he was a goner. He should have owned up to it that night, and he should have gotten down on his knees and sworn his love last week in the snow. But instead he'd panicked. He'd frozen and run away.

She'd been right. She did deserve better than him because he was the weakest person he'd ever met. He was a coward.

A mental image of Caitlyn baring her soul in her living room seared his brain and brought with it the now familiar stab of gut-wrenching pain. What Caitlyn had done—now that was strong. That was courageous, even.

And he'd hurt her.

She was the best thing that had ever happened to him, and for some unknown, unimaginable reason, she had fallen for him. Of course he didn't deserve her but who was he to question a miracle? Life had gone and handed him a cool, sweet glass of lemonade and he'd somehow managed to turn it into a pile of rotting, sour lemons. Well done.

What are you going to do about it?

The little part of him that wasn't wallowing in self-pity demanded action. A restlessness stirred in him, making it impossible to sit still and take part in any more idle chitchat.

He'd made a mess of everything and he'd hurt Caitlyn... Now it was up to him to fix it. A little voice cautioned that he might still hurt her but he silenced it. It was a risk, sure, but it was a risk she was willing to take. So what was his excuse? If she could take a chance on them, why couldn't he? They both had a lot to lose, mainly their hearts, but wouldn't it be better to try? If she could be courageous, then so could he.

Ben leaped out of his chair quickly. Too quickly, judging by the shocked expressions on the faces surrounding him.

"Are you okay?" Natalie whispered in a loud voice.

"Yeah, I, uh..." He surveyed the upturned faces. Oh hell, he didn't have time for diplomacy. "I've got to tell a girl I love her."

He ignored the gasps and whispers as he grabbed his jacket and headed toward the door. Only Natalie's triumphant whoop reached him as he headed toward the restaurant's exit.

He just hoped and prayed that Caitlyn would give him another chance.

Chapter 17

Ben ran out the restaurant door to the curb. He'd wasted precious days letting her believe that he didn't care, and the thought that she might spend one more second under that misapprehension was unbearable. He had to make this right and he had to do it now.

Hailing a cab was a hopeless cause. It was a Friday night and it was freezing outside. He stood there waving like a madman as one unlit cab after another breezed by. No nearby subways or buses would take him to the heart of the Lower East Side and the sense of urgency to get to her was overwhelming.

Muttering curses under his breath, he started the long, cold walk to the theater. The walk turned into a jog and then into a full-on sprint until he finally spotted the weathered marquee.

He paused in front of the entrance for a moment to catch his breath and rehearse what he would say. He'd had a nice long run to conjure up a speech that would win her back yet somehow it all kept coming back to one thing—he was an idiot and he wanted her back. Here's hoping Caitlyn wasn't one to hold grudges.

"Hey there, sailor."

Ben's head shot up and he spotted Alice leaning against the far side of the ticket booth talking to some guy who looked vaguely familiar. He took a step toward them warily. Alice had been the first to warn him about hurting Caitlyn. And now that he thought about it, she'd been the first to realize that he was in as much danger, if not more, of getting hurt. She'd seen right through his crass, tough-guy routine from the start.

Now she was eyeing him, her expression unreadable. Decked out in her costume, she was the spitting image of Rita Hayward. "Gilda?" he asked.

She tipped her chin in acknowledgement and a little smirk tugged at her lips. The guy she was talking to had apparently not received the message that the theme was old movies because his costume was a pair of green hospital scrubs.

He waited for the lecture, the angry yelling—whatever Caitlyn's friend could dish out, he could take it. He deserved it, all of it. But impatience was eating at him. He had to see Caitlyn and make this right before another moment passed. He didn't want to live another second without her in his life.

Alice must have seen some of the desperation on his face because she jerked her head toward the entrance to the lobby. "What are you waiting for? Go on and win back your girl."

His girl. A brief flicker of hope lightened the anxious weight in his chest that made it hard to breathe. The fact that one of her closest friends didn't think his quest was impossible was heartening. Maybe he hadn't destroyed everything completely. He could salvage this; he knew he could. That was all he needed to pounce on the door.

The lobby was crowded, filled with men and women in old-timey attire, some more elaborate than others. But he didn't care about these people. It took everything in him not to shove them out of the way as he maneuvered through the crowd to find her. Maybe he could scream her name over the jazz music that underscored the rumble of partygoers talking and laughing.

He moved past a woman with a giant feathered hat and then there she was on the far side of the dimly lit lobby. At the first sight of Caitlyn, Ben stopped breathing. He'd seen her coming out of the shower wrapped in nothing but a towel, he'd seen her in his T-shirt that hung down to her thighs—he'd even seen her in skimpy lingerie once. But never had he seen her more heart-stoppingly beautiful. She was decked out in a 30s-era dress that fit her curves to a tee, her hair was done up in an intricate, curled style, and her lips were a bright red. She was gorgeous. But it was the fact that she was there, in his life, when he'd been trying to get used to the fact that he would never see her again, that made her more beautiful and precious than anything he'd ever seen.

If she gave him a second chance, he would make her happy. He would devote his life to making sure she felt cherished and adored each and every day.

She caught him gawking and her eyes widened in surprise at the sight of him. He was dimly aware of her friends nearby, all of whom had stopped what they were doing to stare at him as though he'd just crashed through the window.

She seemed frozen in place as he moved toward her. When he stood directly in front of her, so close he could smell her shampoo and could reach out and touch her if he dared, she asked, "What are you doing here?"

* * * *

She was dreaming. She had to be dreaming. She'd fantasized about Ben coming back into her life so many times over the past week and a half that she had finally crossed the line from daydream to hallucination.

"What are you doing here?" Was that her voice? She hadn't intended to speak. He was so close she could smell his soap and feel the cold coming off his coat. Why would he be here? A flickering of hope filled her chest but she did her best to squelch it. *Don't jump to conclusions.* She didn't think she could live through another rejection. Best to go into this situation with eyes open. No expectations. No hope. He'd made his feelings clear.

He cleared his throat and Caitlyn realized with a start that he was nervous. Ben—Mr. Say-whatever-is-on-his-mind-and-screw-the-consequences—was actually nervous. That made her feel oddly calm.

His voice was low when he spoke and her friends around her all stopped speaking so they could hear. "Sometimes, when I've been a complete and utter ass, I like to ask myself one question. WWCGD?"

WWCGD? What the hell? But then the rest of his words sank in and Caitlyn's chest tightened. He admitted that he'd been an ass. Was he admitting he was wrong? The surge of hope that filled her heart was terrifying—she was setting herself up to have her heart broken. Again. Because he didn't love her, she reminded herself. He would never love her.

Yet that flicker of hope seemed determined to stay alive.

The silence around her seemed to be spreading as the crowd caught on that a scene was unfolding before them, and when Caitlyn spoke, it was for a large audience. "Excuse me?" The words came out on a shaky breath.

"WWCGD," Ben repeated. And then, as though explaining to a child, he said, "What would Cary Grant do."

A little laugh was startled out of her at that and Ben seemed to gain some confidence.

"But since I am obviously no Cary Grant, it might be easier to say what he would not do." Caitlyn was watching him with fascination, her mind reeling. What did this mean?

Ben cleared his throat. "He would not be a blind asshat when confronted with genuine emotions. He would not be so fucking oblivious that he can't see real happiness when it slaps him in the face. Most of all, Cary Grant would not walk away from the woman he loves. He wouldn't—"

Caitlyn's breath caught in her throat and her entire body started to tremble. "What did you say?" The words were still echoing in her ears but she couldn't believe that he'd said them. *He loved her.* Or was that hope playing tricks with her mind?

He took a step closer so they were nearly touching. The room was deathly quiet as the crowd listened in.

The look in Ben's eyes was so sweet and tender it took her breath away. But there was something more there—there was a hint of fear.

"Ben, if you're doing this because you're afraid you hurt me—" she felt compelled to say.

He cut her off by taking her hands in his and pulling her toward him so she was pressed against his chest, and they were the only people in that room and quite possibly inhabiting planet Earth.

His eyes met hers and the depth of emotions she saw there made her knees weak. "I love you, Caitlyn."

Caitlyn's heart stopped beating as the words coursed through her, giving her a heady, dreamlike feeling. *He loved her.*

"I know I don't deserve you. I know I'm not good enough to be with you but I promise you I'm trying to be. You make me want to be a better man. You make me want to be Cary-bloody-Grant."

The happiness she'd been afraid to trust exploded inside of her as his words sank in. *He loved her.* Tears were threatening to fall and the words came out in a wobbly voice. "You already are my Cary Grant."

He raised his brows in amused disbelief.

"You're funny," she offered.

"I'm sarcastic."

"You're sardonic," she corrected, which made him laugh. God, she'd missed his laugh.

He gave her a rueful smile as he leaned in even closer. "I'm apologizing. You're not supposed to be defending me."

"Sorry." She bit her lip to keep from laughing aloud.

"I have a long list to get through here," he informed her. He drew in a deep breath. "Cary Grant would never walk in on you while you're getting dressed just to see you naked, he would never leave dirty dishes on the coffee table, or change the channel when—"

"I love you, Ben."

The words she'd been thinking for weeks finally came out of her mouth and it was such a relief. Like a weight had been removed from her chest and the tendrils of hope that had been flickering inside her burst into the open. He loved her. And she loved him. They were really doing this. Hearing the words and saying them herself was magic, but nothing could compare to the look of pure joy on Ben's face as he scooped her into his arms.

He crushed her lips beneath his in a searing kiss that branded them both. She wrapped her arms around his neck and held on for dear life as his lips moved over her cheeks, her eyelids, her ear, jaw, and neck.

"I want to move back in," he said against her neck.

She pulled back with a breathless laugh. "Easy, tiger. That's moving a little fast, don't you think?"

"You're right. You deserve to be wooed."

"I'm already wooed."

"Oh, you ain't seen anything yet. Get ready to be dated by the master. Get ready to be dated by the man who loves you and adores you and—"

She cut him off with a kiss.

When he spoke again, his lips pressed against her ear and his voice was so low that only she could hear. "I want to make love with you. And then, after we're well and truly satiated, I want to sleep with you. In your bed. And I want to wake up—in your bed. And I want to repeat that sequence of events pretty much every night for the rest of our lives."

Caitlyn couldn't imagine a more perfect proposition.

* * * *

Ben was convinced the party would never end. He'd wanted to scoop her up in his arms and get her out of the theater, into a cab, and back to her apartment. But his plan was thwarted was by her friends.

It seemed Alice had taken off without warning, throwing everyone into a panic. Since she was the organizer, someone needed to stick around to make sure the caterers and staff were paid and all the details taken care of. Meg and her husband had gone to see if Alice was all right, and Tamara was stuck answering questions about the theater for the patrons who were interested in its history. Which meant Caitlyn had been stuck making sure the party ended without a hitch.

And Ben was left to watch her from the corner. Which wasn't so much a hardship, really, as he was happy to ogle his new girlfriend any time day or night. But he only had so much patience, and so help him God if he had to watch her smile and sashay across the lobby much longer, he would turn into King Kong and throw her over his shoulder.

"You do know you look like a stalker standing over here leering like that, don't you?"

Ben spun around in surprise to find Gregory standing beside him. "What are you doing here?"

Dressed in a tux with his hair slicked back, his friend looked disarmingly like a matinee idol from back in the day. Gregory lifted his drink to gesture toward Ben. "Thanks to the favor I did for you, I am this theater's biggest champion. How could I refuse an invite when this is my new pet project?"

"Have I said thank you yet for that favor?"

"Only about twenty times," Gregory said. He gave Ben a little smile. "Don't worry about it. Besides, you were right. This place does have character."

Ben watched Gregory take in everything from the faded carpeting to the ornate sconces with the eye of a real estate mogul. But then Gregory's gaze stopped, fixated by something on the far side of the lobby. "Who's that?"

Ben followed his gaze to a small group of costume-clad women gathered near the bar. "Which one?"

"The blonde."

Ben squinted at the woman who was the spitting image of Veronica Lake...albeit pint-sized. "I don't know—oh wait. Is that?" He leaned in a little closer. Well, hell, she cleaned up well. "That's Tamara. She runs this place."

He watched his friend stare for a little while longer. "Who's leering now?"

That got Gregory's attention back but he ignored the jab. Instead, he kept up his steady perusal. "This place has potential. You were right to help save it."

Ben shrugged off the compliment. It still felt a bit odd to be putting emotions ahead of business.

His gaze was caught by Caitlyn as she flashed a brilliant smile at the bartender. Something told him he'd get used to it. From here on out, she was priority number one.

"It was a risk," Gregory added. "But it looks like it could pay off."

Ben smiled at that. A risk? Killing the development deal was nothing compared to the risk he'd just taken. But that had paid off better than his wildest dreams.

Gregory must have seen his attention turn back to Caitlyn. "So you finally woke up and saw what was right in front of your face." Gregory's smug grin couldn't put a damper on Ben's night.

"I was an idiot," Ben admitted happily. "But now that I've realized how much I need her, I'm never letting go."

Gregory paused, his drink hovering in front of his mouth. But once the shock passed, he slapped Ben on the back. "Good man."

It wasn't until later—much later—that Ben was able to show Caitlyn in exquisite detail exactly how much she meant to him.

Curled up in bed, thoroughly satisfied at last, Ben held Caitlyn in his arms. Warm and contented, she was snuggled up against his side, her head tucked beneath his chin. "So what would the perfect boyfriend do now?"

"Mmm, you're doing it," she mumbled sleepily.

He stroked her back with one hand while tightening his grip with his other arm. She should have the best of everything. She deserved that and so much more. A little pang of unease threatened the perfect calm and happiness he'd been reveling in. Shifting a bit, he said, "I promised you Mr. Perfect."

Her hands started to roam over his chest and shoulders and the snuggling became decidedly less sweet.

He heard her quiet laugh as she tipped her head up and planted a kiss on his lips. "You are Mr. Perfect," she said, her voice husky and soft and re-awakening his desire. Before he could argue, she added, "For me."

Her words had hit a spot in his heart he hadn't known existed until that moment. When he tugged her so she was firmly wrapped in his arms, he vowed then and there that he would never let go.

Epilogue

Ben led Caitlyn to the restaurant and stopped in front of the door, gesturing to the sign like a model on *The Price is Right*. "Ta da!"

Caitlyn took one look at the place and started to laugh. "Really? We're returning to the scene of the crime?"

After much debate about where to bring Caitlyn for their celebratory dinner, he'd finally settled on the spot where they'd had their first date. There was a symmetry to it, a way of seeing just how far they'd come in a relatively short amount of time.

He grabbed the handle to open the door for her and leaned down to whisper, "Let's just hope the waiter doesn't remember me," as she passed in front of him.

Her answering giggle helped to calm some of his nerves as they followed the maître d' to their table. On cue, the waiter brought over a bottle of champagne that Ben had ordered beforehand.

"You shouldn't have," Caitlyn said but she wore a huge smile that made her eyes sparkle and his heart tighten.

For a moment Ben was speechless in the face of her happiness. *Shit. Words don't fail me now. Not tonight of all nights.* But the enormity of what he was doing—what he was feeling—struck him anew. And that was when he knew—he was the luckiest man alive. "We're celebrating tonight," Ben said as he raised a glass for a toast. "To you and your new book."

Caitlyn's blush gave her a glow as she clinked her glass against his. Her first book of knitting patterns had been released that day and he couldn't have been prouder.

"Thank you." Tilting her head to the side, she took in the champagne, the flowers he'd surprised her with earlier, and the suit he was wearing. "You really didn't have to go to all this trouble, but I appreciate it."

This was nothing. There was a whole surprise party waiting for her at Cagney's, but first, he'd wanted a chance to celebrate alone.

"I owe it all to you," she said. She reached across the table and took his hand, entwining her fingers with his. "If you hadn't pushed me to take a risk and try it, I may never have gotten the nerve. You made me brave."

Ben choked on laughter. "Are you kidding?" Caitlyn may have underestimated herself and her talents when he'd first met her, but she had always been brave in the ways that counted the most. She wasn't afraid to put her heart on the line and make herself vulnerable—all in the name of love. That was a lesson she'd taught him and thankfully his stubborn ass had learned it. Leaning over, he squeezed her hand in his. "You're the bravest person I know. You always have been."

"I learned it from you," she said, her eyes glimmering with a happiness that made his heart feel whole. He wanted to see that happiness in her eyes every day of his life—and he wanted to be the one who put it there.

"I'm not brave, I've just got swagger." He waggled his eyebrows, making her giggle.

"I don't know," she drawled. "You've been pretty brave these past few months."

It was true. Having overcome his biggest cowardice and admitting that he loved her, a gate had opened in his heart, making it easier and easier to take leaps of faith into the unknown. Like inviting her to move in with him in his new condo. It had been a no-brainer. It was something that would have terrified him in the past. But from the moment he'd moved in he'd known it wouldn't feel like home unless Caitlyn was there with him.

She'd been worried they were moving too quickly but he harassed and nagged until she'd finally caved, and they'd been blissfully cohabitating ever since.

As if reading his thoughts, she said, "Asking me to move in, I'd say that was pretty brave."

That's nothing compared to this. He met her eyes and matched her grin but the thought of what he was about to do had his palms sweating and he inhaled deeply.

Before he could launch into his well-rehearsed speech, Caitlyn noticed that something was off. Of course she did, his girlfriend knew him inside out—better than anyone. But now, that particular insight was working to his disadvantage. Her eyes narrowed. "Is everything okay?"

He smiled at the concern in her eyes. "Everything is great. I just want tonight to be perfect, that's all."

She rolled her eyes. "I thought we agreed—perfection is overrated."

"*You* agreed," he said, turning her hand over in his to trace patterns along her palm. She shivered, her lips parting on a gasp.

"You're such a tease," she whispered.

"You agreed," he said again, ignoring her protest. "*I* still think you deserve only the best. You deserve your—"

Caitlyn threw up her free hand in warning. "I swear to God, if you say Cary Grant—"

"You deserve your Cary Grant," he continued as if she hadn't interrupted. Her lips were twitching as she tried to hold back a laugh.

His girlfriend really was the most fun to tease.

She leaned over the table as if to tell him a secret. "I've changed my mind."

He cocked an eyebrow. "Oh yeah?"

She gave a quick nod. "Yeah. Cary Grant is no longer my ideal leading man."

His eyes widened as he feigned shock. "No?"

She shook her head. "He's been replaced. That particular role has already been filled." Her eyes softened and the love he saw there was nearly his undoing. "By you," she added softly.

This was it. The moment he'd been waiting for. Not even Cary Grant could ask for a better cue. As he got down on bended knee, his breathing steadied and the nerves subsided. This was not a risk—this was trust. This was love and respect and commitment and everything he'd never known he'd wanted. But it was everything he needed and it was what he desired for them both. A future together. Forever.

And don't miss Maggie Dallen's A Chance Romance series.

The Accidental Engagement

Oops . . .

It started as a regular night for New York City restaurant hostess Ivy Sinclair, until a rowdy customer turned out to be world famous playboy Jack Everett. Thanks to the paparazzi, now the world thinks they're a couple—which couldn't be farther from the truth. But when a brooding, sexy businessman offers her a simply irresistible proposition . . .

Uh oh . . .

Just when cutthroat venture capitalist Daniel Gladwell thought he'd never close the deal with an Italian conglomerate, a simple mistake becomes the perfect opportunity. All he has to do is convince Ivy to pretend to be Jack's fiancée while on a business trip to Italy to offset Jack's bad-boy reputation. As long as Daniel doesn't sabotage the plan by claiming the tempting waitress for himself . . .

Oh yes!

It was supposed to be a business-only arrangement. But in the magic of the Tuscan countryside, neither Ivy nor Daniel can fight the attraction building between them. In the world's most romantic setting, the line between business and pleasure is one that begs to be crossed . . .

Chapter 1

Ivy Sinclair thought she'd seen it all as a hostess at a hotel bar—but when a young man came running up to her with a look of panic before diving behind her hostess stand—well, now she'd really seen everything.

"Excuse me, can I help you?" she asked, looking down at the top of his head as he crouched beside her.

The young man barely looked at her. He was too busy peering around the edge of the stand toward the door. He muttered a curse as a large, brutish man wearing an intimidating scowl walked in.

"I'm not here," the young man at her feet whispered. "Excuse me?" "Please," he added. His eyes widened and filled with panic. Ivy couldn't help but take pity. The large man, who looked ready to kill, zeroed in on her. "Where is he?" She swallowed a lump of fear at the aggressive tone. "Where is who?"

Ivy tried to keep her voice innocent but it came out as a squeak. She cleared her throat and tried again. "I'm afraid I don't know to whom you're referring." He leaned in closer and Ivy fought the impulse to run. "Where is Everett?" he growled. Ivy stared down the oversized thug who was leaning over the hostess stand. She tried not to flinch even as his hot, rancid breath hit her square in the face.

"As I said before, sir, I have no idea what you're talking about."

Several guests had paused in the hotel lobby, en route to the restaurant,alb to watch the drama unfold. The giant didn't seem to mind the attention but this job was Ivy's only source of income and she could repeat the manager's lecture on courtesy and service verbatim. But above all else, her job was to be discreet.

Ivy had to believe that meant covering for the well-dressed, albeit rumpled, young man who was currently crouching behind the hostess stand, uncomfortably close to her legs. She didn't know what the hidden man had done but she couldn't blame him for hiding from the heavyset giant who loomed over her—he looked like a man who was capable of causing serious pain.

And at this particular moment he looked like he would throttle her given the slightest provocation. Ivy was a good foot shorter than the brute, with a petite frame—not exactly an even match. She tried to keep her voice soft but stern—the same tone she used to cajole Otis, her parents' German Shepherd, into his cage when it was time to visit the vet.

"I don't know what this Mr.—uh—" "Everett. Jack Everett," the man sneered. The name caused even more passersby to stop in their tracks. *Why did that name sound familiar?*

"I don't know what Mr. Everett has done, but I assure you I have not seen the man you described come into this restaurant."

His frown deepened into a menacing glare and she added, "If Mr. Everett comes looking for you, I'd be happy to pass along a message, Mr.—"

He leaned in even closer. "You tell Jack that if I see him with my wife again, he's a dead man."

Ivy's hands clenched at her side. That was it. She couldn't have people making death threats in her restaurant. She drew a deep breath and mustered her courage. "If you don't leave immediately, I'm afraid I'll be forced to call the police."

The burly man slammed a fist against the podium. "Listen, lady, I'll do whatever I—" His voice cut off abruptly when she snatched up the phone and started dialing, keeping eye contact all the while.

The man muttered a curse, shook his head, and backed toward the door. "You tell that little bastard I'm coming for him."

When she was certain the man was gone from view, Ivy let out a deep breath and looked down at the young man.

"You are my hero," he said with a grin.

Ivy rolled her eyes and reached out a hand to help him to his feet. "You're Jack, I presume?"

The young man paused on his knees, a lock of floppy brown hair partially covering eyes that were filled with mischief.

"If I were you, I would get out of here quick, before he comes back," she said.

He ignored her advice and grasped her hands in his. "I'm serious, I owe you my life. That guy was going to kill me."

Ivy stifled a laugh at his melodramatic tone. He looked to be around the same age as her—most likely in his late twenties—but everything from his laughing eyes to his mussed hair said he was a little boy in a grown man's body.

"In case you didn't hear, that nice gentleman would prefer that you stay away from his wife. I hope you take his advice," she added, allowing honesty to outweigh discretion for a moment.

His look was sheepish and he gave her an adorable lopsided grin but he made no attempt to deny the accusations. The man had the face of a movie star and clearly the charm and confidence to go with it. She shouldn't be surprised that he was a ladies' man. Working in a hotel restaurant she'd witnessed more than her fair share of adulterous rendezvous. She'd thought she was worldly-wise when she'd first started working at the hotel. She was no longer fresh off the bus from her tiny hometown in Ohio, but she'd still been shocked by the constant and casual affairs. Now, after two years in one of New York's swankiest hotels her scandalized disgust had given way to weary disapproval.

The young man was still on his knees and resisted her insistent tug. She was horrified to realize that the crowd of people who'd gathered to witness the earlier scene were now watching *her*—with more than a little amusement. Heat flooded her cheeks and she dipped her head. "Please stand up," she muttered.

He flashed her a wicked grin. "Not until you accept my sincere gratitude—"

"Fine, you're welcome. Now stand up, please." "And tell me how I can repay you," he finished. "You can repay me by standing up." Whether it was her pleading tone or the red cheeks, he did stand up—and planted a sloppy kiss on her lips. Sputtering with surprise and embarrassment, she pushed him away and turned her face from the people who were now laughing and clapping. Ivy ducked her head, trying to hide her flaming cheeks behind a curtain of hair. She grabbed Jack by the hand and dragged him into the hallway leading to the restrooms, away from the prying eyes of strangers. "What do you think you're doing?" "Sorry," he drawled. "I just wanted to say thank you." His eyes were wide with innocence but the unapologetic grin told her that he found her distress entertaining.

"You've said it," Ivy said with a scowl. She tugged her hand out of his and crossed her arms into her chest.

His lips twitched in what she assumed was a valiant attempt to keep from laughing. "Do you know who I am?"

Ivy blinked at the sudden turn in conversation. "According to your friend who was just here, I'd assume you're Jack Everett."

He crossed his arms and leaned back, his eyes searching her face, waiting for something—some sort of recognition, no doubt. The hotel where she worked was one of the most exclusive in the city; nearly every guest thought they were famous as well as rich. They were almost always wrong.

"Should that mean something to me?" she asked.

"Nothing," he said with a laugh. "Nothing at all. So now that we've established my name, why don't you tell me yours?"

"Ivy Sinclair." "As in poison ivy?" "As in The Holly and the Ivy." At his raised eyebrow, she explained.

"My mom has a thing for Christmas." "Don't tell me you have a sister named Holly," he teased. She gave a sheepish shrug and he burst out laughing. He gave a jaunty salute as he walked back toward the hotel lobby.

"Thank you for saving my life, Ivy Sinclair. I'll be in touch."

* * * *

Word had spread quickly in the hotel and less than twenty minutes after Jack left, Ivy had been summoned to the manager's office. Franklin Webster was known for being a tough boss but he kept his mouth shut through the entire tale, giving her a chance to fully explain her side of the story.

Ivy cleared her throat and forced herself to continue despite Franklin's intimidating frown. "So you see, sir, I really didn't intend to cause such a scene. I was trying my best to keep the situation under wraps. But this young man...well, I'm afraid he was a bit of a ham and he sort of made me—er, *us*—the center of attention."

When she'd finished explaining, he took his time polishing his glasses and made a show of straightening his tie. Ivy tried not to squirm in her seat. Every time she was called into Franklin's office she couldn't help but feel like she'd been called in to see the principal. More nerve-wracking since the only times she was called on to speak to the principal were when her sister Holly was in trouble.

"Ivy, do you have any idea who Jack Everett is?"

Ivy's eyes widened in surprise. "Uh, no sir."

Franklin sighed. He handed her a copy of one of the tabloids that were sold in the hotel's gift shop.

Ivy stared at the front cover, momentarily speechless. There he was—the man who'd huddled by her feet while she fended off an angry husband. He was flashing the camera that now-familiar cocky grin, one hand on the back of a supermodel as they made their way toward a waiting limo. "Tech Mogul Out on the Town," the headline read. Ivy had never taken much interest in gossip columns or celebrities and today her willful ignorance was on display.

When she looked up she saw that Franklin was watching her with a tight-lipped look of disapproval. "I'd say your Mr. Everett has a tendency to find the spotlight. Or rather, the spotlight has a tendency to find him."

Ivy let out a pent-up breath. "So you're not angry?"

"No, I'm not angry. I think you handled the whole thing quite well, considering...."

"Oh, thank you, Mr. Webster," Ivy interrupted.

Franklin's lips twisted into a rare hint of a smile. "Of course. And if Mr. Everett should be true to his offer and come back to the hotel, I know you will do everything in your power to keep him...*entertained.*"

The suggestion made Ivy's skin crawl but her smile didn't falter. It remained frozen in place as her stomach churned. She had heard stories about coworkers being urged to dress more provocatively or to flirt with the guests but she never believed them to be true. She struggled to keep her voice even. "Excuse me?"

His expression remained coy. "I think you know what I mean, my dear." His gaze lowered and he studied her figure as though appraising a piece of art at auction. "My sources tell me you were quite a hit with the young man."

She forced a joking tone as she held the tabloid up before her. "From what I gather, most women are a hit with that young man."

Franklin let out a cackle that made her jump in her seat. Franklin Webster did not laugh. Everyone knew that. But at least he wasn't eyeing her like a piece of meat anymore.

He settled back into his seat. "I like you, Ivy. You're smart and you're a go-getter. This is a tough business and there aren't a lot of openings in the areas where you show an interest..." His voice trailed off and he seemed to be weighing how best to phrase the next statement. "You'll soon learn that to be considered for promotion, an employee must show that he or she is willing to go above and beyond for the company."

Bile rose in her throat. She was going to be sick. She knew exactly what he was insinuating but feigned confusion. "Mr. Webster, are you suggesting that I get involved in a romantic relationship with Mr. Everett for the sake of my job?"

Franklin's mouth opened and closed to resemble a guppy as he protested the coarse accusation. "Of course not. I would never suggest such a thing."

"Of course not," she repeated—*because that would be illegal.*

Feeling a twinge of success at having the last word, she made a move to leave the office but he stopped her.

"No one would ever make such a crass suggestion at this hotel," he said. "But I hope you keep in mind, my dear, that there are a limited number of jobs at this hotel and there is no room for employees who aren't team players."

She stopped in her tracks halfway to the door with her back to the manager. The threat could hardly be called "veiled."

Panic warred with disgust. She needed this job.

She heard the crinkle of the tabloid when he picked it up. "We're willing to overlook your antics this afternoon because we know that you are a team player. Am I making myself clear?"

Ivy resisted the urge to spin around and tell the old man where he could shove the tabloid and her job. But that couldn't happen. She could barely afford to pay this month's rent and she was drowning in debt from her stint on unemployment. And there was no way she could turn to her parents. They had enough on their plate trying to keep their house. The last thing they needed was another mouth to feed.

It was only the thought of having to run back to her parents that gave her the strength to turn around and force a smile. "Understood, Mr. Webster."

* * * *

Ivy's studio apartment in Brooklyn was tiny, but it was all hers, and for that she was eternally grateful. Particularly that evening when all she wanted was a hot bath and a glass of wine.

Hours had passed and she still couldn't get rid of the disgusted feeling. Not even a hot bath could wash it away. For what felt like the millionth time that week, Ivy considered quitting. Oh, it would feel so good. She sank further into the tub and let herself daydream about all the ways she could give her notice. In reality, she would go to bed, wake up, and do it all over again.

She'd moved to the city right after college because she'd landed a great job in an up-and-coming ad agency. But less than two years into the great new job, the recession had hit, and Ivy's entire office had been liquidated. Hers was a small branch of a large company and the closure of their office had been a necessary sacrifice for the greater good—or so she'd been told.

The hostess gig wasn't exactly her dream job but it paid the bills and it was steady work after a series of temp jobs. And it wasn't *all* bad. More and more lately she'd been called in to help the assistant manager with event planning for the hotel and she'd discovered it was something she really enjoyed. She knew there was an opening for an events manager at the hotel. If she could just keep her head down and hold her tongue with Franklin, the job could be hers.

She sighed and sipped her wine. That was a very big "if."

The front door buzzer rang just as she was stepping out of the tub. Her elderly neighbor Edith liked to stop in for a cup of tea and a chat often and she always seemed to show up at a time when Ivy craved solitude. Sleepy and wet from the bath, she threw on a robe and went to answer the door. She tried to summon a smile for her elderly friend.

"Hi Ed—" The name stuck in her throat as she faced the stranger in her doorway.

This visitor was *not* a harmless old woman.

Ivy's mouth gaped as she took in the tall man with dark hair and even darker eyes. His shoulders were broad and he wore a well-tailored suit that looked incongruous in the dingy hallway of her apartment building. Behind him stood a nondescript man with an earpiece and ramrod posture.

"Miss Sinclair?" The tall man before her smiled, causing his eyes to crinkle and eased the intimidation factor only slightly.

"Yes?" Ivy cinched her robe tighter. She was keenly aware of the fact that she wore nothing beneath her flimsy robe.

"I'm Daniel Gladwell, I work with Jack Everett. I believe you met him this afternoon?"

Ivy nodded, unable to take her eyes off of the man before her. He had the kind of chiseled features that were usually reserved for statues or actors portraying James Bond. She made a futile attempt to swipe away some of the unruly auburn curls that had escaped from the loose bun atop her head.

She closed the door a little behind her and took a step into the hallway, wary now that the surprise of finding a gorgeous man in her doorway had worn off.

"Can I help you with something?"

The man's smile grew and he tilted his chin in a charming sort of aw-shucks way, but it was all show—the look in his eyes was strictly business. "Actually, I believe you can. May I come in?"

Ivy hesitated; her small town politeness warred with practical street smarts. "I'd rather not invite strange men into my apartment."

"Of course." If he was surprised to be denied, he didn't let on. "I apologize for the late hour. Jack just informed me of this afternoon's *interaction* and I wanted to speak with you immediately."

Now Ivy was truly intrigued. "Is something the matter? Is Jack okay?"

"Oh no, he's fine. Thanks in no small part to you." Heat flooded her cheeks under his watchful gaze. Despite his warm smile and easy demeanor, his eyes were calculating and observant. They seemed to take in everything, from her bare feet to the damp tendrils clinging to her neck.

"That's actually why I'm here, Miss Sinclair." "Call me Ivy, please." "I wanted to thank you in person for your assistance today. I'm sure you're aware of Jack's fame and fortune—he's easy fodder for the tabloids."

Ivy nodded, but she was sure some of the confusion she felt was evident. *Where on earth was he going with this?* She shifted from one foot to the other.

"I came here tonight because I'd like to show you how appreciative we are...."

"We?"

"My business partners and I. There is a lot invested in Jack, and his reputation."

"I see," Ivy said politely.

"We'd like to show you our appreciation for your help today and for your discretion in the future." He was watching her closely for some sort of reaction and it took several moments for Ivy to fully grasp what he was implying.

"You want to pay me to keep my mouth shut?" The words slipped out before she could stop herself.

Only a slight widening of the eyes revealed Daniel's surprise at her outburst but he recovered quickly. "Well, that's one way of putting it, I suppose."

Daniel gave her a lopsided grin, the first genuine smile she'd seen, and Ivy was very nearly charmed off of her feet.

For a moment she just stared at the man before her, unsure of how she should react. She didn't know whether she was offended or amused. Amusement won out and she startled both men in her hallway when she burst out with a great peal of laughter.

She slapped a hand over her mouth and let out a little snort as she tried to contain her giggles. "Oh, I'm so sorry, this is just too much." She waved her hand toward Daniel and the silent man behind him who was watching her with no expression. "I feel like I just stepped into a movie or something. I mean, are you seriously trying to pay me off? If I don't take it am I going to swim with the fishes?" She giggled again at her own joke.

"Ms. Sin—Ivy, I hope I haven't offended you."

"No, no, why would I be offended?" she said, still smothering a laugh. She took a step back into her apartment and started to close her door.

"Thank you for the laugh, Daniel, but you don't need to pay me. I won't say a word." She held up three fingers in salute. "Scout's honor."

His forehead creased in concern as he gave her a doubtful look that said he wasn't convinced. He opened his mouth to protest, but she held up a hand to stop him.

"Look, I understand where you're coming from, I really do. But believe me when I say I have absolutely no interest in that sort of fame. And if you don't believe that, then maybe you'll understand this—the hotel has very strict rules about not speaking to the press about their guests. If I break that rule, I'd be out of a job. If you don't trust my girl scout's honor—which is sacred, by the way—then believe me when I say I would never jeopardize my job."

He studied her for a moment longer and was apparently satisfied with whatever he saw there. "I'm sorry I disturbed you, Ivy. Have a good night."

* * * *

Ivy didn't even have a chance to hang up her coat when she arrived at work the next day; she was summoned to the manager's office the moment she walked through the door.

She was stunned to find Daniel there, leaning against the manager's desk when she walked in. Both he and Franklin turned to look at her when she entered. Ivy's stomach sank. This could not be good.

Franklin was the first to react to her arrival. He threw down a copy of that morning's paper and beckoned her over to take a look. She cautiously edged toward the desk and glanced at the paper spread before her—it was open to the gossip section. Both men seemed to be waiting for a reaction so she took a step closer and looked down.

Ivy's stomach dropped and she leaned in closer, unable to believe what she was seeing. It couldn't be. There was a large color photo in the center of the page that showed Jack on his knees before her with a caption that read, "Renowned bachelor Jack Everett may finally have found his bride. Everyone wants to know—who is the lucky lady?" As if that wasn't bad enough, there was another picture just below that perfectly captured Jack's ridiculous kiss. "Brilliant billionaire smitten with his mystery woman," the caption read.

There was a little blurb beside the pictures but Ivy couldn't tear her gaze away from the image of herself looking like a woman in love. Like a woman being proposed to, no less. This couldn't be happening.... A rush of adrenaline flooded through her, leaving her shaky and lightheaded. The words blurred before her eyes. She had a feeling she didn't want to read whatever they'd printed anyways. There was no way there would be one hint of truth to any of it.

"Franklin, may I have a private word with Ivy, please?" Daniel asked.

It wasn't so much a request as an order. Ivy couldn't believe anyone would dare to kick the old manager out of his own office but Daniel seemed to be the type to take control of every room he was in. The older man, who normally put the fear of God into Ivy, looked weak and nervous beside him. Franklin nodded and hurried toward the door. Daniel's face gave nothing away but Franklin's tight-lipped grimace was more than enough to tell her that she was in trouble. When he passed her on the way out of his office he shot out a hand and gripped her arm roughly. "You will do whatever he says to make this right, do you understand me?"

Ivy nodded and swallowed. This was it—she was going to lose her job.

Daniel leaned against the desk, one leg crossed in front of the other. He was wearing another perfectly tailored suit. This one was a dark gray as opposed to the jet-black suit he'd worn the night before in her hallway but it fit just as well. He was perfectly groomed from the tidy hair to the shined designer shoes. Unlike most men she knew, he looked like he was comfortable in formal attire as though he had been born and raised wearing designer business suits.

He was watching her. His dark eyes scrutinized her every move, and despite his relaxed posture, or maybe because of it, Ivy grew unbearably tense until she had to do something.

The words came spilling out of her mouth. "I had nothing to do with that," she said, pointing to the newspaper. Her shaking hand seemed to betray her, making her look guilty rather than what she was—horrified. She instantly regretted the outburst. She hated how defensive she sounded.

Daniel nodded, his expression unreadable. "I know."

Ivy shifted uncomfortably. Well, at least he knew she wasn't the enemy here. "If you'd like for me to call the newspaper, explain what happened...."

Daniel shook his head. "Unfortunately, the situation is a little too complicated for that."

Ivy's face scrunched up in confusion. "Too complicated for the truth?"

She thought she saw a flicker of amusement in his eyes but it was fleeting. He gestured to the chair in front of him. "Please, have a seat and I'll explain."

Ivy hesitated for a moment before squaring her shoulders and perching on the edge of the chair. She tried to discreetly pull down the hem of her skirt, which suddenly felt much too short under his scrutinizing gaze.

He sat across from her and leaned over the desk with his hands folded. Every gesture, every move, was precise. This was a man who thought through everything—nothing was unintentional or improvised. Everything was planned. And the way he was looking at her now? It was clear he had a plan for her.

"As I mentioned last night, my company has a lot at stake, and it's all riding on Jack. He is the face of EverTech and his reputation has a direct impact on the business."

Ivy nodded and tried not to shift in her seat. *Just get to the point already.* "I won't beat around the bush, Ivy." *Oh God, could he read minds?*

"I am in the middle of negotiating a very sensitive merger with a company that could either make or break EverTech." When he paused Ivy wondered if she was supposed to speak. She opened her mouth, about to ask what any of this had to do with her but he continued before she could get the words out.

"The owner of the other company, Gianni Brunelli—well, he's a bit old-fashioned. He's made it clear that he doesn't approve of Jack's current lifestyle and this latest stunt...."

He gestured to the newspaper with a pained look. When he turned back to her, she was caught in his gaze. His dark eyes were focused on her with an intensity that was frightening. She couldn't look away.

Ivy squirmed in her seat. Was he trying to torture her? She had no idea what he was getting at but the way he was looking at her, you'd think she single-handedly maneuvered the latest "stunt," as he put it. Ivy gripped the edge of her chair to keep calm but she was growing impatient with nerves. She'd already offered to call the newspaper, to try to explain the situation.

"I'm not sure how I can help you," she hedged.

"The only way Brunelli will move forward with this is if I can convince him that Jack has changed. That he's a new man."

There was a brief pause and Ivy wondered if she was supposed to know what he was getting at. She found herself holding her breath as she waited for him to continue but he was either extremely fond of awkward silences or was waiting for her to respond. His eyes were studying her expression though his face was a polite mask, no emotions to be found. He was waiting for a reaction of some sort, that much was clear, but she had no idea where this was heading—only that it couldn't be good.

"Okaaay..." she stalled.

Silence broken, Daniel stood and moved to the front of the desk so he was looming over her. He crossed his arms in front of his chest and fixed his eyes on her. "You see, Brunelli doesn't want to get into bed with someone who's 'not faithful in his private life'—those are his words not mine," Daniel said.

Judging by his smirk, it was clear that this man didn't put much stock in Brunelli's beliefs or his old-fashioned values.

She blinked up at him in the silence that followed. "So, what do you want from me?"

Daniel's laugh took her by surprise. It was a deep rumble that Ivy could feel all the way to her toes. Her breath caught in her throat at the genuine smile that caused his eyes to crinkle and made him seem less intimidating but far more dangerous.

"You're a straight shooter, Ivy. I like that."

She wished his words of approval didn't affect her but she couldn't deny the warm glow that spread through her chest and left her slightly breathless.

He looked her straight in the eye. "I want you to go along with a lie, Ivy. I want you to tell the world that you and Jack are engaged and I want you to play the part of the happy fiancée until this deal is signed."

Ivy found herself staring up at Daniel and for the life of her she was unable to come up with any words. Her brain had turned to mush in her shock and she had the odd sensation that time stood still. The hum of the air-conditioner was temporarily washed out by the sound of her own heartbeat in her ears.

Daniel was eyeing her warily, his gaze fixed on her, and for a moment she thought she saw a hint of concern in his eyes. Those dark eyes that still held her captive.

He was gorgeous. Now was not the time to be thinking about this man's sex appeal, but there it was. Her heart was racing and she was no longer certain if that was due to shock or sexual attraction.

Focus, Ivy. This man wanted her to lie for him—about her entire life.

His voice startled her back to the moment. "I can see my proposition has taken you by surprise." He relaxed his intimidating stance and leaned against the desk with his hands in his pockets as though they were discussing the weather and not her life. "Don't get me wrong, we are not asking you to do anything illegal or anything that would jeopardize your values. You will be handsomely rewarded in return—my investors and I are more than willing to ensure that you are very comfortable financially in return for this favor."

"Other than lie." The words slipped out of her mouth.

Her words put a dent in Daniel's perfectly poised sales pitch. She couldn't help it. Her mother's face loomed in her mind's eye at the mere thought of lying. Her parents had thoroughly ingrained their children with the need to tell the truth, the whole truth, and nothing but the truth.

He paused and raised his brows in polite inquiry. "I'm sorry?"

She cleared her throat. "I said 'other than lie'. You said 'we're not asking you to do anything that would jeopardize your values.' And I said 'other than lie.'"

Oh Lord, she was babbling. She was repeating their conversation like a court reporter. His forehead wrinkled as if in thought for a moment but again she couldn't tell if he was amused or annoyed. Or both.

"Yes, you have a point there. I'm sure lying to your friends and family will not be pleasant but unfortunately, we can't afford to take any chances on anyone slipping up. It would be more difficult for you as well if the truth were to come out. It would not paint you in a flattering light, I'm afraid."

Panic made Ivy's heart rate accelerate. He was talking as though she'd already agreed to go along with this stunt. She shook her head. "I'm sorry, Daniel, but I'm really not a very good liar and I'm not much of an actress. I don't think I could pull it off."

"Unfortunately for us, we don't have much of a choice in who will play the lead in this particular farce." He gestured toward the newspaper. "But you will have a team of people at your beck and call to help you—I am absolutely positive you will get through this little façade with flying colors."

Ivy bristled at his know-it-all tone. Was he really trying to steamroll her into telling a life-altering lie just because it was convenient for him?

He wasn't even pretending to frame it as a question—as though it was understood that she would comply.

"Do people always do what you say?" she snapped.

The charming smile faltered. It was slight but she caught it. His perfectly poised demeanor slipped—just for an instant, but it was enough to give Ivy a sense of triumph. She had a feeling that Daniel Gladwell was rarely taken by surprise.

He recovered quickly though and his answer was brutally honest. "Yes, Miss Sinclair. They typically do." *If they know what's good for them.* He didn't say the words but he didn't have to.

Gone was the polite smile and Ivy found herself face to face with Daniel Gladwell, the ruthless business tycoon. His jaw clenched and his eyes hardened, holding her captive yet again in a disarmingly direct glare.

He looked like a gladiator ready for battle. The look he gave her was so intense, she swallowed her clever retort—this was not a man to mess with.

"Honestly, Mr. Gladwell, I'd really rather go back my job—"

"Your job will not be waiting for you should you refuse my offer." He stood up straight and moved to stand behind the desk. His tone was cool and collected, at odds with the harsh words.

She tried to ignore the uncomfortable sting of unshed tears as his words sank in. She couldn't go back to being unemployed. She'd worked so hard to get where she was. She couldn't start over. And she couldn't go home. Bad investments and a housing market collapse had left her parents teetering on the edge of bankruptcy at an age when they should be planning for retirement. If she lost her job they'd feel compelled to help her but they could barely help themselves.

"That's not fair, you can't do that." Ivy's voice shook. She swallowed and tried again. "The hotel has no reason to dismiss me. I've been a great employee. Ask anyone, ask Mr. Webster."

"It's not a matter of how well you've done your job, Miss Sinclair. The hotel can't keep someone on who acts irresponsibly with the hotel guests. Not to mention, employees here are expected to be team players."

"I am responsible. And I *am* a team player." She tried to keep the tremor out of her voice. She felt like she was on the wrong end of a steamroller. She had to regain control.

She tilted her chin up and straightened her shoulders. Who did he think he was to come to her place of work and threaten her job? Maybe Franklin wasn't in her corner, but there had to be people above him.

Standing, she faced Daniel who had returned to his seat behind the desk. "You can't fire me, Mr. Gladwell. I'm sure Mr. Webster doesn't even have the final say and you have *no* say in the matter so—"

Daniel cut off her tirade before she could even gain steam. "Actually I do have quite a bit of say. My company is the majority owner of this hotel."

His words were like a punch in the gut. Her mind struggled to make sense of this new information. It couldn't be possible—could it? Maybe he was kidding. But even as she thought it, she dismissed it. The man before her clearly didn't have a sense of humor. She stared at him with wide eyes, trying to think of something to say, but she was rendered speechless. She flopped back in her seat like a deflated balloon.

With astonishing speed his cold businesslike demeanor was once again replaced by the charming smile that Ivy was beginning to know well. It was the smile of a predator before it ate its prey. "Listen, Ivy, it doesn't have to be this way. I don't want to lose you as an employee. But

I also can't allow yesterday's incident to ruin a multi-billion dollar deal that I've been working on for the past two years. You can understand that, can't you?"

Ivy just stared back at him. Her mind was racing as she considered her options. She could try her luck in an unemployment office once again and pray that she'd find a new position before she lost everything. She could go back home and try to find a job there—but no, that wasn't an option. The job market in her hometown was far worse than the city and she couldn't allow her parents to help her.

"How much?" she asked. "How much would you pay me if I go along with this?"

For a moment she thought he was ignoring her. He picked up a pen and jotted something down on a piece of paper. He pushed it her way and when she picked it up, a series of zeros stared back at her. The six-figure number took her breath away. That was enough to pay her rent for the year and still have plenty left over to help her parents.

"And of course you'll get a promotion, which comes with a raise," Daniel added.

"I don't want a promotion if I haven't earned one," Ivy said, sitting up straight. She may be desperate for money, but she still had some morals.

She thought she saw a hint of a genuine smile again. Good Lord, this man's lips were hypnotic.

"On the contrary, Miss Sinclair. I've had a long talk with Franklin and it seems you have been long overdue for the promotion. I plan to have a talk with him about that." His look of disapproval actually made Ivy nervous on Franklin's behalf.

"So, do I take it we have a deal?"

Ivy swallowed down the feeling that she was taking a leap off of a high dive without checking to see if there was water below.

"We have a deal."

Meet the Author

Maggie Dallen is a huge fan of happily-ever-afters. She writes contemporary and YA romance and has been known to rewrite the endings to classic love stories to ensure that they end on a happy note. In Maggie's version, Ingrid Bergman does not get on the plane. She lives in Northern California and works at a yarn store to support her knitting addiction. For more info please visit maggiedallen.com.

Follow her on Twitter @Mag_Dallen.
Or connect with her on Facebook.